MONSTER VICE

MONSTER VICE

George P. Saunders

iUniverse, Inc.
New York Bloomington

Monster Vice

iUniverse books may be ordered through booksellers or by contacting:

iUniverse
1663 Liberty Drive
Bloomington, IN 47403
www.iuniverse.com
1-800-Authors (1-800-288-4677)

ISBN: 978-1-4401-8449-9 (sc)
ISBN: 978-1-4401-8450-5 (hc)
ISBN: 978-1-4401-8451-2 (ebook)

Printed in the United States of America

iUniverse rev. date: 11/20/2009

With an *homage* nod to David Foster Wallace, and for Rose
... without whom, all this would never be. All my love to you
forever.

CHAPTER ONE

▼

At the moment, I'm not fixated on sex.

Unusual for me, because even though I don't do a lot of Hokey-Pokey-Roll-Roll In-The-Whiskered-Bunny-Fun-Hole at present, I'm always much immersed in the pursuit of The Ejaculation Behind The Curtain. There's a reason why ... but I'll get to that later.

For now, though, I enjoy briefly what is here and now, tangible and tasty. A walk in Echo Park, and yummy treats in hand.

I'm a cop with a cop's appetites, no denying it, no sir. The Hostess Twinkies I hold in my mitts are twin rolls of golden magic, laced with hydrogenised vegetable oil, and enough Red Dye No. 5 to kill your basic lab rat. I am cognizant of these carcinogenic facts, yet I chomp down on Twinkie Number 1 and chew happily — realizing that this will be the highlight of my night.

Name is Dick Pitts, Special Agent to Task Force Monster Vice, Los Angeles Police Department. My shift begins in half an hour. I'm ahead of schedule, and contemplate stopping off at Nicky's Bar for a quick nip. I walk the park in my down-time like this sometimes just to see if there is something evil that needs killing. My hobby, my pass-time. My *métier*.

And then she appears. From behind a tree, a succubus, young, teeth like razors, perfect tits, and piercing black eyes. She is virtually naked, and I cannot ignore the shaved mons between her legs. Nor the bat-like wings flapping that stick out from her back. She smiles.

"Wanna fuck, handsome?

I sigh, and take out my Beretta.

"Always wanna fuck," I say. "Just not you, sweetheart."

I pull the trigger, and the demon-chick's head blows apart.

Ho-hum. This stuff happens a lot. Strolls in the parks, semen-hungry succubae, various other low-life predators of the supernatural. Routine, really. Same ol', same ol'. Yawn.

I continue walking, enjoying the night air, scarfing down the last twinkie.

My cell suddenly rings. I reach for it, and flip open the speaker.

"Pitts here," I mumble.

"Dick, it's Bill," my brother says in a strange voice I have not heard before.

"You okay, bro?" I ask.

"Gotta see you. Right now."

I check my watch. My brother's house, annexed to his church, is only a few blocks away. Very do-able. "Sure, I'll be right over --"

"No, not the house. Please," he says, his voice raspy, gravelly, tired. "The park. Okay?"

"Bill, you don't sound good."

"I'm *not* good, that's why. You have a gun?"

The question takes me momentarily off guard. "Of course," I answer.

"Good. See you in a few." He hangs up.

And I am now worried.

✻   ✻   ✻   ✻

My brother Bill always tells me: "Take stock of your life, Dick — know when to walk away from a losing proposition." My brother is an Episcopalian minister, a walking-talking advertisement for good sense and moderation in all things. I love him for that, yet I know that he can afford to be moderate — I cannot.

He doesn't do what I do for a living.

And sometimes walking away from a losing proposition isn't an option. Running, maybe. But walking? Rarely.

Walking away gets you killed faster.

Still, I think of his benign adage as I move down the cracked sidewalk that comprises Alvarado Street and Northrop. I suddenly step in something hot and yielding. I look down in disgust and with familiar horror - perennial constants in my chosen career.

Werewolf shit. Not good.

The wolf droppings, fresh and still steaming on cool asphalt, tell me that I'm seconds away from either a good clean Kill — or a tail-tangle with evil I may not survive. The stench is foul. It assaults my senses full force. I lift my foot and stare down at the intestinal residue of my sworn enemy, the Lycker (a werewolf slang term we in Monster Vice use for the beast's Greek etymological origins re *Lycanthropy*). The fecal mass glows green in the moonlight, steam rising off something that I can determine is part of an undigested human toe. This sucker has already fed tonight, which means I will be attacked for different reasons other than hunger. The smell gets worse. My stomach does the Funky Chicken and I almost bring back dinner, a questionable mix of Carl's Junior (The Five Dollar Burger) and day-old Tai, followed hard upon, of course, by the Twinkies. I quell the imminent rise of bile in my throat, and try to remember the most basic mathematical constant in differential calculus or the Latin term for female orgasm.

By which I mean to say, I search in panic for a mental distraction — anything, anything at all to replace the visual reminder of the unholy excrement now glued to my over worn Reeboks.

I lumber off the concrete, and onto the green grass, covered in a glowing veneer of evening dew. I try to focus on the positive.

I breathe and look around the immediate vicinity. My brother has not yet arrived. I pray that he is running late, no matter what the nature of his personal emergency.

I was not expecting a Lycker confrontation.

I continue to scan the night. The good news is that Echo Park appears deserted this evening. No bums, perverts, same-sex jerkers, or homeless vagabonds haunt the usual spots. We are alone.

Myself and the werewolf, that is.

Mental sound bytes suddenly loom in my mind from past conversations with my brother.

"You should surround yourself with beauty, Dick," Bill would advise on our Sunday beer outings together. "Don't embrace the Ugly — embrace the Divine. It's all around you, if you look carefully."

On those lovely afternoons, I drink more beer and shrug, nodding in acquiescence, as if my nod meant to say: well, yeah, you're right, I guess, kind of ... except I just killed something last night that had four legs, six eyes and perchloric acid for urine. Just another day at the office.

I of course don't "go there" with my minister brother, Bill. He wouldn't understand. No, sir, he wouldn't understand one little bit.

Another growl. Translated: *You're about to die horribly, Dick.*

My weapon of choice for this evening is a Beretta 92F Nine Millimeter, with a magazine capacity of fifteen shots. If the wolf gets the jump on me, and I fire too late, it wouldn't matter if I were Captain Kirk loaded with an arsenal of radioactive fart-photon torpedoes. I'd be a human finger sandwich for the Lycker. Worse still, within the hour, I'd start sprouting fur and a nasty overbite, along with an insatiable peckish taste for human flesh. Such are the vagaries and downsides to being bitten by a werewolf in modern day Los Angeles.

Something growls again. Something, my ass — I know *exactly* what snarls in the dark.

It.

The Thing.

A Creature Of The Night. I refer to it simply as The Target, but such a definition in and of itself is almost laughingly inadequate. What lies in wait, just ahead, shouldn't even exist.

The target has spotted me, and lurks just a hundred yards ahead in within a reticular wall of hedges. I could, of course, begin firing blindly, hoping, praying for a bulls-eye, a miracle if I get a direct hit to the heart or brain — the only surefire way to terminate a full-on charging lycanthropic wet dream with a bad, bad attitude. Experience and pragmatism, however, urge me to restrain myself. It doesn't help of course that I am trembling with terror. Even after so many years, so many encounters, I'm a big scared baby when it comes to this kind of thing.

This kind of thing, of course, is what I arguably do to bring home the bacon. Chase Monsters, that is. At one point we thought it couldn't get any worse than 9/11. Wrong, kids. It did.

"You were so good with women's clothing and design," Bill constantly reminds me on our Sunday get-togethers. "Soft knits, tweeds, a sense of color. You had such a gift. What happened?"

When I was very young, you see, I wanted to be a dress designer. It's what our father did, with great success. He was the King of Women's' Fashions. Arnie's Dress Shop Just Around The Corner. That's what it was called. Truly. And I had a talent for style, color and accessorizing.

This was all very early in my life, you see — before I discovered what I was *really* great at: whacking bad guys ... and then much later ... whacking monsters.

"Should have followed your real calling," Bill still tells me every Sunday. "What is it you do now?"

"I'm a cop," I always reply amiably. Bill *knows* I'm a cop, but that's his favorite rhetorical question: *What is it you do now?*

"That's right," he says, as if perhaps he's just remembered the last verse to a lost poem by Keats. "Some kind of violent crime division."

"Monster Vice," I remind him … as I always do.

I usually take a sip of beer and wait for this bonding moment between brothers to pass. Bill doesn't mean to, but he gets under my skin every time he pursues this line of conversation.

"I can't see it," he says sincerely. "I've watched you through the years, and still can't believe you've chosen this line of work."

Fair enough, I think. Neither can I.

"Well, remember … it's never too late to quit," he'd advise, as he has done so for these past fifteen years. "Sooner or later, it all turns into a losing proposition."

We usually laugh. It's a running joke.

Quit. Get back into clothes and tweeds. Imagine.

Ha, ha, ha.

Another growl. A rustle of leaves, the smell of damp fur, and then I see it. *The eyes.* Green laser-like beacons of pure hate stare at me through the darkness. The mouth to which the eyes belong opens, and the glow of ebony white fangs, emblazoned in a glowing red drool, is clearly delineated against the black of night. I have an uncontrollable urge to lose my bladder just about now, followed by the fight or flight response of my species — the one designed to save life and limb when faced with immediate peril. But I am a creature of duty. I have trained hard for this kind of work, and my rational mind wins the wrestling match with the Panic Drive to get the hell out of here, now, and be right quick about it because I'm about to be something's dinner. I bring my weapon up, pointed at the picture of hell ahead of me, and take aim.

The eyes suddenly vanish, as do the teeth. The growls echo off into an eerie silence, and I am again faced with nothing more than the still of night. Which by the way, chills my bones to the marrow. The wolf has decided to play a waiting game. It's in stalk-mode now, and I put my chances of coming out of this un-munched at about one in ten. Crappy odds to be sure, and I again entertain the notion of running like a broke-dick schoolboy out of this park.

Right about now, I think: Perhaps I have been doing this for too long. Perhaps it is time to retire after all, move out to the country, kick back, get married, get a life. I've been a cop now for almost two decades, a Special Field Inspector for Monster Vice as of 27 months ago. The old days of Homicide work are over. What I do now, on almost every level, defies description and strains credulity. You're curious, so go ahead and ask. Go ahead. Just try. You would probably begin quite politely:

Hey, Dick, how was your day?

And I'd reply just as cordially: *Not bad. Thanks for asking. Let's see, for starters, killed a few vampires, slew a few dragons, whacked a few wolves. The corpse of a nineteen-year-old automobile crash victim began to scuttle about on shorn legs in the County Morgue, had to brain it and dissolve it in a corrosive acid solution, then bury it in hallowed ground. Oh, there was the exorcism over at Disneyland; one of the rides was haunted by a flesh-eating thing from hell. Broke for lunch around two pm, and I'd rather not talk about the rest of the afternoon. 'Nother day, another dollar. The usual.*

There'd be an awkward silence, before you found your tongue.

Uh ... well, great. Don't overdo it, Dick. All work and no play, you know ... Ha, ha, ha.

Maybe we'd have a group hug, shoot the shit for another microsecond, then you'd run off giggling, thinking: guy's a loon. And you might be right.

How was your day?

Don't ask.

Even so, get that question from people all the time. And though everyone knows about the current pandemic horror sweeping across Planet Earth, what I do seems to the Average Joe as being ... unreal. I don't blame anyone. The question is natural, though the answer is somewhat not.

Because what I do, by necessity, *is* unreal.

I take out my ever-ready flask of good old American Jack Daniels and suck down a toke of liquid courage. You might say this is rash, unprofessional, unwise, given the fact that I'm facing a supernatural nightmare with one-inch fangs. Sure, it could conceivably slow my response time, attenuate vital reflexes, put my life in mortal peril where precious seconds might mean the difference between my survival or my potential for becoming human Hamburger Helper. I might concede that you have a point. But I've been doing this for awhile, and sometimes the only way I get through this kind of thing, is to fortify myself with a buzz. Okay, it numbs the senses a bit, dulls the judgment, but at this stage of the game, it doesn't matter. I'm either going to kill this furry piece of fuckery with one shot (one shot being all I will get), or I join the ranks of The Evil Dead.

More rustles. More growls hiss my ways. Pretty standard stuff so far from the Lycker. I feel emboldened, revitalized, a Shit-Kicking Soldier For All Things Right, Good and True. The Jack warms up my belly, and I am filled with a desire for hand-to-paw combat.

"You're not a spring chicken anymore," Bill told me last Sunday. "The kind of work you do — it's for younger cats." My brother, though one year my junior, and a Man of the Cloth, occasionally commutes into the language of Black Panther Gangstah' when he wants to make a point.

I took offense at the age thing.

Something moves. A shadow?

Oh, shit, what's that blur of motion --

Whoa, that hurt, and now I'm a topsy-turvy fun-ball flying through space. Clearly, the wolf has charged and hit me hard, though it is an atypical attack, as I am still airborne, proving to those who might doubt the obvious, that Man in some instances was born to fly. I hit the ground hard, rolling, rolling, rolling, just keep that doggy rolling — and yes, praise the lord ... let there be pain. I see stars, and they are in stellar meltdown just behind my eyeballs. I taste blood, my own, and also feel dampness near by knee. I am prone on the ground, and see that my pant leg is torn, the result of a substantial impact with concrete — but amazingly, I am not bitten or mauled.

He's playing with me.

Playing with the food.

This pisses me off. I'm on my feet, the buzz from Jack instantly obliterated, my gun firing blindly into the night. My erratic attack is not fear-motivated, but rather a responsive ire to being toyed with. I think with a false sense of courage: Yo, Wolf! You shitting slab of fur who mocks me with a rhino-like bump in the butt that sends me flying — you will taste my fury, know my wrath, beg for mercy! Y'hear? Your days of Slobber and Slaughter are finished.

He's toast, I continue my inward, self-fortifying litany of coaching enthusiasm. Yeah. Right on. Dead meat. Wolf-burger. I'll get him --

— that is if he doesn't get me first.

"Do unto others as they do unto you," my brother often would repeat scripture to me in my most depressed moments. Bill worries about me, that I drink too much, that I'm prone to moments of almost clinical apathy. "I see violence in your heart, brother. Violence and hatred. No wonder you feel so down."

I asked Bill once what he thought of the monster epidemic swarming over the planet.

"It's the Devil making his last play for Planet Earth," he said easily. "The monsters are just locusts. Nothing serious in terms of what is <u>really</u> coming."

Nothing serious, he says.

Right.

Like what the Vatican said about the Nazis back in 1933. Just a passing phase.

Something hits me once again. Hard. Pain radiates from my lower back to the top of my head, and I again defy gravity. At this rate, I'll have more flying miles to my name than Lindbergh. I am in the air so long, I wonder if there's a flight attendant on her way to bring me a frosty adult beverage -- something, anything, to help me wile away the comfy hours at a cruising altitude of just under ten feet.

Oh, but the magic ends abruptly, because I am again in contact with Mother Earth. This time there is blood seeping into my eyes and I realize that my head has connected rather lovingly, if not jarringly, with the bark of some innocent tree.

This has, I feel, gone on long enough.

My dancing partner, Mr. I-Couldn't-Be-Hairier-And-More-Hideous-Than-You-Could-Possibly-Imagine, growls once more into the otherwise beneficent night. Though I literally see red, and my head spins wildly, I can now visualize the werewolf loping toward me at nine o'clock. He thinks he's got me off-balance, and obviously, with this near-frontal attack, the drooling motherfucker has lost a sense of fun for the game. He wants to end it quickly now, grab a quick bite, then move on to another victim — SOP for your basic werewolf.

While I am considerably far from up to par, I have the heart of an old soldier, and training of decades deeply ingrained in every muscle, every neuron of my being. My gun comes up, a sluggish move that is accompanied with waves of pain through my shoulder, and a cascading inner surf of nausea. I do not have time to aim, nor time to pray, yet some inner voice calls out for help to the great Unknown.

"Die, cocksucker," a gentle mewling oath floats over the evening air, and I recognize the voice as my own.

The Beretta sings its familiar song, a one note kind of song at that, but I will have few complaints if the bullet does not sing true. I close my eyes, wondering vaguely if there is Jack Daniels in heaven or hell.

"And what is <u>really</u> coming, worse than the monsters?" I asked Bill just last week.

He smiled at me. "Promise of salvation," he said softly. "It will come in the night and bear a false name. Look to it, brother. And kill it, if you can."

"Ah, a false prophet," I surmised.

"A false *something*," Bill said.

Always walk away from a losing proposition.

My brother is right — and I hope I have the opportunity to tell him so one day. I realize that the chances are slim to none of this happening, and prepare for the inevitable flesh rending to come.

Silence.

Something tells me, miraculously, that my bullet has found its mark. Yet I am surprised. There is no scream, no snarl of shocked agony. I open my eyes and see an amazing sight. The cocksucking wolf in question lies in a heap, just ten feet in front of me. Blood pools around its motionless form, telling me the shot must have ruptured the aorta. I am shaking with joy, my mouth an arid desert of desiccated, smacking flesh, searching for anything remotely resembling saliva. I blubber some nameless thanks to whatever gods may be and my eyes are probably big old teapots of astonishment.

Predictably (and sadly), the werewolf begins to transform in front of me.

I wait for the inevitable, the insidious transformation from snarling beast to ravaged human. I feel remorse and horror for the metamorphosised victim before me — some poor bastard buggered by the fates, subjected to an unholy end by someone like me. Someone's father, someone's son, probably, who was in the wrong place, wrong time when another wolf somewhere had hit him and hit him hard.

Fur turns to flesh, paws to hands, haunch to human thigh.

The victim is male, Caucasian.

I stare at the face.

In recognition.

My brother.

I swallow hard and look at my watch, a carryover from my days in homicide. T.O.D. (Time of Death), 10:42 p.m. I put my call into Monster Vice.

"MV, this is Pitts, 106, On Station," I say dully. "I'm in Echo Park, south-southwest corner, Alvarado and Union. I need a meat wagon, ASAP."

"Roger, that, 106," Dispatch responds dispassionately. "On its way, Dick."

I nod, then drop to my knees and begin to sob.

CHAPTER TWO

▼

The ME wagon comes and goes. I stand alone now, looking up into the night. Bill is gone. I will see him no more. The thought leaves me indescribably empty.

My dispatch pager suddenly goes off: "We have Fangs, 209-niner, downtown, Sector B. All Points."

I hate Fang Detail.

We call your basic vampire a Tuti -- (a truncated pseudonym from the arguably Romanian etymological origin *Nosferatu* or the Greek alternative *nosophorus* meaning "not breathing"). More than one Tuti and we here in Monster Vice ascribe the term "Multiples." Fang Detail means going out into the world and Staking a herd of MVIs (Multiple Vampire Infestations) before they become a threat to the general public.

Multiples are the worst. One Bloodsucker is bad enough -- by definition, a pissed off, degenerate slab of undead cocksuckery with no sense of humor, homicidal to the extreme, with zero latitude for reasonable negotiation. More than one Tuti and you knew the night was going to turn butt-ugly fast. I mention this because Dispatch called in five minutes earlier with the dreaded "Fang-Detail 209" designation. Somewhere nearby, a bunch of bloodsuckers were up to no good.

I put my recent personal tragedy behind me. There is work to be done. I call my partner, Hanson, who picks me up within two minutes. I do not tell him about my brother.

I hate Fang Detail. Not so, my partner. Mel "the Plug" Hanson, kind of digs FDs. They call him the Plug because he has a registered Stake (or Plug) kill ratio for the Fangs of fifty-four. Not bad, considering that LAPD's Monster Vice division has only been in existence for a few years – about the time when the dead walked and the world turned topsy-turvy bug-shit insane. By way of a little background, the vampires are the worst, mainly because they're the smartest. They're also organized, and they're mean. The Lyckers (werewolves) are next on the shit-list, followed by a close and loving third, the collective Everything Else contingent, which include, but are not limited to, incubi, succubae, spooks, goblins, ghosts, ghouls, and zombies -- things that go bump in the night, but are not necessarily lethal on every encounter … and some of which are downright benevolent. PDs in New York, Chicago, Miami and Houston have it almost as bad, but LA is still King of Crap when it comes to Monster Infestation. I blame it on Hollywood, a completely irrational prejudice, but what the hell. There has to be a reason why we're statistically more plagued than any other city on the planet. Probably all those movies -- Frankenstein, Dracula, etc. … harmless by comparison, when you think about it … when you think about the fact that the real McCoys are god awful nightmares a thousand times worse than any celluloid version of your mythical monster. Scratch that. A million times.

Anyway, Hanson has fifty-four kills to my fifty-three. It's been a running gag down at Rampart MV who would win the Christmas pool, only one week away. Hanson is the favorite, for obvious reasons, his score a horse-nose better than mine. That, and he really loves the whole Stake and Bake process. He'll sing a Christmas carol while drilling a Tuti, the thought of sending the wretched bloodsucker to hell in a heartbeat almost sexually arousing for him. I like Hanson, mind you, but when it comes to nailing Tutis, the guy is a veritable Prince of Darkness With A Hard-On for vampire butchery. I've always been a believer in Love Your Work, but Hanson takes it to the extreme. Me, I'm just happy to be breathing and have 6 quarts of good old American hemoglobin still racing through my veins after a Fang Detail. That being said, tonight could be the night for me to catch up to and/or surpass Hanson's lead in the Plug Department. Fun, in theory, to contemplate ... but not when you realize that you might end up dead trying to leap-frog the competition.

Notwithstanding Hanson's love of the hunt, and my own ambivalent, yet obsessively professional commitment to duty, Fang Detail is historically the most dangerous call you can get. More good Blues and P-Clothes have ended up paws up and Staked themselves after a vampire rumble. Hanson and I are the oldest vets in Monster Vice. Most of the guys who signed on some 27 months ago are now dead, staked and buried, not necessarily in that order.

We're three minutes into the call when I remember that my life is in danger. That, and my immortal soul.

The location of the alert is downtown, near Grand, in some warehouse between Olympic and 7th. Dark part of the city, not good, no sir, not good at all. Backup has been called in from Central, and we are told two SWAT divisions are on the way with choppers. Excellent. We'll need every edge we can get; it's a Full Moon, and that means the Tutis will be meaner than usual, and famished. I wonder vaguely who made the call — who had survived long enough to dial 666 — the direct Emergency Line for Monster Vice. I wonder if that poor party is still alive — or munched by a group of savage Multiples.

Two minutes until we're On Station, racing south on the Hollywood 101 Freeway, about to turn off on the 110 Harbor going south. I have a bad feeling about this call, don't ask me why. My weaponry has changed. The Beretta is gone. I now check my Stakes, hanging from either chest-strap; my Holy Water is easily accessible on my standard-issue PD waist belt and every bullet in my customized .357 Magnum is silver, mercury tipped, with the "Jesus Loves Me" logo embossed across the base. A sentimental touch. The Little Carpenter may or may not be My Personal Savior, but I take no chances. The Tutis hate the cross, per legend, and this officer of the law is comforted by that fact nevertheless.

I'm ready for bear, or more accurately (and this is a reflection of the world we live in today), I am ready for the Creatures of the Night.

Oh ... perhaps I should back up a bit and explain that part about losing my life and soul. Seeing as I have a bit of time before I face a multiple colony of unholy impossibilities, thirsting for human blood, all minus a heartbeat. Fine. The night is clear, the moon is full, and in case I haven't mentioned it for the third time ...

I hate Fang Detail.

✴   ✴   ✴   ✴

So, trekking down memory lane, what I'm about to tell you happened about a year back.

I was jumped by a Fang just outside of Ralph's on Sunset. It was a stray Fresh Kill - some poor gal who had already been Sucked, and left for dead by a Feeder, i.e., a full fledged, hands-down, no-bullshit, *vampire*. She was drained nearly dry. When she awoke, she was technically *undead*. The Change had occurred within the hour, but the pathogenic effect within the FK (That's Fresh Kill, to those in the technish know) was at ninety percent, thus the contamination she could pass on to a prospective victim was equally toxic. If she Hit and Bit someone, *anyone*, they'd Go Over within an hour, unless immediate treatment was administered. As for the girl herself ... she was Dead Meat at the end of the day, poor dear. *Nada* that anyone could do for her. End of story, life's a bitch and then you're Staked.

It just so happened, however, that Mrs. Nelson Pitts' dumbest eldest son, Richard Bartholomew Pitts (that's me) had been that Someone/Anyone that the Fresh Kill would hit that night.

I didn't even see her coming. Usually, I'm on guard, even after the shift. Old habit from my days in Homicide when all we had to worry about were *human* monsters. Before the new century, before a time when the planet decided to support fun and feisty new forms of life, like Nosferatus, Lyckenthropes and Demonicus Smellicus. So, there I was, tired and looking forward to home and hearth after a hellish day of a Staker down in Compton, a Lycker collar outside of Cantor's deli on Fairfax, and a flying Homunculus decapitation (which, as you can imagine, really takes the wind out of you. I had wing-burn after that one, and believe you me, that kind of thing smarts.)

In retrospect, the girl wasn't that fast — I was just careless. Must be getting old. She had been lurking near the telephone booths, near the south alley; if memory serves me, she looked to me like an average young woman of twenty-one, probably doing some late night, if ill advised, shopping. I had just punched out of MV, tired, my mind on milk for the cat, as well as some much needed Jack Daniels to take the edge off the day. There had been other shoppers, mainly single guys like me -- guys with no wife at home, no respectable profession by the light of day, no other better thing to be doing at almost two a.m. in the morning. As an MV Inspector to the Rampart Division, I qualified as the aforementioned kind of late night, wandering Mug With No Life. I assumed this was the case with the girl, albeit she *was* female, unlike the majority of other Ralph's patrons that night. I assumed she was an anomaly, a nice gal by herself, picking up a few things at the local grocer, perhaps a little too late if prudence had its way. In other words, I assumed nothing strange.

More fool I.

She was on me within seconds, biting hard, sucking, wolfing down my blood like a puppy going for a chew-toy. It all took less than a minute. She was strong (they all were after the "Suck and

Screw" festivities generously dispensed by your basic vampire -- a term we came up with at PD that was perfectly accurate. Let's face it, after you were Sucked, you were generally Screwed thereafter, permanently, end of story, go sweetly into the night, you poor bastard) and I was tired. Not only that, but a Fresh Kill is imbued with ten times normal strength once dead and awakened.

At the end of the S&S, I was lying face down in a pool of my own red, feeling like the Undead proper. Lucky for me that a few off-duty Blues found me; the FK snarled at them, warning them away. Mistake. And typical of an FK's lack of practical experience once reanimated. Not her lucky night in general, because one of the Blues, a big guy by the name of Winston Mustafa Delecroix had gone through MV training six months earlier, and thus was Stake Qualified. He nailed her fast with a blessed two-by-four standing upright in a nearby trasher.

Lucky he had his pocketsize St. James version on hand.

The Feeder, once impaled, steamed, screamed, then melted in a few seconds — typical catalytic response to a Two Points, Slam Dunk, Stake-In Plug. I owed Winston. The FK was about to come back for seconds just as Delacroix and the others arrived. Had that happened, my blood wasn't the only thing she would have sucked...

Anyway, I was transported to Vermont Presbyterian, examined and assessed — it was too late for conventional treatment, an injection of Holy Water and 1000 ccs of Bioxypenicillan. Thus, I was what they euphemistically referred to as a Trooper Gone Home. In other words, I was a virtual Changeover, and would probably have to be terminated within twelve hours. Rampart was notified, along with my partner, Hanson, who shed a bitter tear. I was lying there on the hospital gurney, contemplating eating Stake, when suddenly my final blood specs came back with some very favorable numbers.

I was eligible for the Tungsten Maneuver. Treatment would be lifelong in terms of administration and if I missed a day, I would probably go into Change-Mode, posthaste, within the hour.

Which brings me to my current dilemma, the one about being in dire jeopardy of losing my life and immortal soul.

See, the Tungsten Maneuver was not really anything more than a discovery by the brilliant biochemist, DeLion Tungsten, three months into the monster infestation. He learned that the only way to stop the Tuti-toxic effects of vampiric transformation, in immediate victims, i.e., those "just sucked" was to generate a massive flow of brain neurochemical responses involving something called prolactin. Through flushing the entire endocrinal system with prolactin, which gives rise to a chain reaction of other meaningful brain activity, a good dose of this biochemical manna from heaven neutralizes for a 24 hour duration, the Tuti-toxic cellular bite-factor infection. Alright, you ask: How do you generate sufficient levels of prolactin to ensure you don't turn into a vampire?

Answer, sports fans, and don't touch that bat channel, lest you miss the magic: The only sufficient biochemical response to Tuti-Transformation is by induced sexual ejaculation (women don't clearly need to ejaculate, but orgasmic climax guarantees prolactin intervention, and this is a very fortunate thing for the gentle sex, believe you me). [1]

---

[1]   The aforementioned anti-vampire manna from heaven, Prolactin, is a typical neuroendocrine response originating in the cerebrocortical areas of the hypothalamus, thalamus, caudate nucleus, and inferior and superior temporal gyri.

Brain mechanisms that control human sexual behavior in general, and ejaculation in particular, are poorly understood. Positron emission tomography was used to measure increases in regional cerebral blood flow (rCBF) during ejaculation in heterosexual male volunteers. Manual penile stimulation was performed by the volunteer's female partner. Primary activation was found in the mesodiencephalic transition zone, including the ventral tegmental area, which is involved in a wide variety of rewarding behaviors. Parallels are

That's right. The "P Response" can only be activated by sexual stimulation, originating of course in the brain, and concluding, naturally, in one's nether regions, explosively and with predictable short-term finality. Let me translate that another way: for the rest of my life, it will be necessary for me to have at least one orgasm a day. Kind of like the need for you to have an apple, just to keep the doctor away. If I miss my Wad Moment, I'm as good as Stake Food for anyone of my associates at Monster Vice.[2]

Since my girl left six months ago, I take care of this basic need myself. Even when I don't feel like it. I turn 43 in a week ... I hope my desire doesn't diminish with middle age. I'd be in trouble then.

---

drawn between ejaculation and a 'man, oh, man, am I fucked up on a cool heroin rush" kinda feeling. No one knows why.

[2]   Orgasm, in case your alien leaders have not informed you thus, is the conclusion of the plateau phase of the sexual response cycle, shared by both men and women. During orgasm, both men and women experience quick cycles of muscle contraction in the lower pelvic muscles, which surround both the anus and the primary sexual organs. Orgasms in both men and women are often associated with other involuntary actions, including vocalizations and muscular spasms in other areas of the body. Also, a generally euphoric sensation is associated with orgasm. Sometimes orgasm results in little screaming creatures called babies, whose primary function in the first year of life is to defecate on everything imaginable, and turn your fond memories of orgasm into a sublimely tortuous recollection involving a series of god-awful bad decisions for which you will pay dearly for the rest of your meaningless little life. Along those lines, orgasm can lead to divorce (preceded by marriage of course – or not), and cost some poor male his house, his financial accumulation and his sanity.

Why the gods decided to tease Mankind with the need to 'spooge oneself silly' in order to survive a vampire attack and subsequent infection, is anyone's guess. Certain police officers embrace a philosophy that perhaps god(s) is a sadistic pervert that would always like to have a guy, once bitten, continuously walk that precarious line of agony and ecstasy, just to watch him squirm like a worm in a bait box with having to remember daily to beat-off to survive and not go Tuti.

Which brings me back to my current dilemma.

I've gone the whole day without Spanking Monkey Meat. Okay, fine, laugh — to your average teen-age kid with a four-inch boner, it's damn amusing. But for me, it's a daily necessity. Strike that — it's a spiritual and physical imperative.

As we head off of the 4th Street exit, making the slow semicircle into the deserted downtown area, my mind wanders on a most critical question: When will I have time to Bat the Baby and get that Prolactin flushed through my system. I was already two hours late — I try and initiate my Beat-Off ritual at precisely the same time, day in and day out. I like to stay regular, so to speak.

I chide myself for my delinquency today. Now, going into a 209 Multiple Fang Detail, I am in danger of possibly joining the opposition if I don't shoot my requisite load at least before midnight.

I hate Fang Detail.

As I contemplate the issue of my mandatory Choke The Chicken session (don't ask when, don't ask where!), we arrive to the Call In All Alerts Location. Three black and whites are already there, minus driver and partner. So far, it's just Hanson and myself. Not good.

We look miserably at the warehouse before us. The SWAT choppers are nowhere to be seen as yet. The heretofore mentioned backup was ominously absent. The bad feeling tingling on the short hairs of my gonads is palpable, visceral. I look to Hanson, the back of my mind spinning with images of sugarplums and last month's issue of Playboy's Lingerie Teen-Tigress Special. The impelling urge, you see, to Whack Winkie has still not diminished, and forget about the fact that we may very well be fodder for Nosferatu in the next few moments.

"We should go in," he says, about as enthusiastic as a cobra contemplating swing dancing with a herd of mongooses.

"I got a bad feeling about this," I mutter, glancing at my K-Mart Rolex look-alike watch that tells me the time in Zaire and the theoretical surface temperature on Venus.

"Back-up should be here any minute," Hanson says, stalling for time.

"Yeah, but the Call was a Distress, and it's five minutes old. There's a chance someone is still alive in there," I say ruefully. Not strictly true — I lay better odds of Jerking Off using the Force, with no hands, then seeing anyone still breathing and un-Bit. Still, that's what we do: We're the few, the proud, Fang Cops of Monster Vice.

"Okay, we go in," Hanson says, reaching for his stakes and pump-action .48 repeater.

We exit our '99 Mercury Sedan — a piece-o'-shit hand me down from Homicide that we're forced to use due to cutbacks on every departmental level. We hear no screams, no howls, no characteristic and anticipated preternatural hiss from any Tutis, either from high above, or street level. For this relief, much thanks. It tells us one thing certain: The Bloodsuckers have opted to remain inside, versus take to the streets. They realize that Monster Vice will converge on this spot shortly, in its damn near entirety; better odds at conducting tactical maneuvers from within the dark, nefarious interior than deal with an army on the outside. Better for us, too. If we keep the Tutis contained, here, now, there's a chance we can wipe out this multiple infestation in one fell swoop.

Down side, of course, is that it's kinda like going inside the hive of a bunch of really nasty hornets. Still, public safety is first and foremost. To protect and to serve.

I glance at my watch again. I've got eleven thirty on the dot. I'm pushing it in terms of Boner Blast-off. I'm on the edge tonight. I hope we wrap this up, right quick. Else I might have to excuse myself, mid-siege, and take care of business in the damn car. I wonder if I should share this with Hanson, but decide against it. Tension is already high.

We move like a single unit for the main entrance, which we see, to our great consternation, is partially open. Probably left so by the other four cops that no doubt already entered for prelim Intel. I tap my communications link-up.

"Units four and six, this is MV-12, on the perimeter," I say, in a half whisper. "You guys okay in there?"

No answer. Not good.

"I repeat, four and six, this is Monster Vice, number 12, On Station, come in," I repeated fervently.

Hanson stops. So do I. We listen. Nothing.

"They're dead," he says and I tend to agree.

Somewhere, distantly, I hear the tak-tak-tak of the SWAT choppers moving in on our position. A rotating swathe of light suddenly appears, as Miller and Brokowsky in car five, screech around the corner. They're young, been in Vice now for about a month, full of piss and shitting steel to kill as may Tutis and Lyckers they can shake a Stake at. So far, they've collared some Corpse Eaters and a few Reanimators, but that's it.

This will be their first Fang Detail.

Regis and Kellerman (the latter a rather fine piece of female police officer I would have no objections indoctrinating into the fine art of Tellerman's Maneuver) arrive next, quieter, without the fanfare of the two youngsters parking next to our POS Sedan.

All officers exit their vehicles, and flank us, standing operating procedure for Siege Assault.

Everyone looks to me. I'm the oldest guy in Vice. The Senior Honcho. Hansen, with a gut the size of Rhode Island courtesy of Burger King and Anheuser Busch looks ten years my senior, but he won't see 42 for another three months.

As it turns out, after tonight, he won't see 42 at all.

The SWAT choppers hover overhead, looking to me for some kind of signal. I again gaze at the entrance looming before me, an abyss of horror, a chasm of certain death and fates worse than death.

Seven minutes have passed since Monster Vice got the 666 call.

Someone may still (conceivably, unbelievably) be alive in this warehouse. Frightened, hiding, fearful and rightfully so, of things that should exist only in nightmares, but now have been translated into bloodsucking reality. A security guard, perhaps, some poor stray cleaning lady, maybe a kid ... having the bad luck or poor judgment to be in the wrong place, at the wrong time, when the herd of Tutis decided to wing in and set up shop.

It's eleven thirty seven, and I have twenty minutes within which to safely secure this location and Shoot My Load, lest I transform into one of the enemy and turn everyone's night into Shit On A Bloody Stick.

"It's time," I say with false conviction. "Hanson, on my right, everyone else, on rear point. Let's go Stake some Fangs."

CHAPTER THREE

▼

I sound braver than I feel.

When I was younger, when the world was sane, when I dealt with mere mortal men and women who also happened to be murderers, deviants and/or sexual predators, I seemed to possess more intestinal fortitude. I had no equal, I was A Number One, Captain Courageous. Compared to me, Dirty Harry was a girlie-man, Tofu-eating fairy, whining for his .44. Han Solo was a space faring pansy who secretly mated with Chewey when he wasn't running away from the mean old Empire. And John Wayne -- well, he was nothing more than a limp-wristed, bow-legged, horse-buggering cross-dresser who sat to pee.

You get the picture -- these guys couldn't touch me in the Balls department. I could eat them all for breakfast.

I was Tops.

I was He Who Knew No Fear.

I was Big Dog of LAPD Homicide — youngest, hottest Inspector on the block. I had thirty collars under my belt by New Years 24 months ago and had four silver stars (with cluster) from the Mayor of Los Angeles for Courage Under Fire. Lightning shot out of my ass when I walked the streets; women dreamed of me, men yearned to be cloned after my likeness.

I was a Star.

And then the world changed. The Popov Meteor Shower ended the party a little over two years ago. Twenty-four hours of atmospheric pyrotechnics, coupled with a bizarro solar flare, and the next morning, The Dead Walked. Vampires came out of nowhere, sucking whole populations dead, thus creating other vampires, Fresh Kills that murdered and plundered without purpose. Werewolves, once a Lon Chaney chuckle on Late Nite USA, stormed the land, literally "wolfing" down the good people of America (and abroad). These were the New Killers (Osama was history), The Most Recent Bad Boys On The Block, and conventional law enforcement was at first hamstrung by the epidemic and overwhelming tide of supernatural evil that cloaked the globe like a shroud. The lesser evils followed; Demons from Hell, Walking Corpses, Ghouls, and others — but none were so vile, so directly a threat to human existence, as the Nosferatu (Tutis) and the Lycanthropes (Lyckers). The Tuti/Lyckers killed indiscriminately and for pleasure, as much as for survival. Later, as the Tutis fed, their collective intelligence soared, making them the most dangerous life form on Earth.

Now, in every city on the planet, local law enforcement, state and federal protection agencies have special divisions to deal with the Monster Situation, which has become a globally endemic nightmare. In the beginning, it was generally thought that Armageddon had arrived -- the end of all Mankind.

I didn't share that notion. Not at first.

I was a King. I was Super Dick. Six feet of Bad-Ass Kicking Hell on Two Feet. I moved from Homicide into Monster Vice with the speed of an ICBM full-tilt boogey for its primary target, still possessed of the old one-two, simply ready to kick a different kind of Bad Guy's ass. I called the Monster Bluff, and I called it loud: Look out Nosferatu, Dick Pitts is your new nightmare in town. And as for you, Lycker slobbering bastards, well ... the Wolf-Bullshit is over, finished and done with. The drool stops here.

That was then. This is now.

My bravado has been tempered by time, experience and personal tragedy. I have been Bit, and I have gazed into the Maw of Evil. My very life, my very continuance as a human being, is contingent on the timely effectiveness (and sometimes, imaginative technique) of Swat The Salami, a critical function to be performed every twenty-four hours before midnight. I have lost friends and associates on the battlefield of this new kind of campaign against the Undead. It is a war we are losing, albeit slowly, and the knowledge troubles me to the core.

I am a soldier.

But I no longer feel brave.

And on occasion, after a particularly bad night of Fang Detail, I sit to pee.

There was a time I would say proudly: I am Homicide.

But now, I am Monster Vice. And Monster Vice is my home, the last bastion of personal sanity, a sanctuary of work and purpose. I fight the good fight. But I do so with fear in my heart.

I enter the warehouse and my blood freezes.

Like my need to Flog Little Freddie, not for the first time.

*   *   *   *

The Fangs throw four Fresh Kills at us right off.

The four cops, in fact, that had arrived On Station first. They're pretty well gnawed, insane from the death experience and the re-animation - an inevitable curse to being fed on by Nosferatu. The poor bastards don't have a soul anymore; they are starved chunks of cold vicious meat, fueled by a mysterious cosmic evil that defies conventional science, Newtonian physics and any kind of basic Cartesian reality. Their eyes are balls of wide, bloodshot jelly, inflamed in the sockets; their torn throats, replete with hanging shards of chewed flesh and severed arteries, dangle pitifully as they charge us. Their smell is the most offensive, the galvanizingly worst part of this whole insanity. Once Bit, the Fresh Kills issue an ammonia-based gas, pungent with the commingled odors of sulfur dioxide and glucose. It's one big Shit-O-Rama in here — and on top of it all, I've got an inexplicable standing erection. Probably my close proximity to Kellerman, who I have (forgive the crass colloquialism) wanted to bone from Day One.

Thoughts of coupling with Kellerman are dashed in a microsecond as one of the Fresh Kills tackles her from the right, slashing her throat with his newly grown two inch incisors. I cry for her pain, I cry in fury; we're two feet in the door, and already sustaining unacceptable casualties.

"Lay down a suppressing fire, ASAP!" I yell, hoping my people are together enough to follow orders.

I fire into one of the Fresh Kills, aiming for the head. My aim is good and true, and brains paint the wall nearest me. Hanson has taken out another FK, while the two rookies deal with the remaining lot. I call into the SWAT Unit overhead.

"Officer down. We need Medical Evac," I yell, as another sound begins to drown out my own voice. A sound that fills all of us with a deep terror, a primal terror that defies experience and time in the Kill Zone of Combat.

The hiss. The chilling whine of things with no pulse, and teeth the length of my dick. We don't see them yet, but they are here. Around us. Not just two, three or four. No, we sense Multiples, taken to the next exponential level of fun and horror, courtesy of Popov's Meteor Extravaganza two years back.

"Heads up," I call out, though the warning is superfluous. Everyone is frosty, on the watch. I continue to hold Kellerman's head in my hands, as she stares at me in astonishment and pain. Regis, her partner, gazes at me with an uncharacteristically dull, bovine and hopeful expression on his face ... as if perhaps I held the power to Eternal Life in my palms. I return the helpless gaze, and a moment later, as if to confirm my painful inadequacy as God Almighty, Kellerman dies. The physical damage is too great to hope for any kind of treatment; her carotid and jugular veins are masticated cords of useless tissue. Blood cascades out of her body like the Great Niagara. Death is a certainty. Yet with this in mind, I take one of my stakes and make the sign of the cross. Regis makes a sound reminiscent of a whimper, then takes a step back.

I drive my Stake into Kellerman's heart. Her eyes open suddenly, and they are no longer the eyes of a human being. Nor is the scream that explodes from her mouth, further chilling my blood, and by the way, shrinking my ten-dollar Hard-On of moments before into a frightened little pup that's gone to hide. I'll have to lure that bad boy out with crackers later and the thought reminds me that I have a deadline to Pound Porky, lest I become one of Legion with a peckish hankering for human plasma.

I despair as Kellerman dies (again). Her protestations at my stake sticking out of her chest, like some erstwhile new appendage that astonishes her, are minimal. She jerks and jolts beneath my grip, attempting a feeble paw at my hands, but that is all. Another moment, and there is only a shudder and a rattle, then nothing. Kellerman is gone. I will flirt with her nor more in the halls of Rampart's Monster Vice. I will lust no more after that splendid body nor dream of a candlelight dinner with her on some nameless night in a brighter future. Rather, I will weep when I think of the beautiful young officer on this most horrible of nights.

"Dick," Hanson calls out to me. "I make two, maybe three Tutis on the upper level. We gotta move, buddy."

There are tears in my eyes, and I wipe them clean. I look to Hanson, and he nods. Pure, unabashed empathy stares back at me. There is no shame in weeping for a fallen comrade, a doomed officer, a friend. We cry openly in Monster Vice, as do we drink, smoke, shoot up if necessary. It's not strictly By The Book, but IA never quips on us about that.

They know what we do.

And what we deal with.

"Everyone else clean?" I ask, hoping the answer is in the affirmative.

My people nod. No one is Bit. Not even a scratch.
Only Kellerman.

I hate Fang Detail. Really.

"Let's move out," I say tonelessly.

I have fifteen minutes before Masturbation Mania.
Wonder if I'll make it.

$$\ast \quad \ast \quad \ast \quad \ast$$

Our comlinks crackle. Dispatch notifies us that we have
substantial backup out front, also in the rear. The warehouse
is completely surrounded. Nothing leaves unless it flies — and
if one of the Tutis even tries to "bat out" the SWAT choppers
would torch it. We ostensibly have our bloodsucking friends
outnumbered twenty to one ... assuming, of course, there are
only three or four of them hiding here inside. Vampires don't
travel in huge groups, a single nest of them never exceeding half
a dozen.

Three or four is enough, believe me. Six months back in
Macy's, one vampire killed five Monster Vice officers inside of
five minutes. I feel my hand tighten on my Stakes, remembering
the carnage well. I was the only survivor that night.

The rookies finish staking the remaining Fresh Kills that
attacked us. I listen to the accompanying hiss and gurgle of
vampire disintegration, wondering vaguely, from someplace far
away, how I came to be in such a grizzly line of work.

A shadow moves on an upper level, and my attention snaps to
the blur of motion. I then begin to hear hissing. Coming from
nigh on above us.

"Somebody's home," Hanson mutters, eyes focused
upwards.

I nod, then look to the remaining three officers in back of
Hanson.

"Let's spread out, people," I say in a low whisper. "Watch
your necks." MV humor. Ha, ha, ha. No one laughs.

I then see the green stream of iridescent smoke tendril out from around a corner on the level above us. It moves as if it is alive, probing, thinking, understanding. I know what it is, so does Hanson.

"Oh, Jesus," he mutters and I shudder, truly fucking petrified.

"What is it?" one of the rookies ask, fascinated by the twinkling mass of steam.

"It's a Master," I say, choking on the last word.

One of the rookies is familiar with the term. He stops in his tracks, looks at me, courage and bravado draining out of his face. "Maybe we should withdraw and just level the place."

The idea is appealing to me. One good Comp B incendiary bomb, and everything for a square block roasts for half an hour. I know it is not realistically an option. Whoever made the Monster Vice call may still be in here, alive, in need of our help. The ominous green contrail continues to snake downward.

"What's a Master?" the other rookie presses.

"Master Vampire," I say quickly. "A shape changer. He can move through walls, become any animal he pleases. And he has the strength of a baby dinosaur."

Hanson has already pulled a Stake. "This could get ugly."

I say nothing. Whenever a Monster Vice team has confronted a Master Vampire in the past ... that squad has been wiped out to a man. Our best recourse would be to run now, before the Master has a chance to reincorporate into solid form. Still, standing orders, even with Masters, are clear: Kill, kill, kill. We look above, and see three Tutis, hovering together, snarling at us. Females. The Master's harem. I again wonder who made the initial Distress call to MV.

The serpentine stream of smoke — the supernatural essence of the Master Vampire — continues to rove deliberately down the staircase. Leisurely, without hurry.

"Don't fire until he forms completely," I advise.

I glance at the rookies, their eyes blazing with the thrill of an impending kill. Regis, eyes tear stained from the loss of his partner, Kellerman, looks to me and swallows hard. Hanson's eyes remain fixed on the hypnotically fascinating smoke stream of the discorporated Master Vampire.

I glance at my watch. I have five minutes to kill a Master Vampire, along with his snarling entourage of bloodsucking bitches upstairs, then find a nice corner someplace to beat off. I am not overly optimistic about being able to accomplish these tasks in that time frame.

The smoke stream stops about ten feet away. It begins to fluctuate in place, expanding, contracting, pulsating.

"Here he comes," Hanson announces, fury in his voice.

I bark commands. "Cartwright, you and Regis watch the stairs. The girls may want to come down and help."

Cartwright is one of the rookies, and he looks disappointed. Clearly, he wanted a shot at the Master. But he's a fine young officer and doesn't hesitate in following orders. He and Regis move close to the base of the stairs, glancing up at the females, who gesticulate wildly with claws fully extended. This means that it's me, Jennings (the other rookie), and Hanson who will take on Old Smokey.

Things happen quickly and tragically.

The Master Vampire's transformation finishes sooner than I anticipated. He's enormous, standing six foot nine and easily weighing four hundred pounds on the hoof. Wingspan is twenty feet, easy, maybe more. He doesn't wait to study his surroundings. Hanson fires first, his pump-action repeater rifle blazing. The Master takes three good slugs in the chest, and is lifted bodily off the ground and slammed into the nearest wall. Which is where, unfortunately for them, Jennings and Cartwright are positioned. The Master Vampire lands hard, and without missing a beat, slashes outward, his arm almost mystically extending beyond the limits of its socket. The move disembowels Cartwright, as he sinks to his knees, suddenly finding his hands filled with his own intestines. A mask of gray agony covers his face, his mouth open in a silent scream. In the same motion, Regis's head is severed from his body. It flies through the air and lands at my feet. Regis' mouth and eyes still move, and I realize horribly that his brain remains alive, so instantaneous is the decapitation. His eyes tell me that he's afraid and astonished. Is this really happening? the eyes seem to say.

I fire the .357, hitting the Master in each infernal eye. The Master screams, blinded, but he is on his feet again, bearing down on Jennings, who now opens fire with his own 9 Millimeter, screaming in fury. Each bullet has been blessed, and steam hisses out of the Master's gut with each impact, but it does not slow him down. Sensing Jennings' close proximity, the Master lunges blindly forward, tackling Jennings. Vampire and man hit the floor rolling.

The Master takes Jennings by the chest and groin and tears him in half. Jennings' screams echo through the warehouse interior, as flesh and internal organs fly out at us. Cartwright, distracted by his own essence slipping out of his body, sits in a yoga position, trying vainly to shove several feet of his small intestine back into a massive cavity that has sprouted from his midsection.

I run and dive onto the Master's back, driving a Stake into his skull. The Master screams, dropping Jennings from two massive claws. He tries to slash at me, but I dodge the claw, already driving my second stake into the Master's back.

Hanson comes around the front, driving a stake into the approximate location of the monster's heart. Damn near hits it, too, except damn near isn't good enough with a Master. Hanson reaches for a second stake. The Master throws me off his back and I am suddenly flying (look, Ma, no hands!), ass over tea-cups, landing ten yards on the other side of the room. I'm not hurt so much as terrified for my partner Hanson, who now faces the Master alone.

Blinded, furious, in agony, the Master slashes wildly at Hanson. But Hanson, fat loveable fool that he is, manages to sidestep every attack and even manages to drive in a second stake. The blow is fatal, hitting the Master's heart dead on. The Master screams and pitches forward, disintegrating a second later.

I am almost beside myself with glee and don't mind of course that Hanson will win the Christmas pool for Stake and Plug number fifty-five. He looks at me and winks, covered in goo and blood. My smile fades abruptly. Good reason.

We have both forgotten something.

The other vampires.

I'm on my feet, yelling: "Behind you!"

Hanson realizes what I'm saying a split second after my smile turns to a grimace. He turns. The three bitch-suckers descend on him en masse. Hanson doesn't have time to scream. My .357 becomes a living, breathing Angel of Death. I fire into the throng of writhing, chewing evil. The vampires scream in pain and fury. One turns toward me, lunges. I Stake her on the fly and she screams, dissolving in mid-air.

Other Monster Vice officers come running toward Hanson and the two remaining vampires. I get there first, dragging one bitch by the hair, off of Hanson's neck. She snaps her head toward me and spits a wad of blood into my eyes. I see only red, and she thinks she has me. She then looks down at her chest, as one of my Stakes drives deep. She dissolves and steams in my arms, and I scream in pain, as the acid-like dissolution of her demise burns through my body armor. I tear off the melting armor, praying that the corrosive blood and flesh of the vampire doesn't beat me to the punch and eat into my arms. I beat the clock. The last vampire, the smallest, is backed into a corner by a dozen officers. The Stakes come out and I only hear screams, as the beast is impaled repeatedly.

Hanson is at my feet, his eyes meeting mine. He has been bitten, but more than that, his chest has been torn open. His heart, now almost fully exposed, beats outside of his body, a torn, bludgeoned muscle that pumps desperately. Hanson is not yet dead, but his death is a certainty.

Amazingly, he can still talk.

"Time — to move on, pardner," he quips, coughing blood.

"Fuck you," I say without inflection. I turn and scream out into the darkness. "Medic!"

He reaches for me with an arm partially chewed off. His hand grips my shoulder. I see that three fingers are gone.

"We — just made history tonight," he whispers.

I know what me means. We've defeated a Master Vampire.

"You're — gonna be famous," he says, coughing again. He's right. I am, again, the only survivor to madness.

I try to smile. I realize I am crying again.

Hanson looks sleepy. He takes one big breath, then looks at me with big, rheumy eyes that bespeak volumes of sadness. "You do it, pardner. No one else, okay?"

I nod. "Sure."

He dies a second later. There is a smile on his lips.

I keep my promise and remove the last Stake in my possession. By this time, the second unit Monster Vice officers have finished with the remaining vampire and now all stare at me. I recognize Bollino, Tippet, Clark a few others. Sirens wail outside and I hear the SWAT choppers landing on the roof.

I drive the Stake deep into Hanson's fully exposed heart. His eyes burst open, the red horror of Take Over crimson and staring at me with hate, but I understand that this is no longer Hanson. What stares at me is something from Beyond, a force of maniacal evil that will never know the joy of murder and mayhem. Not in this body, anyway.

I stand and watch Hanson disintegrate. I am reminded that I have one final duty to perform tonight and check my watch.

One minute to midnight.

Wordlessly, I walk past my fellow officers and exit the warehouse. I pass through the throng of other Monster Vice soldiers milling about outside, and turn the corner, disappearing into an alley. All eyes are on me, a thousand questions begging to be asked from fellow colleagues. Yet they give me room and time, seeing that I need to be alone. Presumably to deal with the loss of so many comrades. A moment of silence, time to grieve.

The alley is dark, clammy, foreboding, but I am not disturbed. I unzip my trousers and take out the angry python that is my prick and begin the soulful session of jerk, jerk, jerk.

When I come, I find that I can hardly breathe.

It takes me a second to realize that I have been sobbing uncontrollably.

I have fought the good fight.

I have lost my partner and friend.

I hate Fang Detail now more than ever.

I look at the pitiful wad of spunk in my hand. I have forestalled, for one more day at least, the danger of my own embrace with vampirism. I flick off Old Faithful and put him back into the cage. I look up into the night and see the moon, staring down at me, an uncaring, unconscious ball of light — the only witness to my session of Shuck The Sausage.

It has been a bad, crazy night.

I close my eyes, hoping that when I open them, this has all been a dream.

Something moves directly behind me. I turn, my .357 out, pointed and cocked.

"Please, mister. Don't shoot," a voice calls out from the darkness.

"Who's there?" I growl.

A grate moves in the shadows, then falls to the ground. It is a vent grate on the warehouse wall. A form of a female crawls out. She is limping, her arms in the air.

"Please don't shoot me," she says again.

My gun does not lower. The girl comes into the light, a combination luminosity from a lone street light and the moon blaring down. I see that she is around twenty five years old, black, pretty, yet disheveled. Her dress has been torn, shredded more accurately, and there is blood on her arms and legs.

"Who are you?" I ask.

The girl looks at me for a moment, her face a blank, as if the question just asked was one that applied to differential calculus. Then she brightens, nodding.

"Mona," she said. "I'm Mona."

My gun lowers, and her arms come down, though a hand comes up to her neck. Something is irritating her there, or causing pain.

"Are they gone?" she asks me.

I am not as sharp as I should be. "Who?"

"The vampires," she says and I see her visibly shudder. Her neck continues to bother her, and I suddenly put together an unpleasant equation.

"Yes. They're dead. What's wrong with your neck?"

She begins to cry. Only one word comes out. "Bit."

I step forward. She steps back, eyeing me warily, or more specifically, the monster gun I still clutch. I replace the pistol, then gently take her hand away from the afflicted area on her neck. As I fear, and as she has already affirmed, she has indeed by bitten. I am immediately baffled by the very slight severity of bite; more baffled by the girl's appearance, which aside from evidencing a bloody struggle of sorts, is not representative of a full on Tuti attack.

Something about her made the Tuti stop feeding.

"Why were you doing that?" she suddenly asked.

"I needed to see how badly you were attacked," I answered, assuming she meant my examination of her wound.

"No, I mean the other thing," she said.

I am again foggy. My mind is not exactly going at warp speed. She takes her hand and mimes my act of masturbation. I realize that she has been a percipient witness to my ejaculatory campaign against vampirism. I am instantly humiliated and embarrassed, depantsed on every conceivable level.

"You — saw me?" I groan.

"Didn't mean to stare, but you don't see a cop do that every day. Not in a back alley, anyway."

Oh, come now, I found myself fencing with her mentally. *We butch cops always whack off in dark alleys, and at the oddest times. It's a man-thing, dear, you wouldn't understand.*

I close my eyes, fighting for composure. Okay, she saw me Spurt-Slush Myself Silly in the dark. Big deal. There were bigger fish to fry at the moment. The girl needed treatment, and fast.

"I have to get you to a hospital," I said, reaching for her arm. She allowed me this and walked beside me quietly for a second.

"I didn't mean to stare," she said. "I was just trying to hide from them and the only place I thought they'd never get me was in that vent."

"Smart," I say and mean it.

"You sure got here fast," she said.

I stop, look at her. "You're the one."

She stares, again blankly.

"You called Monster Vice, right?"

She nods, understanding. "There's a payphone inside."

"What were you doing in there anyway?"

Mona looks down and begins to cry. "My husband and I got into a fight. Tonight he hit me. I left him. I ain't going back, either."

She sniffs, and we begin walking again. The lights from the MV contingent just outside the alley illuminate everything in sight.

"I was just wandering. It got chilly so I came into this building. The door was open, I was only planning on staying a few minutes," she said. She looked at me with huge, tearful eyes. "Then they came."

"Well, they're dead now," I say comfortingly. I do not add that my partner and best friend is also among the deceased. The thought fills me instantly with a bone chilling depression. My prick tingles from the recent bout of Bangin' Bozo and I am sullen that my life has not turned out happier, after all is said and done.

"Pitts," a familiar face and voice hails me from the Monster Vice Crime Scene, now an army strong. It is Captain Zelig. He walks toward me, a human mountain of muscle and scar tissue; he looks angry. Correction, he *is* angry. I can't imagine why ... except that my entire platoon is now dead. Dozens of Forensic Vampire Specialists usher in and out of the warehouse, like drone ants on pre-selected missions, eyes either down on some critical piece of evidence linked to the most recent scenario of horror, or directly ahead, in search of a M.M.F.V (Mobile Monster Forensic Vehicle). On site analysis is standard operating procedure, and a good one, but tonight I wish everyone would just disappear.

"Goddamn it, Pitts," Zelig is snarling at me, eyeballing the girl next to me for about a micro second. "I am getting very tired of losing good people on these raids."

"No less am I," I reply elegantly, and with as little inflection as possible. This is my seventh such raid on Tutis; up until tonight, Hanson and myself had emerged relatively unscarred. That record is now held, of course, only by myself.

Zelig looks like he wants to spit poison at me, but then takes a breath, and looks at the warehouse. Bodybags are seen; my people, good officers, solid men and women. Flushed out of existence by supernatural sewage.

"Jesus," is all he can say.

I look to the girl. "This young lady needs DeCon, ASAP."

Zelig nods, then whistles to two Medi-Vac Techs. The girl looks to me, her eyes frightened. I know what she is thinking.

"Don't worry. They'll help you. And if they can't --"

"I don't want to be one of *them*," she says in a whisper.

I want to cry again (Dick Pitts, Prince of Homicide, Top Dog, One Time Crime busting King, now a little schoolgirl, whah, whah, whah). Must be hormonal, no doubt linked to my compulsory need to Pound the Pickle every twenty four hours.

"You won't turn," I say emphatically, though I do not know for sure if this is the case. I do however feel that her prognosis is pretty good; like myself, she'll have to commit herself to the rigorous daily regimen of cherotonin flush.

She reaches for my hand and holds it tight. The Med-Techs arrive, waiting patiently for our emotional moment to play through. They then lead her away from Zelig and myself, to an M.E. Van nearby. Zelig now turns to me, his eyes red, rheumy, tired.

"You ran into a Master," he says evenly.

"That's right," I reply. I look at my watch and see that it is quarter after midnight. I want to go home and drink my body weight in Jack Daniels. I want to mourn my partner. And my brother. I want to sleep.

"Mind if I get a report out of you tonight?" Zelig prompts.

"Tomorrow," I say. I refuse to go into the office. Won't do it, no way.

"I'd like you to meet your new partner," Zelig is persistent.

I am stunned that such a thought would be forthcoming from Zelig. He and Hanson went back through the years, graduating in the same class out of LAPD at the Academy. I came in through the Marine Corps a long time ago, bypassed the Academy, went directly into Tactical, then Homicide. Hanson and Zelig had gone the mile together.

"Hanson isn't even cold, Captain," I reply stonily. "Can't this wait?"

"Afraid not," Zelig's reply is near instantaneous. "I need coverage. Hanson would understand."

Sure, I think. Hanson probably would. But I'm tired, and not feeling all that understanding at the moment.

"My brother was killed tonight, Zelig. Add more fun to the festivities of just five minutes ago."

Zelig stares at me for a moment, then closes his eyes. He nods, whispers.

"Dick, I'm sorry."

"He was Lycker-bit. We'll talk more about it another time, okay?"

Zelig puts up a hand, nods once again. "Go home. Take some time. Be in my office at nine a.m. on Friday. Okay, buddy?"

"Okay," I say.

Zelig stomps off, muttering, the last phrase I hear going something like this: "Goddamn vampires. When's it gonna end?"

A Med-Vac approaches me, his face sheepish, almost embarrassed. I recognize him as one of the guys I just handed the girl Mona over to.

"Inspector Pitts," he calls out. "Thought you'd like to know, sir."

"Yeah?"

"The girl. She'll be fine," he says, genuinely happy. "We got her in time."

I nod. The price was high enough, I thought. Eight dead officers, my partner included.

"The attack looked atypical," I say, and the young Medic nods, as if this was the next item he had been planning to address before I beat him to the punch.

"Yeah, we saw that, too. There's a reason. Ran a blood gas analysis on her." He paused her for emphasis. "Kid's got Sickle Cell. Must have left a damn nasty taste in their mouths."

I am mildly bemused. Traditionally, vampires avoid humans with terminable blood conditions, and the fact that Mona is afflicted with Sickle Cell Anemia lends itself to a consistency in Tuti behavioral psychology. I wonder distantly if I should develop leukemia or hypoglycemia in the near future as a remedial deterrent to potential attack. I decide against these radical vampire defenses within seconds. My life is complicated enough, what with remembering to Placate Mr. Wriggles once a day.

"Thanks," I tell the young medic.

I turn and walk toward my sedan. I open the door, and get in, turning on the ignition. I cannot bear to look to the right, where I am accustomed to seeing Hanson, or at least hear him breathe (wheeze, was more like it, with the gut he was carrying). He will breathe and wheeze no more.

I am crying again.

Lately, it is what I do best.

That ... and survive.

CHAPTER FOUR

▼

Though it's been a pretty busy night thus far, and I've done my obligatory homage to massaging the old Trouser Mouse, my fatigue is dissipating, replaced instead by a kind of odd nervousness and disoriented high. This frustrates me, because I know in my heart that sleep is the best remedy for post-traumatic horror. My feelings are disparate, erratic, jumbled, an amalgam of sorrow, guilt, self-loathing and fear. I have survived the unsurvivable — a confrontation with a Master Vampire. Once again, I live, though others have died, horribly at that. A part of me feels invincible, my old self again, Big Dick Pitts of Homicide.

I listen to the cackle of multiple Dispatch and All Unit transmissions. My name is on every lip, in every precinct. The Big Show ended badly tonight, for both Monster Vice and Vampire alike, but Pitts again emerges unscathed. I will assume some kind of legendary status (again!), though at this point in my life and career, I will derive no joy from such acclamation. My friend and partner is dead tonight. Another victim, one of many. Hanson's death has shattered a previously held belief system, inviolate as long as he was alive, that somehow we were both blessed - that somehow, after all "this" was over, we'd look back at our days in MV and thank whatever guardian angels watched over us that we alone would survive the carnage of the age. I am inconsolable and feel the need to drink heavily.

And this comes as no small wonder, as I am reminded that I have also lost my brother this evening. Just one of those god-awful days that never seems to end.

So, rather than head for home and bed, I head down to the Morgue. One last duty to perform before I surrender to sleep and an oblivion hopefully devoid of dreams.

*   *   *   *

Because I am a decorated officer of Monster Vice, the rigmarole of beaurocratic machination is eliminated in terms of retrieving my brother's body. The forensic guys of course would love to cut him up, another specimen to study in the War Against Witchery, but I have pulled the necessary political strings and saved my brother's corpse the indignity of dissection and post-mortem skullduggery.

Thus, the funeral takes place the following day. Mindy, Bill's wife, holds my hand as I watch my brother's casket lowered into the ground. His two sons, Gary and Todd, twins of five years each, stand on my right side, their faces blank with non-comprehension. Bill – dad – is gone, this much they know, but that's all that's really understood in the Child's Big Picture of the moment. His will indicated that he wanted to be buried in his own churchyard. My brother had many friends and the ceremony is crowded with mourning parishioners.

Though my heart is filled with sorrow, I am thinking of other things at the moment. Mindy has indicated to me that Bill had remained in the church property that evening, to leave at dinner only for, in his words "a quick walk around the block." I tell her of course that he must have left church grounds at one point — a werewolf was unable to do anything on hallowed ground. Mindy assures me that Bill was at his desk in the rectory, probably when he had called me as well. But remembering his voice on that call – the agitation, the raspiness, the pain which it held – convinces me even now that Bill had made that call once already bitten by the Lycker. Which still does nothing to alleviate my overriding concern: For I am forced to entertain the notion that somewhere out there is a werewolf with no compunction to killing on hallowed ground. I do not see how this is logically possible; historically, werewolves and vampires simply cannot survive within a blessed environment.

As I have been given a few days off for bereavement, I take it upon myself to investigate the circumstances surrounding my brother's death. Mindy does not try to cling to me, nor keep me close by for comfort. She knows how I am – a kind of come and go guy, tarry not too long in any place for long. I say that will visit her and the kids in a few days, but that there is work to be done – work germane to Bill and his gruesome passing. Mindy tells me to go, and I do.

I ponder Bill's werewolf scenario in earnest, and try to dissect his case with professional detachment. So. If he was attacked, presumably near his church, then logic would dictate that the "biter" who got to him was local. Werewolves, unlike the Nosferatu, were not roving creatures, generally speaking. If they found a shelter that suited them over the course of weeks or months, generally they would not wander far, especially when it came to feeding.

I drove to the church, directly after the funeral, opting to skip the post-ceremonial festivities that Bill's wife was overseeing. I was never great at wakes. Instead, I thought I might have myself a little look-see around the neighborhood.

The church was surrounded by generally low-income tenements. Not much traffic to speak of ... and not a lot of activity on the streets. I tried to pick out potential "hot spots" for Lycker infestation, and found only one prime piece of property: an abandoned four story house at the end of the street, doors and windows boarded up, the gate padlocked to the gills.

As soon as I spotted the house, the back of my neck began to tingle. Now if that wasn't a Lycker stomping ground, then I didn't know dirt about werewolves.

I was about to act on a foolish impulse.

I was going to investigate the house, alone, without backup.

Unlike the Tutis, Lyckers could move about during the day. Which made my little piece of decision making presently all the more questionable. If I were to be cornered in that dump of a structure with a pissed-off Lycker, I could pretty well just kiss it all good-bye. My hope was, that if indeed there was a "biter" inside, I could find it napping, or off guard, and dispense with it quickly and antiseptically. A hope, anyway.

I took a peripheral glance around the area; no one was about, no kids, nada. Good. This could conceivably go by the numbers, and by the way, vengeance would be mine against the piece of shit wolf that killed my brother.

My thoughts returned to the night I was forced to put a bullet into Bill, and end his suffering. Yet born from that loathsome memory came other images from my past ... and questions as to what kind of future lay before me. How long could I, for instance, continue this existence? A career Monster Killer. Not a lot of promise for comfortable retirement, much less surviving another evening. Was it time to call it a day? Was it too late to try and find some meaning to my life? Get married, maybe ... have a kid or two. Step into the day rather than spend most of my waking hours in the dark, battling creatures that had no right to exist, yet <u>did</u> ...

I'm not generally predisposed to looking back – to analyze the decisions, right or wrong, that had brought me to this instant in time (i.e., a jaded Boogey Man Cop who had to Pound the Python 24/7 at least once a day). I tended to live in the present, dealing with immediate issues (usually, trying not to be eaten by something foul and evil), moving past those, and onto subsequent challenges. I was a creature of the moment, like the muse Terpsichore – a dancing blur of motion against an endless sea of activity that has no beginning and no end.

But sometimes ... just sometimes ... the questions loom high, like a huge wall of water approaching that you know can only drown you in sorrow and despair.

Boy, with thoughts like this flying about the ether, I don't envy the wolf running into *me* today. I'm in no mood.

The sun has suddenly disappeared behind a dense cloud cover. I look up and note that it is about to rain. Great. No umbrella, a heavy heart, and a werewolf just five minutes away, up the stairs, and god knows where. My mind went on its own private acid trip for a moment, recalling some lines from Omar Kayam.

A loaf of bread, a jug of wine, and thee.

My gun hand starts to shake – never a good sign. I thought I had rested sufficiently, but I realized this was good old American self-denial. I had drunk my body weight in whiskey since Bill died, and was still nurturing the proverbial Hangover from Hell. My mouth was dry, and tremors of paranoia seized every fiber anatomically possible.

What the fuck was I doing?! Go back, asshole. The fur-prick in that house is going vivisect you in a minute flat, rate you're going.

Ah, the sweet, rational voice of reason. But would I listen?

I cocked my piece.

I searched half-boarded windows for the glow of watching eyes. Even at the height of day, the eerie luminescence of the Lycker gaze could not be missed. But there was only blackness in and between those ancient planks. Which made my body temperature drop yet another point on the old Fahrenheit constant of 98.6.

My arms and legs ached, and between my badly tremulous grip on the Beretta and my fairly weak-kneed approach toward the house, I was almost beginning to believe that I was alcoholic. That perhaps to compensate for a life so unnatural, I had reconciled myself to the downward spiral of the doomed and drunk. Such cheerful philosophical ruminations came to an abrupt halt when I heard it.

A low, purring growl.

It was waiting for me, had probably seen me coming now these past five minutes.

Probably sending out Christmas cards to all the other wolfies in Wolfendom that a human finger sandwich had been delivered, real personal like, and with no need to tip the delivery boy. Food's a comin', kids. Drool freely.

Alright, I must stop this, I chide myself gently, as an unspecified twinge of pain seizes the right hand side of my stomach, slightly up, and just under the ribs. I wonder dimly if I'm slowly dying of cirrhosis, or some other suppurating disease that, in the great scheme of things, I probably rightfully deserve.

Another growl. I again shake uncontrollably, and this time I know that the genesis of these spasms are pure fear related. I give this a 9.5 on the Poop Your Pants scale of terror. And yet … I push on.

Why? Because Dick Pitts eats fear for lunch.

The front door now opens. Invitingly.

Come to mamma. Come on, cop-burger. It's grits and vittles time, with a dash of human brain and a healthy serving of human hemoglobin.

I surmise that the wolf is testing my mettle. Or my clear lack of an appreciable intelligence quotient – depending on what gets me through the door first.

The idea of turning, running back toward my car at a brisk sprint, taunts me with common sense and an inner voice that says: *Pitts, you dumb fuck, leave now. This is a no-win situation for you. Okay? Are you listening? Do you want me to translate it in the Cyrillic? Maybe hieroglyphics? Ancient Coptic?*

No need. I get it. Leaving would be a good move.

I kick the gate open and approach the door.

No more growls now. Just an eerie creak from the hinges, shifting slightly to and fro, as a breeze comes in from the north.

I approach the darkness. And then I do what any normal mental paraplegic would do under the circumstances.

I enter the house.

I expect some warning growls. Maybe even a growl of barely suppressed joy and triumph. Because, you see, after all, the wolf has me on its terrain. Sure, there's the fact that I have the gun, but really, when you get down to brass tacks, it's Wolf Team 10, Dick Pitts 0. And this is even before the first pitch is thrown.

I dig for courage deep within myself. I am an Alpha Dog. Leader of the pack. Head high, nose wet, my muzzle *not* sniffing another mutt's bung-hole because I couldn't hack it as Head Canine. No sir. I reminded myself who I was, what I had done of late.

And then the wolf howled.

I took a step back, my blood instantly turning to something as gently viscous as ice water. I run into the edge of the door, which, as luck would have it, slams shut behind me. A draft? The wind? Sure. And I've got a 24 inch schlong, and that's from the floor up.

My gun darts to all points on the compass. Right, left, in front of me, and up, toward the stairs. The light is bad in here, very bad. I squint into the fetid blackness, sniffing the residue of age and dry rot.

I feel that the Lycker is near.

Usually you can at least hear the fucks breathe, or gnash their teeth – twitchy, yet predictable, idiosyncrasies to being a werewolf. But this one is quiet, very quiet. So quiet you could hear a bird fart, and then, hear it echo.

"Foolish thing," a dreadful voice comes out of the dark.

I cannot, no shit, sports fans, believe what I am hearing.

Unless I am grossly mistaken, the wolf is actually *speaking* to me. You think that's strange?

But let me tell you why.

Werewolves *don't* talk.

"But very brave," the horrendous, raspy voice chortles.

I continue to have no more than a foot's clear visibility in any direction.

"Who are you?" I venture, and I hear my voice quaver.

"No one special." And I detect a note of wry amusement in its tone. "But I know who you are."

"Why don't you come out and show yourself?" I ask.

"Put your gun away, and I will," it says.

I almost chuckle at that.

"Yeah, that's gonna happen," I snort.

"I give you my word I won't attack you."

I think about this. When you get right down to the straight poop, had the wolf gone for a full-frontal attack, I would have been dead by now. Lyckers are exceptionally fast, with speeds exceeding that (and this is clocked) of a jaguar.

My fear has been subsumed by abject curiosity. I slowly replace my weapon in its holster. And wait.

Silence, at first. And then a dragging rustle from just under the massive staircase.

The eyes, of course, are the first visible evidence of the wolf's close proximity. They glow green and bright. Staring at me with a commingled sense of hate and ravenous desire. But there is intelligence beyond these particular eyes – a distinctly *human-like* patience that is highly disconcerting.

A list of possibilities automatically list themselves in my mind as to how a werewolf has achieved the power of speech. A mutant? A new form of advanced Lycker? The product of top-secret government experimentation? A rogue anomaly?

None of these scenarios strikes a chord of definitive truth in my soul.

No, this is something else.

This is something truly, fucking scary.

The wolf does me the unnecessary courtesy of keeping a respectful distance. It stops near the stairs, cocking its head toward me, fangs flashing at me with disturbing regularity.

I decide to open up the dialogue.

"You mind telling me how you can talk?" I ask.

The question has little interest for my furry friend, based on what he next says. "You are here because of your brother, n'est pas?"

And now it's speaking fucking French to me! I nearly soil myself where I stand. The Lycker isn't even playing hard to get.

"Yeah," I almost choke.

"You think I attacked him," the wolf continues to surmise with eerie confidence.

"Yep, that about sums it up."

"It was not me. It was the Grand Master."

And from some remote and distant place in my mind ... I believe the wolf. Moreover, I must continue to remind myself that this thing can kill me within a few seconds, and forget about all this pleasant banter. It has *chosen* to impart information to me. But why?

The answer is simple: complete fearlessness. It has nothing to lose.

Or ... it enjoys telling me something that is absolutely true, and stick it, Dick, if you don't like it.

And then the words begin to penetrate into the psyche.

The Grand Master?

"Who the hell is that?" I ask the Lycker, trying not to let my voice quaver and quake with each forced syllable.

The Lycker begins to laugh, a truly abhorrent thing to hear and witness, given it looks more like a large dog choking on food too hastily (forgive the pun) – *wolfed* down.

"He is who he is. He is bat, he is wolf, he is snake – he has no limitations on what he is or manifests. He is perfection personified," the Lycker says. And I gotta kind of hand it to the drooling fuckstick of a monster – it had a certain sense of poetic nuance.

"And this Grand Master killed my brother," I say again.

"Two nights ago," the wolf affirms. "In the church."

So my worse fears are confirmed: something out there, of the non-human persuasion, is able to exist and kill on holy ground. This is, my fellow fang-fighters, very bad news indeed.

"How is that possible?" I ask, feeling very much out of my league at the moment. "How can a vampire transform someone into a werewolf, and function on hallowed ground?"

"And how is it that I can speak?" the wolf replies. "A gift from the Grand Master. He has no limitations. And your hallowed ground security blanket … you can kiss that good bye, meat pie."

"Love to meet this big, bad Master of yours," I bait the Lycker.

It smiles back at me … an indulgent, almost benevolent expression in its eyes.

"You will. *Especially* you!"

"Why especially me?"

The wolf takes one step forward, and its grin is gone.

"You have killed so many of our kind. And *his!* He will extract his revenge against you slowly."

I also take a step forward, my patience dwindling.

"Your kind and his started this war. And you've murdered thousands."

"We have always fed off of you through the centuries. But there were so few of us … now … it is different."

I hold the Lycker's eyes in my gaze.

"Tell your Master I'll be waiting for him," I say, all fear suddenly drained away.

"And on that day, you die," the wolf whispers back. It does not trundle off into the dark – as if perhaps it is undecided about whether it might not be a fine and dandy idea after all to just kill me where I stand.

Then I am suddenly aware of another presence in the room.

The wolf senses it, too, and it curls its lips in feral anger, this time backing up.

Down the stairs, the translucent apparition of a young woman descends; I recognize it as a simple Haunting – a Ghost – an individual who may or may not be aware of anyone else aside from her own despair and confusion, her spirit temporarily trapped on some plane between heaven and hell.

The Lycker glances at me, a furtive glance, and hisses out of sight. Werewolves hate ghosts, always have. Like cats hating the water. Or vampires detesting crosses and garlic.

I watch the girl continue to descend; quite beautiful, really … and her eyes stare directly into mine.

"You should leave now," she says in a soft, dulcet tone. "When I go, the creature may return to hurt you."

I instinctively take a step backwards, but I am not afraid of this gentle entity. The Popov Meteor Shower had produced benign side-effects to the world of the Living and Dead, and this girl's soul was evidence of that.

"You're right," I say. But I cannot immediately take my eyes off of her. She is already beginning to dissolve into a misty, fog of ectoplasm.

"Go. Now," she whispers again.

I nod, and exit the house.

CHAPTER FIVE

▼

The panic attack hits me like a ton of bricks as soon as I'm outside the gate. I actually enjoy the luxury of yarking up what little I had eaten that morning for breakfast, choking on bile and other tasty afterthoughts to acid reflux.

I spin quickly on myself, wondering if the werewolf was still entertaining second thoughts about having me "stay for dinner", as it were.

But there is no wolf.

And the beautiful spectral vision of the girl is gone.

Only a light drizzle annoys me, which by the looks of things, will graduate nicely into a fairly respectable thunderstorm. I am not so casual in my retreat from the house. I back up, gun out once again, not one to trust a Lycker on any occasion, albeit one that talked and warned me of an impending grizzly death by something called The Grand Master.

Monster Vice is not going to enjoy my report tomorrow. No, sir. Vampires can now hang out in churches and with complete impunity and beyond that, turn human beings into werewolves. Hell, this Grand Master could probably take First Communion and mix Holy Water with J&B and then invite dancing girls, for all that danger that apparently was *keenly* missing in your basic vampire's terror of churches, missions and hallowed ground.

And he was coming after me.

I had also inferred that the Grand Master was probably just as powerful, if not more so, than mere Masters. Masters could control the females, and shape-shift ... this Top Dog in the vampire community obviously was capable of much more – like letting a werewolf acquire speech and *parlez* the *Francaise*.

The ramifications of all this was just too shitty to dwell on. I decided to head for home, lock myself in my apartment, and watch reruns of Mr. Ed.

Sure, I say that now ...

Ah, to be that cavalier about the whole thing...

Instead, I feel tempted to speed my way toward Monster Vice at Rampart, head back for the house near my brother's church, waste the Talking Wolf, then track down this Grand Master with a vengeance.

But I realize with increasing fatigue that these are all pretty dumb options. Best thing to do is get some sleep and be sharp and frosty by tomorrow morning early.

Of course, I have just now come to the conclusion that the Grand Master could easily pop over to my place and snuff me out in my sleep. However, I put this pretty low on the probability scale – this King of the Hill Bloodsucker wants to nail me big time, but real slow. No, I suspect he'll wait for some theatrical moment.

I live in a walk-up, rattrap just off of Melrose Blvd. and Vine, about two blocks west of Paramount Studios. The neighborhood has that gentle ambient quality of the Port Authority Bus Terminal, replete with unconscious transients, and the usual suspect lot of bottom dwellers one might expect to find in a post-Millennium ghetto. I am one of the few gainfully employed residences of this urban Mecca; in fact, I am one of the few residences, period, in this part of town, given the close proximity to Hollywood Cemetery just a short distance south. The cemetery is a constant source of problems, inasmuch as it is a traditional haunt for the Lyckers, Tutis and unburied dead hanging out ready to reanimate into something flesh-eating and generally unpleasant. Though

Monster Vice has a special "Cleansing Unit" that does regular drive-buys to clean out whatever vermin ensconces itself there, no amount of diligent housekeeping gets ride of the pests one hundred percent. Monsters are like houseflies in L.A. — plenty of them, hard to kill them all, and they seem to replicate by fission or through spontaneous generation.

Really, I should move one of these days. I got a raise last December and could easily afford the more plush, and infinitely more attractive digs in West Hollywood or even Beverly Hills adjacent. Why do I stay, then? Up until two nights ago, I told myself it was because my brother lived nearby. His church, like my apartment, was literally situated in No-Man's land part of Hollywood. We always used to go back and forth, mutually urging one another to relocate, to find a safer place to live. His reasoning for staying was wholly epistemological in nature: his sheep, his congregation *lived* here, and thus he would remain until a clearer vision for his future was offered.

My reason was more prosaic in nature: I liked to stay close to the shit, on the off chance that every day I terminated a vampire or werewolf in this neck of the woods, someone's grandmother was safe for another day, someone's daughter need not fear walking the family dog just around the corner come nightfall. Even off-duty, I was still "on."

So here I am. It's late, I'm tired, and with a terrible thirst for Jack Daniels in my soul. I turn the corner and am about to enter my apartment.

That's when I see her.

Mirabelle. She's there most nights – a vaporous vision that never fails.

"Hey, big guy," she says to me, smiling. As she always does, I should add.

"Hi, Mirabelle."

"Now you always blow me off, but can I persuade you into some action tonight?" she asks me … as she always does.

Mirabelle, by the way, is a ghost. I have on every occasion thus far declined her kind invitation to ectoplasmic sex – whatever that may entail, however that may be accomplished. I somehow imagined the whole experience on a theoretical level to be somewhat ... unsatisfying ... from a very corporeal point of view. I could not even imagine what the experience would be like for her, given the clear lack of friction for either party.

Thus, no, no, no, was my courteous litany and response to her invite.

But tonight, I don't say no.

"Sure, come on up," I say.

Mirabelle was a murdered prostitute 15 months ago, around age 30, and drop dead gorgeous. Since the Popov Meteor Shower, she can't find much rest, like so many others – like the beneficent vision today in the Wolf's lair. She hangs in this part of the hood because I was the guy who arrested and then subsequently shot her pimp (who had killed her one week earlier). It's all pretty sordid, but the bottom line is that she likes me ... and can't escape this part of the universe.

So, she hangs near my door, just about this time every night. Always very cordial ... always offering me "a little slice of joy" as she puts it. Don't have a clue how she could possibly make me happy, being dead and all, and have never had the curiosity or inclination to ask her – but tonight, I'm lonely. I'm single, so is she (albeit dead), and I decide to have a date.

She follows me up the stairs, though I cannot see, hear or smell her (because, again, she's dead), but I know she's there.

"How was your day?" she asks.

Without turning, I shrug. "Same old. Met a talking werewolf."

"Oh, no. Those are nasty."

"You have no idea," I say, meaning it.

"I float around town a lot, and I gotta tell you, there's a lot of wolves. And vampires."

"No, really?" I am flip with her and don't mean to be.

"Yeah. And they hate you."

"Yep, right"

"Not you, personally. Just ... you know ..."

"Ah, the *living*?" I say at last.

She shrugs and nods.

"It's a strange world," she says.

I couldn't agree more, as I pull out my key and open the door.

"This is the first time you've invited me up, Dick," Mirabelle says.

"You don't mind, I hope."

She smiles at me and winks – and it is a sweet, sincere wink, not the least bit filled with lasciviousness.

"No, I'm glad."

I smile at her, and leave the door open, though I know she could pass through it, no problema.

She watches me as I go to the kitchen, and take out the Jack, first things first. I don't bother to reach for a glass, I simply take off the cap, and ... well, drink. Yeah, right from the bottle, sports fans. The liquor goes down hard and fast, and I close my eyes.

Little Prick, my mutt of a cat, yowls at me, rubbing himself against my calf. His message is clear: I'm fucking hungry, where have you been? The cat hisses very quietly at Mirabelle, but Little Prick's more culinary priorities outweigh his need to protest the pretty spook's presence.

I tear open some kitti-vittles, pour them onto a plate, and let Little Prick go mad. He dives into the food, purring all the while, as I continue to chug down Jack.

Mirabelle watches me without judgment. When I open my eyes, she is still there, hovering, waiting for me to do something.

"Please, sit," I say, as she floats more or less at the entrance of my kitchen.

"Thanks," she says, and manages to coax herself down to the nearest sofa. She is actually not so transparent anymore, and has even acquired a kind of corporeal appearance – flesh tones, a rather fetching aroma, and even detail in her hair. I find it quite becoming.

Ghosts, you see, after the Popov Meteor Event (as they call it), are able to sometimes mimic or, temporarily at least, assume tangible form ... don't ask me how or why (that's for the scientists at the CDC), but it happens. Trans-something or other, coupled with the discorporate effect of life to death –as they call it.

"Any idea when you'll be moving on?" I ask her. Moving on, meaning, of course, that she doesn't have to stay in this cesspool of a world any longer – that she can move to the next level, or dimension, or whatever other shithole/heaven might exist after life on planet Earth.

"Don't know," she shrugs. "I don't mind, really."

I'm surprised to hear this. "Why"

"Because I love you. And I get to be near you every day."

I'm a bit flummoxed. I've always been fond of Mirabelle (as much as one can be fond of a ghost), and she's always been very sweet ... but to hear a declaration like this ... well, my breath is taken away.

"Honey – " I begin to say.

"It's okay," she says. "I know you don't love me. That's not part of the deal. But you helped me when I was in trouble, and you saved my life. Before Ernie killed me, that is. I can't help but love you. Please say you don't mind..."

I am both touched and saddened. I think I could have fallen in love with Mirabelle when she was alive; it's cliché, I know – the whore with a golden heart, but in her case, the sentiment and virtue was genuine.

"I don't mind, dear. In fact ... you don't know how much I needed to hear that after today."

She is momentarily silent, and then a grim expression crosses over her face.

"I'm sorry about your brother."

I look up at her, dumbfounded. "How did you know?"

"He passed my way, very quickly, the other night," she says solemnly. She then gives me a gentle smile. "But he was able to move on."

A tear stings my eye. So my brother is okay, not to be trapped here by the supernatural magnetic that keeps so many souls, like Mirabelle, in a perpetual state of limbo. On to whatever may come hereafter. The thought momentarily fills me with a feeling of euphoria – that perhaps, after all, there is nothing to fear about anything whatsoever. I hope I can call upon these fuzzy feelings when I sooner or later meet the Grand Fucking Master.

"Thank you, Mirabelle," I croak, then turn away, and again imbibe from the bottle of Jack.

Mirabelle rises off of the couch and approaches me. Very slowly, she takes my hand – and I feel flesh, substance. She is not as cold as I imagine, in fact … not cold at all.

She leads me into my bedroom. She takes off my jacket, no hurriedly, but with great care – as if I were a patient with a painful wound that needed special, gentle treatment in undressing. I allow her this intimacy, as I am suddenly exhausted to the bone, almost unable to move.

She unbuttons my shirt, slips it off my shoulders, then urges me to sit on the bed, which I do. She then takes off my Reebocks, socks to follow. She begins to rub my feet, and that is when I begin to feel Mr. Stick-Boy has sudden interest in things to come.

She unzips my pants, and I assist her in the taking-off process. At this point, Mirabelle removes her own light skirt and blouse – the very clothes she was murdered in, and slips next to me. She reaches for the blankets and covers us both.

She is unbelievably warm – either that, or my imagination has taken a turn for the wholly creative.

I kiss her and do not much time spend on foreplay – though I suspect that Mirabelle doesn't mind. I slip into her easily and am momentarily aghast at how human she feels. And she responds in kind, until our passion is spent after five furious minutes of sweat, scratch and scream.

We lay there afterwards in each other's arms, not saying a word. She even mimics breath – and her breath is warm, delicious. I am morbidly curious as to how she is able to replicate being human again so effectively, but decide not to ask this question on the nose. Instead, I take a roundabout approach to things in general.

"What was it like?" I ask, nuzzling her ear.

"What was what like?" she kisses me back.

"Dying."

She stops kissing me, and looks off distantly, then rests her head on the pillow, thinking sincerely about the question ... remembering.

"Strange," she says quietly. "Not as painful as you would expect. I was shot –"

"Yes, I know," I say sympathetically.

"I remember a burst of pain in my chest ... and then blackness. Like a blanket had been put over my head. That lasted a few seconds, and then suddenly ..."

"Go on."

"I was outside of your apartment," she says, looking to me, touching my cheek.

"Where do you go when you're not here?" I am truly curious. Do ghosts sleep? Do they hang out at ghost-bars? Shoot ghost-pool? Drink ghost-whiskey?

"I tend to just wander around," Mirabelle says cheerfully. "I like looking at the people. I talk with other ... you know –"

"Ghosts."

"Yeah, them. Best part of my day is in the park, watching the children playing."

"What's the worse thing?"

She doesn't even hesitate. "When I run into a vampire or a wolf. The wolves don't like ghosts, but the vampires tend to snarl at us. It's a bad feeling. They're just plain mean."

"Tell me about it."

She then rolls on top of me in a surprising burst of spontaneity. "Know what I miss most about being alive?"

"Tell me."

She closes her eyes and sighs. "Eating and drinking. We don't have to do that, you know."

"I kinda guessed."

"Wine, pasta, hamburgers, chili. Boy, oh boy. You eat that kind of stuff?"

"All the time," I respond, and I hope my voice is not too pinched with sadness for her.

"And I miss my daughter," she says with a sense of finality.

I am again caught by surprise. "You had a daughter?"

She nods, and I can tell she's fighting off tears. "About two years before I died. I gave her up to the an orphanage downtown because I couldn't afford to care for her."

"What was her name?"

Mirabelle takes a moment to get control of her emotions. "Jennifer."

I am familiar with the orphanage. I collared and killed a Lycker a block from there about six months ago. Furry bastard was actually chasing one of the nurses and some children when I arrived on the scene, teasing them, terrorizing them. I took him out with a silver bullet through the throat. Best part of my day, that one.

"Have you been by there since?" I ask.

Mirabelle nods. "Every time I try to go to the orphanage, I suddenly find myself back here. It's as if there's some kind of wall keeping me from her. I don't understand it."

I actually do, from my limited understanding of ghostly lore. Hauntings (which Mirabelle technically constitutes) are unable to revisit certain locations due to guilt or trauma, thus are forever consigned to occupy one spot as a kind of homeroom to the afterlife, in this case, outside my apartment. She is permitted to roam locally, but for the most part, not beyond a 10 block radius.

In essence, she will be mostly trapped here in the building until some burden is lifted off of her earthbound spirit, that burden as yet still beyond her scope of understanding.

I make an uncharacteristic offer.

"Mirabelle. If you'd like, I'll go down there and see if your daughter is okay. Sometime this week, alright?"

"No, I couldn't ask that of you," she protests, more out of embarrassment than anything else.

"It's not a big deal. I'd really like to help. And who knows, maybe this is an issue which is keeping you trapped in this place."

Mirabelle considers this for a moment – perhaps she had already deduced as much already. She looks at me, then touches my face.

"Thank you."

I kiss her again, and find myself aroused once more. As I make love to her, there is a place in the back of my mind that asks: how did I arrive here? Having sex with a dead woman … and liking it.

I assume that life is simply too bizarre for definition and continue to fuck my ghostly companion without further ado.

CHAPTER SIX

▼

When I awaken, it is three a.m. in the morning, pitch black out, and Mirabelle is gone. This is not surprising, given the nature of ghosts – she is off on her daily travels, probably compelled to make them by some higher power. I make a mental note to check on the orphanage where her daughter may still be residing. I decide I'll go into Monster Vice early, before the light of day hurts me with its of-late intensity and my increased consumption of alcohol.

I shower quickly, and find myself again crying, thinking of my brother and Hansen. There is still half a bottle of Jack Daniels left, and before I leave, I make myself a stiff bracer. And because I am too lazy to cook, I open one of Little Prick's kitti-vittles bags and begin to munch. Little Prick is still asleep under my sofa, commencing his day, as usual, with non-stop napping. The night is hot, humid, smoggy. I would prefer to dip my dick into acid right now, rather than go into Monster Vice, but again, duty compels me forward.

Los Angeles Rampart Division, home to Monster Vice, is not unlike Las Vegas - it is a place that never sleeps, perpetually active. In fact, since the monster epidemic, it has remained open and ready for business twenty-four hours a day, including Christmas and New Years. The crime rate in L.A. at the end of the century had gone down to an impressive 7 percent, and violent crime down to five percent. With the arrival of the vampires, werewolves and other crawling hobgoblins after the Popov Meteor Storm, the city now enjoyed an 87 percent jump in violent crime. Rape was down, sure ... but wholesale murder, assault and battery and dismemberment had skyrocketed. Consequently, there was always a small contingent of officers on duty at any given point in the day or night.

Word had spread quickly on the warehouse sting three days back. The mood was down, friends had been lost, and the undead had kicked our collective butts again. Not a good week in Mudville, boys and girls, and the atmosphere is so heavy with sorrow it is downright palpable.

"Pitts," Captain Zelig shouts out to me from his half-open office door. "You're early."

"So are you, Captain," I say.

"Come in, come in."

I lumber into my captain's office and take my seat opposite his duty desk. He punches a button on his speakerphone.

"Send Curadal in here."

Zelig then shoved a file toward me. I opened it.

"Attila Curadal, Lieutenant, out of New York as of yesterday," Zelig rattles on professionally. "He's young, sharp, street wise and Tactical in NYPD gave him top marks. Like you, he has the dubious distinction of being the longest sole survivor in Monster Vice East Coast."

"Lucky him," I say, inwardly thinking, poor bastard. He probably has a background similar to mine -- lone survivor to a long string of Fucked Up Beyond All Recognition defensive campaigns against the Undead.

"I really don't need a new partner this soon," I say, though roaming the streets by myself is not an enticing thought.

"I know, tough guy," Zelig nods. "You'd rather go solo. But that's not how we do things around here, remember?"

Zelig is of course fucking with me, which I deserve, because I was fucking with him. I am feeling sentimental and self-pitying, wallowing in grief for my lost partner and brother, which Zelig no doubts appreciates but can ill-afford to indulge longer than a nano-second. So, we've done our political dance and metaphorically finished sucking each other's dicks in tacit commiseration, just in time to turn our attention to the door opening and one Attila Curadal.

"Lieutenant Curadal, meet your new sidekick, Inspector Dick Pitts," Zelig says.

I take Curadal in for just a second. He's my size, slim, black on first appearance ... but not quite. In fact, his skin tone is hard to pinpoint. Zelig says he's young, and there is a youthful quality about him, but one look at the eyes and you know this guy has seen a lot, probably done a lot. I shudder for a second and am surprised. This is one of the good guys, I remind myself.

Yet those eyes ... a piercing blue ... and his hands look like they perform brain surgery, so delicate, even fragile in appearance they seem to be. He extends one of those hands, offering a smile.

"Inspector," he says in a surprisingly deep voice. "My condolences on your losses the other night."

I take the hand, and offer a curt nod, noting that Curadal's grip is powerful, surprisingly so. I am again reminded of Hanson and feel immediate sorrow.

"What brings you to L.A.?" I ask unenthusiastically.

He smiles, not too broadly, and there is a touch of sadness in his eyes when he replies. "Personal reasons, Inspector."

Fuck you, the reply says clearly. Fine. I respect that. None of your goddamned business, Dick, if you don't mind me saying so just at the moment. I realize that I am not dealing with a rookie, rather a seasoned vet who likes conversation about as much as I do. Gotta respect that.

Zelig takes over, and both of us turn to our senior officer.

"It's been a bad bloody week in the City of Angels, gentlemen," he says wearily.

"And along those lines, I've made a few nasty discoveries in my days off," I say.

I then proceed to tell Zelig and my soon-to-be-new-partner about my run-in with the talking wolf and the Grand Master.

Curadal is silent after my declaration, but Zelig is about to have a coronary.

"Holy Christ, that shakes it! Vampires and werewolves on holy ground! We are completely fucked!"

I wish I could disagree. It is Curadal who interjects an unexpected dose of optimism.

"I suggest a special task force to find this Grand Master. Once found, we can attempt capture and find out how he's controlling the Lyckers and circumventing the normal rules of behavior."

"I don't want to be the turd in the punchbowl," I say, "but every regular Master we've run into thus far has had to be killed, and that's with outrageous casualties on our end. It can't be done."

"I captured one in New York," Curadal says.

"You *what*?" I sputter.

"Down in Battery Park, about six months ago," Curadal studies a nail. "He lasted a whole day before I had to stake him."

"You, alone, captured a Master?" I am again dumbfounded.

"Well, with the assistance of my partner. She was most helpful."

"She!" I spew incredulously.

"Yes. She."

Zelig looks to me, and I shake my head in clear skepticism. Curadal doesn't seem to notice, and then looks to Zelig.

"Samantha has moved out with me," he says. "I'd like her to join our task force."

Before I have a chance to offer further protests, Zelig nods. "Okay. You, Pitts and your partner. I'm assigning you to find this Grand Master and get some answers."

Zelig dismisses us in short order, and I am completely dejected. Not only do I have a new partner, I have two new partners. I look to Curadal, who regards me with those two disturbing eyes.

"So when do I get to meet this Samantha person?"

"Now, if you'd like. She's at the house I'm renting."

"It's early."

Curadel just smiles.

I shrug. "No time like the present," I say dryly.

"Then I would suggest that we return to the place where you found the talking Lycker," he says.

I'm looking for a reason to quarrel, but Curadal is right. The wolf may still be in the house, and at the very least, I'll have an opportunity to plug the sonofabitch. I hate talking werewolves.

I drive and Curadal, gratefully, does not try to make small talk. He seems preoccupied. Fine by me, as I am just as distant. Thoughts of Mirabelle spring into mind suddenly; I find that I would like to see her again this evening. Good chance that will happen, too.

Curadal's house is about ten minutes from Monster Vice and it looks downright haunted. Perched on a small hill overlooking what is referred to as Old Hollywood, the place gives me the instantaneous creeps. We park in a gravel driveway and head for the front door.

We enter ... and I see immediately that there is not a chair, sofa or table in sight. I mean, not a stick. Just walls.

"Roomy," I say.

"Yes," Curadal replies. "Needs some furniture, don't you think?"

I nod that it might be a good idea.

"We just hit town a few days ago. You know how that is," Curadel says.

"Sure."

And then I see her.

She is the most beautiful woman I have ever laid eyes on. Bewitching is a term that leaps to mind.

"Samantha, meet Inspector Dick Pitts," Curadal says easily.

She approaches me (more like glides across the floor), so smooth is her movement. She extends her hand, which I take. I am trembling and it's not because of my hangover.

"A great pleasure," Samantha says in a voice that can only be described as musical.

"Likewise," I croak back.

Her eyes are similar (eerily so) to Curadal's – that same piercing intensity. I wonder if this is a New York thing, that perhaps I have gazed into the eyes of too many dead Los Angelians in my day. But most remarkable about Samantha – and I know this is impossible – but she looks no more than seventeen or eighteen years of age. Her skin is like porcelain, and even the feel of her hand is like touching velvet ... or some kind of material that has the light consistency of cotton candy. I must remind myself that this is not some extremely hot teen-ager, a nymph-narf from the Land Beyond Narnia, but a human being, a trained law enforcement 'specialist', as Curadel put it. Still, Samantha's overall demeanor and appearance is disconcerting, especially to a lecherous old beat-walker like myself.

The house is suddenly inexplicably cold. I wonder vaguely if Curadal and Samantha are lovers. They live together, apparently.

"No, we're just friends," Curadal smiles at me. As if he were reading my mind. "I just wanted to clear that up quickly so it doesn't become a factor in our work relationship."

I nod, not venturing forth a word. I am still mesmerized by Samantha – and find myself staring.

"Inspector, I've heard a lot about you," Samantha says.

"Really," I reply.

"You are a bit of a legend on the west coast. You're quite the talk in the Big Apple."

I am, of course, flattered ... though for the wrong reasons. I entertain the dreamy notion of possibly having carnal knowledge of Samantha – this after only one minute of conversation.

"Well … I'm still alive. Maybe that's the secret to legendary status," I say with all the sincere modesty I can muster.

Samantha smiles and her eyes twinkle.

"How charming. Humility. And in one so young…"

I don't exactly know how to take this, as Samantha appears two decades my junior. She talks as if she's a century old. But I am charmed in turn.

Curadal stands silent, watching this little interchange.

"So," I begin, clearing my throat. "Samantha. I take it you are a police officer."

Samantha smiles. "No. I'm what you might call … a specialist."

"Specialist in what?"

"Killing monsters," she says easily. I wait for an explanation. "NYPD contracted me out to assist in their Monster Vice activities."

"What is your background?" I ask.

"Very specialized. We'll talk about it one day, but now I understand there may be a Lycker who has acquired speech," she says brusquely.

I know when not to push. Fine. She'll tell me later. Maybe over wine. Or after sex … okay, I'm getting ahead of myself.

Curadal fills her in (though I'm puzzled as to how she could have known about the Lycker, as I don't recall him even calling her from a cell phone or from Monster Vice). She listens attentively, and I see an expression of concern cross her face.

"This is happening sooner than we expected," she says to Curadal, who simply shrugs.

"I wasn't expecting this *at all*!" I say, somewhat mystified by these two.

Samantha sighs, and puts her hand on my arm. "It's a case of mutation, Inspector. Any existing life form, after some period of time, will evolve into something different, possibly more advanced. I think this is what we're seeing in the werewolves, and most definitely in the vampire community."

"You're talking about the Grand Master," I say.

"That, and the fact that he, and some of the Lyckers, no longer fear holy ground," Samantha says. "It will make our jobs more difficult."

"Boy, is that an understatement," I respond with a whistle.

"Can we take a look at the house where you found the talking wolf?" Curadal asks.

I'm coming to like this guy. A no bullshit kind of cop, right down to brass tacks and let's not waste any more time on pleasantries. He hasn't offered me a drink, or even asked if I need to take a piss – just pick up the girl, and go to work. Fine.

"Let's do it," I say, and move out of the house.

CHAPTER SEVEN

▼

The ride from Curadal's place of legal tender to the Lycker house (my neighborhood) took around ten minutes. During that time in the car, none of us spoke. The night is unusually bright with a beautiful full moon above. When we finally arrived, Samantha glanced to Curadal and whispered.

"This can't take too long," she says, looking up at the sky. "Sun up soon."

Curadal nodded. "We'll be fine."

I glance at them, clear bum-struck curiosity on my face.

My two rambling companions clearly didn't feel the urge to explain their byplay, so I avert my eyes, and focused on the objective of our mission: The Talking Lycker Holiday Inn.

"Dick, things may get a little dangerous in there," Curadal says. "If they do, leave most of the situation to Samantha and myself."

"I can handle my ass, partner," I say defensively. For fuck's sake, I have been doing this for awhile, I was no novice, I took issue with the cherry treatment.

"No doubt," Curadal says. "I didn't mean to offend."

"I'm more worried about the little lady here," I say, glancing at Samantha.

"Don't," Samantha smiles seductively.

Eat me, was her underlying retort, and I got the message loud and clear. Okay, we were all being a little surreptitiously bitchy at the moment, and we should be thinking of other things. Curadal and Samantha seemed to sense what I was thinking, and then moved toward the front door without further preamble and pissing-contest chit-chat.

"You know," I say, suddenly rethinking things, "we could always call in to MV and ask for some support backup, just in case."

"That won't be necessary," Curadal says.

"There could be more than one Lycker now," I say practically. "I just thought –"

"There's only one," Samantha says with unquestionable confidence.

I was getting the distinct impression that I was being treated like a third wheel on a fuck-in-the-car date. Hey, this was my territory after all. Curadal and his hot looking biker chick specialist acted as if they were merely taking me along on this ride as a courtesy. Perhaps they were.

"Well, fuck me," I mutter in a tone of voice so off the human auditory scale that even a well trained German Shepherd would have been hard pressed to hear what I had said.

Samantha turns to me and grins. "Time enough for that later, Dick."

I was simultaneously astonished and aroused. How she could have heard what I said was beyond me. How she had managed to get me to boast half a stalk, nagging at my trousers, was even more niggling. I suddenly found myself wondering if Samantha had a navel ring, and it was at this point that I realized I should really pull the proverbial shit together and get frosty and focused on other things, like say, a talking werewolf that quite possibly may kill us all within the next few minutes.

Curadal reaches for the front door knob and turns it. The knob clicks without resistance and the door opens.

"Showtime," he says softly, and enters the house, followed by Samantha, and yours boner-hard truly, bringing up the rear.

I notice as we all walked in that both Curadal and Samantha do not have guns drawn (and I should have noticed this earlier, had I not been contemplating whether Samantha possessed a shaved or unshaved Pussy-Cat beneath those tight pants). Samantha, I could possibly understand ... but Curadal? A veteran of NYPD-Monster Vice? What the fuck was he thinking?

I was about to make mention of this little observation when I heard the Lycker growl.

"So you have come back, human," it snarls from near the staircase. "And you've brought company."

"I so enjoyed our little chat last time," I say, trying to sound flippant and casual (probably failing miserably). "I just wanted to share the magic. Bond, if you like. Make medicine."

The Lycker snarls. "I should have killed you when I had a chance."

"Missed opportunities can be so humiliating," I say.

The Lycker came out into what little ambient light was available through the boarded windows. It kept its distance, though, which I found odd. I felt certain it would attack, and this worried me when I glanced at Curadal and Samantha, who were simply standing next to me, still as the dead.

"We're looking for the Grand Master," Curadal said, and I was enviously pissed because his voice was steady and smooth – and it wasn't a damned act, either. You could viscerally sense his calm. Brave fucker, I thought, as my own personal sphincter was puckering tight as a drum in suppressed terror.

"He's looking for you, too," the Lycker growled, its eyes on Curadal and Samantha, its interest in me suddenly evaporated. "Even you won't be able to defeat him, bloodsucker. Or your bitch," it said, glancing at Samantha.

"I really don't think we need engage in name-calling," Samantha said, sighing ... sounding almost weary and patronizing. Her voice, also, was oddly calm. Strike that, she, too, had a keen absence of fear or trepidation in her words. Okay, I thought, was I the only scared girlie-man here today, terrified of the mean, nasty werewolf standing only twenty feet in front of us?

Apparently so.

The Lycker turned to me suddenly. "I find it interesting that you are working with vampires," it said, and my mouth nearly dropped in astonishment. "Most unusual. In fact, rather unheard of," the Lycker hissed.

"Vampires?" I said, sounding about as intelligent and articulate as your basic mentally-arthritic parrot.

"You always talk this crazy?" Curadal said to the Lycker.

"Oh, please," the Lycker growled. "I can smell your type two blocks away."

I realized that the Lycker was a bit delusional, or fucking with me, probably the latter.

"Anyway, what do you want with me?" the Lycker snarled once more.

"I thought I was rather clear on that point. But at the risk of repeating myself, I'll try again. Where's the Grand Master?" Curadal said, taking a step forward.

The Lycker (to my great surprise) backed up a step.

"Suppose I don't tell you?" the Lycker hissed. "Suppose it's my little secret?"

"Then your death will be all the more painful," Curadal responded ... and took another step forward.

"Uh, Curadal," I said, clearing my throat. "Gun? Gun out? Now?"

Curadal ignored me. Samantha glanced at me and grinned. "It's okay, Dick. We've got this furry bad boy under control."

Oh, well, excuse me, I thought, completely speechless. We're only dealing with a Lycker that could kill all three of us within seconds, and by the way, only one of us has the horse sense to have his gun out. What was I thinking? Fuck me in the mouth for being, oh, just somewhat prudent.

"I'll ask again, politely," Curadal said. "Where is the Grand Master?"

The Lycker had forgotten where it was (or so it seemed) and found itself backed up against the railing of the staircase. It eyed Curadal in fury, its fangs barred, a contrail of drool producing a puddle of foul ooze on the floorboards.

"Tonight, he will be at the Crazy Pole Pony," it hissed.

"I know that place," I said. "It's a strip joint on Olympic, near Western." I then looked to the Lycker. "What would a fucking vampire want with hot strippers?"

"He ... he's recruiting," the Lycker growled.

Curadal nodded. "Creating a harem, is he, wolf?"

"That's right," the Lycker said. "It's his thing. And he's not only recruiting women."

"What does that mean?" I hiss.

"You'll see. In time," the werewolf replies enigmatically.

No one said (or growled) anything for a moment.

"So now what?" the Lycker broke the silence.

Curadal smiled at this. "Now you die, wolf," he said.

"But it has been fun," Samantha chuckled.

Was it only me who was going quietly insane? I wondered. Who did these people think they were dealing with? Benji? Lassie? Flipper with fangs and fur?

The Lycker's fur began to rise on its back, and it suddenly lowered its belly to the ground, ears folded back on its head, like an angry cat.

"Maybe you'll die instead, vampire," the Lycker said.

"Unlikely, wolf," Curadal said.

"Can we talk about this?" the Lycker hissed ... and this again took me by wha-fuck surprise.

"No, there's really no viable way out, wolf," Curadal continued ... glancing at his watch. "And this is a bit of a time sensitive issue. Sorry. Bad luck."

The Lycker glanced at me. "You know I didn't kill your brother. And I didn't kill you when I had the chance, remember?"

I was momentarily dumbstruck. Was this thing out of a bad Hammer film actually appealing to me for clemency? For mercy? And I found myself appalled that I was actually, if only for a fleeting second, thinking of a reason *not* to kill the poor wolfie.

"Hey," I sputtered. "Don't look at me. I … this is my job. And I'll bet you've munched a few good citizens lately, so don't go looking to me for help. You furry prick."

My mind was reeling. As if the Lycker *needed* to beg for mercy? What was happening here?

The Lycker suddenly howled and lunged directly for me.

I fired at the wolf, and missed by about a light year, my shot slamming into the roof of the house. Within a span of half a second, I felt that my time on planet Earth was about to be instantaneously terminated.

What I witnessed in the other half of that second defied any sense of credulity I had ever possessed or felt.

Curadal had simultaneously lunged at the wolf, and tackled it mid-air. The two hit the floor hard, and rolled. I tried to recover quickly enough to take aim, but before I did, Curadal was on his feet, holding the huge Lycker by the scruff of its neck. Now mind you, the Lycker stood easily five foot ten, give or take a nut-hair, and had to weigh at least a hundred and forty pounds. Curadal was holding it with one hand, as the wolf growled in fury.

He then suddenly tossed it to Samantha, as if it were a rag doll. She caught it with both hands, but then disposed of the wolf with a truly amazing throw that sent the Lycker (poor wolf, I thought from nowhere) against the far wall, where the force of impact was so crushing, I could actually feel the foundation of the house rock.

Curadal practically flew towards the stunned beast (in fact, it looked like he actually *had* flown, but I knew this was impossible), picked it up by one hind leg, and then slammed it once more into the wall, as if the wolf was nothing more than some kind of hairy baseball bat. The Lycker, I could see, looked truly panicked. It eyed me in abject fear, mixed with some residual fury.

Then from some no doubt inner-wolfen strength, it broke free from Curadal by kicking out its free hind leg, striking my partner square in the jaw. Curadal seemed only mildly fazed, but it forced him to release his grip on the wolf's other leg.

The Lycker decided for a completely unexpected (at least to me) tactic.

It loped towards me with stunning velocity.

I didn't even have time to raise my weapon, before it took its front paw, and in an admirable round-house swing, hit me so hard, I again found myself airborne for the second time in two days, the duration of which was substantial, because I crashed through one of the boarded windows, over the weed infested garden, and then over the crickity wooden gate that surrounded the house – and smashing onto the sidewalk. Total flying time and mileage, easily four seconds and sixty feet.

I had, to my stunned and pained amazement, somehow retained a grip on my gun. The world was a topsy-turvy spiral of disorientation and agony, and I fought for breath, which was battling equally with shooting pains in almost every part of my body. My hearing was seemingly unaffected inasmuch as I could still hear the unholy howls and growls of the Lycker within the house, along with what sounded like a bulldozer tearing the place apart.

I found the strength to roll onto my side, and then assume a doggy-style position on all fours, sucking in volumes of oxygen. I was shaking all over, and didn't have the ability to stand, yet I knew I somehow had to get back inside, and help my compatriots, lest they lose to the power of drooling evil. And so, I, Dick Pitts, aka doggy-boy, proceeded to crawl towards the front door, a journey that spanned around thirty seconds. I was just about thirty feet from the entrance when suddenly I heard one howl of unholy agony ... and then silence. I froze.

And I realized that my friends had been murdered.

I looked to the front door, fully expecting to see the Lycker open it and make its final attack against me.

*   *   *   *

I waited, thinking of the end of one of my favorite poems:
Somewhere folks are cheering,
Somewhere children shout,
But nowhere here in Mudville,
Mighty Casey has struck out.

Yep. That was me, right about now, sports fans. Casey and his final moment of truth. So this is how it all ends, I thought, every nerve ending in my body taking seemingly preternatural joy in firing up collectively for one final fuck-fest of Stick It To Dick Day. I stared at the door.

Sure as monkey-spunk on a stick, it opened.

Samantha appeared first, slapping her hands together, then wiping them on her blouse, a look of clear irritation on her face. She had not seen me as yet.

"God, I'm going to have to dry clean this today before it stains," she said. She then looked to me. "Dick!"

She ran down the stairs, and kneeled down next to me. She did not immediately offer to help me up, and I was getting used to being a human woof-woof, just call me Rin Tin Dick, thank you much.

"Are you hurt?" Samantha asked.

I almost laughed. "I'm fine, Sam. You don't mind if I call you Sam?"

"All my friends do," she smiled. "But you're pretty well bunged up, I can tell that much."

I then looked to the front door again. Curadal appeared. He was dragging the Lycker ... a very dead Lycker, behind him, in one hand. He glanced at me and froze in his tracks.

"Dick, I'm so sorry," he said, and the remorse in his voice was one hundred percent sincere.

"For what?" I said, as Samantha pulled me gently up from all fours to a wobbly standing position.

"For letting the wolf attack you," he said. "Very careless of me. I'm inconsolable."

I thought that he was being facetious, but in an instance, I could tell that he was truly apologetic – as if his perceived negligence in allowing the wolf to play Punch the Pitts Pinata was an act of fundamental betrayal by him toward me.

"Don't let it eat you up," I said, feeling my strength slowly returning, though the shakes were in full tilt boogey mode. "Mind if I ask how come you two aren't dead?"

"Told you," Sam said. "We're specialists in this sort of thing."

"You killed a Lycker with your bare hands," I said, shaking my head, all sense of reality just getting up and running away from me at the moment. "No one does that."

"Ever heard of martial arts?" Curadal said.

"You've got to be kidding," I said.

"Let's talk about it over a drink," Samantha said. "You look like you could use one."

I could have married the woman right there on the spot for her sensitivity.

"Mind if we just put this in your car?" Curadal said, referring to the dead werewolf, its hind leg still firmly grasped in his right hand.

I nodded. "I'll pop the trunk."

As the Lycker festers and begins to decompose in the trunk of my car, Curadal and Samantha both insist that we do the drinkie thing at their place. Curadal drives, and by the way, not at moderate speeds. He is continuously looking at the sky as the dawn is close to breaking, and checking his watch, while hauling through side streets at velocities that might suggest he was preparing to taxi and take-off at LAX.

I didn't mind. Samantha has informed me that there is a cold bottle of Stoly in her fridge, and that thought alone keeps me unpanicked as Curadal continues to ground-fly through midtown Los Angeles.

He screeches into the driveway, and hits the brakes, but in a way that seems not the least bit jarring (and I would have been able to tell, as every part of my body still reeled from my recent encounter with the Lycker).

I must have blacked out for a moment, but I did realize that I was being carried. Further, I must have been hallucinating because I could honestly relate that I believe it was lovely Sam herself carrying me. Effortlessly, at that. The next thing I know, I am in a chair which has magically appeared out of nowhere, with a very large, cold glass of vodka in my hand. Sam and Curadal are in two other chairs directly in front of me. They are watching me, and even fucked-up and woozy, I can recognize the looks of worry on their faces.

I look at my glass, then raise it. "Cheers."

"Cheers," they respond together. "And by the way, well done, Dick."

"What?" I said, not comprehending what Curadal is saying.

"Your job back there at the house. One hell of a job. You've earned your rep," he said, again in that tone of voice that was completely and irrevocably heartfelt.

"Yeah," I said, and laughed. "No, I'm getting very good at flying. And falling. And having my ass kicked on a regular basis."

"I was referring to your courage, sir," Curadal said, again almost deadly serious.

I did not have the heart to inform my new partner that each and every time I face these monsters, I have this urge to just go out and buy some Pampers and wear them for those all too necessary and probable moments of terror ka-ka release. But I decide to spare all concerned my innermost thoughts on this issue and merely offer a woozy, grateful smile, which I dare say is the most convincing thing I have done all day.

"Tell me more of this special training," I change gears, wanting to cleanse my mind of scatological distraction.

"Ah, yes," Samantha says, glancing at Curadal. "It is a combination of advanced martial arts and mental discipline, which, when combined, create a powerful mechanism which we find almost quadruples our combat tactic capability."

Wow, I thought. I suddenly feel like former president George W. Bush reading My Pet Goat, and having to listen to the holographic paradigm of tangential dimensional resonance, i.e., not being a Mensa candidate, and barely able not to end a sentence in a preposition, I merely nod in wise, wise silence. That being said, and after a moment of much needed reflection and as George Bush would have it "thought collection", I venture out on the ubiquitous limb of intellectual curiosity [the 'what the fuck are you talking about' retort of the perpetually ignorant] and take a chance with another inquiry: "Uh, can anybody learn this, special training?"

Curadal laughs. "Oh, yes, Dick," he said. "But there is a price for such knowledge."

I do not realize it but I have finished my rather generous frosty libation. I also do not realize that I am moments away from blacking out. With what little coherence remains, I lean forward and look directly into the beautiful eyes of Samantha (just call me Sam) and smile.

"I think … I'd like to do what you were able to do today to the wolf," I mumble.

Then the world suddenly spins and the immortal words of Simon and Garfunkel echo in my booze-bludgeoned brainy-poo.

And hello darkness, my old friend, comes to me now once again…

CHAPTER EIGHT

▼

When I awaken, I am lying on top of a sofa in a room just off to the left of the living room and the front door. My head feels like a baby giraffe has just finished using it for a hoof-conditioner. My mouth tastes like some small, previously unrecognized species of marsupial has taken a dump in it. The world at large spins, as if Earth itself is defying all gravitational laws of physics, and the capper is that my body can be safely catalogued for all posterity as One Big Giant Piece of Aching Condemned Veal.

I stagger to my feet – a Herculean effort which is rewarded by a cascading tidal wave of nausea and the urge to purge … and who cares which end or orifice this purging is to emanate?! I look into the living room, then into the apartment's only other bedroom and kitchen.

Curadal and Samantha are nowhere to be found.

I look outside and see my car, and another vehicle, which I assume belongs to my hosts … yet they are not in the apartment, this much is clear. I decide to wait for a little while, on the assumption that perhaps they have gone out for a walk, or run a chore to the local 7-11. I look at my watch, and see that it is late afternoon, the sun still high in the sky. I had been sleeping for the better part of the day (sleeping … a wonderful euphemism in my case for being passed out, drunk as a skunk).

Half an hour passes, and still I am alone. I make the decision to leave, inasmuch as I should get back home, shower, and prepare for this evening when, according to the dead Lycker in the trunk of my car, the Grand Master will be awaiting our arrival at the stripper club on Olympic. I jot a quick note to Curadal and Sam, asking them to meet me at my place tonight – I am only five minutes from the club, hence, the logic in my apartment being the jumping-off point for the mission to come.

I make the thousand mile journey to my car, sweating, the shakes kicking in full force. I pop open the trunk and see that the dead Lycker is still, happily so, dead. I decide that I will bury it quickly at the Hollywood Cemetery near my place, then hit the showers, and the rest of my Jack Daniels. If Mirabelle is waiting for me, I will have to courteously decline any offers of romp-n'-fun activities.

The drive home is an odyssey into hell, a kind of labyrinthine horror that I feel I will never successfully complete. I have the sweats so bad, I feel I could successfully aerate most of drought-stricken Ethiopia. The world still spins, and it will probably take several thousand Advils to suppress the pain in nearly every part of my body from today's earlier festivities. My heart races so fast, I feel that cardiac arrest may very well be inevitable and immediate. My teeth itch. I look at the cell phone on my seat and realize I should call in to Monster Vice, update them on the status of the day. I decide against it. My brain is so fried I may simply gibber something that sounds like a rare dialectic found only among some timid Amazonian tribe of stick-in-the-lip natives.

I hit the cemetery first, find some small patch of unutilized piece of ground, then prepare the final resting place for the creature responsible for my current agony. When I finish, and though I know that Lyckers don't rise from the dead, I take out one of my holy water vials, and drop it in the grave, along with the corpse. Just for good measure.

Five minutes later, I'm back at home, and in the shower, Jack in one hand, Dial Extra Strength in the other. I am feeling somewhat better, though realize many of these good feelings are lies, inasmuch as I've refortified myself with whiskey and painkillers, and that sooner or later, I will have to pay the piper with a hangover proper.

I then sit down at my computer and check emails for the day. Zelig has contacted me, wondering on my progress with my new partner. I reply briefly that we have a few leads and that Inspector Curadal is a top man (I exclude my assessment of Samantha as being a smoking hot bitch-kitty with a panache for werewolf butchery). Sometimes less is more.

I have also been advised, to my great astonishment, that Zelig has recommended me for Special Grief and Field Counseling with Dr. Lilia Simonhoffer, our departmental psychologist. I have never met the woman before, nor have I ever needed counseling before (to my own knowledge), but Zelig goes on to explain that with the recent loss of both my brother and my partner, he feels this is an excellent prophylactic necessity to forestall any possible battle fatigue or nervous collapse.

Well, shit, I think.

I momentarily consider replying by email to my captain that I do not need counseling, that in fact, I would consider counseling intrusive and distracting – especially since I'm now part of a taskforce trying to ferret out talking werewolves and master vampires. Priorities are priorities. But I resist the impulse to send such an email inasmuch as I could just see Zelig flipping out and taking me off all cases indefinitely, unless I comply with this departmental mandate.

Fine. I'll see the shrink.

I glance at Little Prick, still fast asleep under my sofa, then look at my watch. It is close to five o'clock, and the sun is still high in the sky. No doubt, the Master Vampire we seek will not be rousing until at least sundown, and for sure, would not be terribly active until near midnight. Moreover, I have not yet heard from my partner and Sam. They have my cell and home numbers. I decide that I can kill some time, since I'm already three sheets to the wind (again), why not see the shrink in the next half an hour and get this silliness over with. I feel this is a good call. I dial the number that Zelig has given me for Dr. Simonhoffer. But I hang up as another thought occurs to me.

I shall make the call in five minutes.

First, I reach for some Kleenex and my trusty jar of Vaseline, then head for my *Agapemone,* or Abode of Love, or bedroom, if you'd prefer. It's time to Clean Out The Old Fun Pipes, just in case tonight gets hairy and unpredictable.

CHAPTER NINE

▼

The good doctor was indeed "in", to wit, she had no problems in seeing me as soon as possible. Within half an hour, I was sitting in her office, a recessed cubicle that stood apart from the outer wings of the hustle and bustle of the Situation Room. The world was still spinning, and by polishing off the rest of the Jack, I was now completely and comfortably tanked.

Dr. Simonhoffer is a woman of around forty-five, not unattractive, on the Boner Meter of 1 to 10, an easy 6. For close to a minute, we say nothing, though she does put her elbows on the desk and brings her hands together in a steeple-like configuration, or pyramidal form, which suggests, in conjunct with her penetrating gaze, a concentrated focus of interest on *moi* and only *moi*.

My mind is already wandering to future events of this evening. Though uneasy about confronting the unknown variable presently referred to as a Grand Master, I somehow feel more at ease in the fact that both Curadal and Sam will be at my side. Their "special training" as they referred to it had impressed me greatly. I hope it will hold us all in good stead tonight.

"Inspector Pitts," my counselor says at last. "I want you to know that this is a safe haven for you, here in this office. Everything that is said within this space is sacrosanct, or as they say, *in camera*, and subject to counselor-client privilege and confidentiality."

"I appreciate that, doctor," I reply magnanimously, hoping that I am not slurring my words too noticeably.

"We are here to assist you in a kind of emotional, mental and spiritual rehabilitation in the wake of your recent multiple tragedies. We shall attempt to, in a completely nonjudgmental and non-prejudicial approach, construct a series of restorative and cohesive frameworks by which we can journey freely within a matrix of healing paradigms. Are you with me so far?"

I nod in what I think is a fairly game piece of sincerity, though I don't have a fucking clue as to what she is talking about.

My counselor proceeds to then tell me that by accessing deep, vulnerable, child-like, or puerile, emotions, brutalized by my putative Field of Expertise, [as she calls it] or my 'profession' or 'vocation,' or 'what I do for a living' [and] by life in general, that is to say, resultant from the slings and arrows of outrageous and egregious unfairness subject to the human condition, or perhaps to be more *sur la tete*, or, 'on the head,' she revises, to *my* particular human condition, given what I do to bring home the bacon or 'pay the bills', e.g. terminate supernatural xenomorphs (as she characterizes the monsters sweeping over the land) - that by utilizing proven and documented modalities of therapeutic panaceas, i.e., tried and true methodologies of reconstituting brutalized, traumatized or otherwise bludgeoned psyches, that in this way or manner, or even more accurately, through this form of aggressive, yet inherently compassionate therapy, by which we (she and I) will be peeling away the layers of pain and hurt from my wounded Inner Child, that through these superstructures of scientific application and Good Feelings Positive Outlook Indoctrination (GFPOI), I might once again be able to function in a world I most certainly feel, of late, has dealt me a bitter and crippling blow.

She may very well have translated the basics of Schrodinger's essays on the analysis of plant phylogeny or [*auf Deutsch* –

gartenbau], inasmuch as I still didn't understand a single fucking word she had just said. Dr. Simonhoffer, in case you haven't noticed, has a *penchant* for run-on sentence psycho babble. Even so, I nod diplomatically and say:

"Uh, huh."

She then proceeds to ask me, with eyes that seem to me filled more with avidity than true interest, what exactly comprises my quotidian, or daily routine, within Monster Vice and how I feel about my profession, my chosen *métier*, or *forte*, or my *raison d'etre* here within the magical walls of Monster Vice, and to think "out of the box" for a moment, how I feel in general when I am in the act of suppressing the xenomorph epidemic currently ravaging the cosmopolitan landscape of Los Angeles and contiguous surroundings under MV jurisdiction.

I digest the full extent of her run-on question and then make the decision to dive right in with likewise run-on enthusiasm, and spill everything, [to let forth] to tumble the beans of my discontent (to mix a metaphor), to unleash the origins of my angst, or fury at the horror of it all -- that 'all' being, specifically, the rampaging, verminous infestation of Things That Feed On Blood and Rise From The Dead To Torment Mankind.

I decide to speak her language, focusing on her eyes and glasses as a kind of mnemonic guideline for her particular form of dialectic.

Thus, I commence by describing my days in homicide not so long ago, my passion for rectifying the wrongdoing of the recidivist elements on the streets, or to be more specific, putting down or laying waste to the multitudinous acts of violence which were surfeit and all prevailing - and in effect thereto, those who would *perpetrate* such violence - and in so effectively expunging, eradicating, or in the common street vernacular, 'taking out' or 'lighting up' those individuals prone to heinous, unnatural, inhuman, psychotic and evil wrongdoing, deriving a kind of personal and self-empowering joy, or ecstasy, or even spiritual transcendentalism that is particular only to those who recognize themselves to be Genuine Heroes for everything right, and true, and good, and that by halting, or arresting possible chances for criminality in the making, or by whacking, or in the colloquial, by Kicking Ass, I was able to achieve a kind of internal completeness that was wholly virtuous, in compliance with the *nobles oblige,* tr. "to do what is right for the sake of right alone, i.e., a Noble's Obligation", principles of selflessness and Templar-Knight like self-sacrifice consistent with the manifest destiny of Judeo-Christian love, Doing What A Man Has to Do For The Sake of King and Country, and the American Way, so help me God, and that above and beyond all this [to drive the point fully home] I was just really, really happy whenever I could deliver another lap-dog for Satan back to the Stygian, Cerberus-guarded infernal regions of everlasting damnation.

My counselor smiles. She seems pleased, and asks me to continue.

I feel I am now on a roll. Thus, I plow forward.

I am then compelled to graduate from the real to the surreal (which for me was epiphanic in the extreme) by which I mean to say, to segue from the world of 'What Was' or 'Pre Monster Madness' or 'Back Then' to the new, wacky, fun-filled world of 'Now', or if you'd like, 'Today', as in 'The Present Where Unholiness Rules,' and that by defining this new environment of horror, of the impossible – of an Earth being overrun by monsters of every description – one must necessarily define the transition from the kind of police-work I used to perform to the kind of constabulary duties expected of me presently, and which must be executed in a very different, and even alien venue, by way of a profound shift in my manner of rationally assimilating the gestalt of this New Kind Of War, the sums of which, when combined in toto, defy any kind of previous conceptual framework of reality, or further (and not to Beat A Dead Horse) how *necessary* it was for *me* to be cognizant of, or vigilant to, the ups and downs, the highs and lows, the synergy of unspeakable horror of this Next Level Field of Play, or In Theater Warfare, and that moreover, to dismiss my preconceived or pre-established epistemological belief systems, and that to Get Off The Pot and Accept The Shit For What It Was – all this, concurrent with the requirement that I cross-utilize novel and Trial by Fire tactical mechanisms, coupled with, and as an adjunct to, a whole new subset of skills and expectations and weaponry not previously utilized (nor needed) in the Good Old Days of rape, murder and plunder by your basic cold-blooded, psychotic, albeit *human*, criminal shiteater with an attitude.

I am then asked by Dr. Simonhoffer (and this is a standard question, she assures me, which she has asked many vetted officers of MP, so not to worry) if I have yet to experience any *guilt* in killing, or to take it one step further, *Destroying Completely*, any of the monsters I have encountered thus far, and that if I have, this is expected, and totally understandable, and in no way should precipitate within myself the need for self-recrimination, self-flagellation, or self-excoriation, that this is a perfectly natural reaction to inflicting damage, (or as I would like to put it, Completely Ass-Fucking The Monsters With Everything I've Got), [but], that to hold myself up to any kind of pejorative mental or emotional self-mutilation or harsh self-scrutiny, while wholeheartedly within the acceptable framework of therapeutic comprehension, is unnecessary (for me), and from this point on, Against The Rules.

"Do you understand?" she asks me in a voice I would usually think is reserved for three year old infant paraplegics.

I nod that I do – a member of that most fictile group of policeman who simply wants to please and get this over with as quickly as possible. I note that as the sun is descending over the horizon, Dr. Simonhoffer's face takes on a kind of marzipan quality, or *plastique* in appearance, a sort of deliquescent pallor which tells me that, as the light shifts, this is a lady who wears far too much make up, who looks like she just might melt any second if water was thrown on her, and who is perhaps more than forty-five, and whose overall facial contours now appear somewhat anile and withered. Perhaps, I consider in a rambling sort of way, Dr. Simonhoffer has been doing this 'kind of work' far too long (not unlike certain police officers in Monster Vice, yours truly included).

She smiles at me, almost flirtatiously, as if she was still possessed of the gynecic charms of a young girl, unaware of the 'absence of bloom' in her cheeks, or more specifically, oblivious to the fact that when she smiles, she resembles something that could be most aptly compared to a kind of subsurface predator, or vole, or grub, (maybe more like a leech or a Lyme-tick) a thing that fed on autopilot, with a mouth locked in a sardonic, unmovable half-grin of famishment.

"Now," she continues, leaning back in her chair, "we have finished with the preliminaries. You have told me what your past life was like with the police department, pre Popov Phenomenon, and what your current duties entail, and in fact, how you feel *anent* about your day to day functions as a Monster Killer. All this is vital information, and I'm appreciative of your candor. We must now go further."

"I'm game," I say, and take a grand breath of preparation.

My counselor then proceeds to ask me if I would have any objections to closing my eyes, and concentrating on an image of a calm lake with a very large elephant standing near the shore, with a small poodle simultaneously yapping (as small objectionable dogs tend to do) and nipping at the pachyderm's trunk. I consider the exercise odd, to say the least, but keeping an open mind and feeling that perhaps to close my eyes for a few moments, perhaps to doze through the Jack presently coursing through my bloodstream, was not a bad idea at all.

And so, with visions of water and elephants and rat-like doggies in my minds-eye, I shut down and enter the world of darkness.

My counselor continues to speak. She now asks me to concentrate on [or materialize by force of will] both my brother and Hanson, on either side of the elephant, waving at me and smiling. This produces within me a twinge of instantaneous sadness. Still, for the sake of therapeutic advancement, I do as instructed, creating the images of both Bill and Hanson on either side of the Big Boy Pachyderm. Dr. Simonhoffer now asks me (though she does not request an answer) exactly how I feel about sex, and how I satisfy this basic human need (remembering, again, that no retort to her interrogatory is required). She simply wants me to cogitate, or ruminate, perhaps even meditate on the requested mental imagery. She continues to speak, as I continue to mull over sex, elephants, dead comrades and irritating poodles. I am in the preliminary stages of feeling this is exceptionally weird and stupid, but continue to concentrate nevertheless. She then suggests, or 'puts it to me' that the elephant's trunk is not really a trunk but in actuality, my father's penis. My eyebrows raise at this, and this reaction must be noticeable to her, because she follows up hard upon by saying that while these subliminal images are being manifested by me (through her coaching), I am ostensibly reaching out for, or touching base with, or excising from, the deepest pain within the wellspring of my Inner Child, which if handled with care, or lovingly, *avec quelque chose gentile*, or kindly, there will be noticeable and provocative core emotions released into the ether, or intangible plasma, of psychological reconstitution.

Indeed, the elephant's trunk, a long, swinging crenellated mass of flesh begins to take on the familiar parabolic shape of a penis head, gradually completing transformation to a Full Blown Cock.

I try not to laugh, and choke on some spit that went down the wrong way, though camouflage this admirably, as if perhaps I was merely clearing my throat ... or appearing *choked up* [emotionally, of course] - (the latter, I thought, would fairly fill my counselor with Inner Joy).

My counselor then asks me if I ever loved my father. I reply that my father and I always had a very amicable relationship, even when I decided to abandon my career in womens clothing.

Dr. Simonhoffer then asks if he was supportive of my decision to become a police officer. I reply that he was very supportive, inasmuch as the decision to become a police officer was predicated upon an incident that happened one night at my father's dress warehouse in Santa Monica, wherein three men entered the structure and threatened my father at gunpoint, demanding money, and that, quite beyond the three assailants' awareness, I was hiding nearby with my father's .38 Police Special (which my father always kept in a cabinet for possible occurrences such as the one he was presently experiencing), and that when pushed came to shove, I decided it was probably best to simply shoot the three attackers with the gun at my father's head, and then address the consequences of my actions at a point further down the line. Inasmuch as I successfully killed all three of the intruding fuck-sticks, with my father suffering not a scratch throughout the entire, very brief fray, he was henceforth delighted that I had found something 'I was truly gifted at' as he put it. Mind you, I have never enjoyed killing, but sometimes one doesn't have a choice, if you know what I mean (I tell my counselor) and I think you do [I conclude with a certain amount of emphasis].

There is a moment of silence (thought I sense, as promised by Dr. Simonhoffer, it is a silence bereft of judgment or prejudice).

"Well," she says in a tone of voice which suggests that 'this explains so much' or 'ah, perhaps we are on the brink of some great discovery.'

She then returns to the subject of sex. The Q and A goes something like this:

Q. Are you currently involved in a relationship?
A. Not really.
   (I have not yet decided to speak candidly about my priapic romps with Mirabelle, despite assurances of *in camera* confidentiality).
Q. How long has it been since your last significant relationship?
A. About six months.

Q. Do you have any other outlet, or release, vis a vis sexual tension?

A. I don't think I understand –

Q. Do you masturbate?

(I do not immediately answer. Then:

A. Does this have something to do with my Inner Child?

Q. Answer the question, Inspector.

A. Uh, okay. Yes. I … sometimes.

Q. How often?

A. Now and then.

Q. Define now and then.

A. Once a day.

Q. Do you enjoy watching pornography?

(I am again momentarily lost in the moment of self-exploration and promised discovery, wondering how this is going to ameliorate my grief and soul-weary sadness for lost friends and family).

Q. Please, Dick. Do you enjoy smut?

A. On occasion.

Q. Have you been in touch with your latent homosexuality for a long time, or has this been a recent *fait accompli*?)

By my stunned silence, my counselor proceeds to adduce, that is to say *pace* my resistance to reply, that I have, through hatred of my father, and coupled with my own seemingly insatiable impulses to 'kill,' or 'snuff out life,' or 'murder,' notwithstanding mitigating circumstances in my favor, that by my obsession with self-abuse, or as the saying goes 'masturbating,' or Flogging Freddy, or Jacking Off, and my very clear (by all accounts from colleagues and Captain Zelig) closeness with my dead partner Hanson, that these factors, reviewed in the collective, could only point toward the obvious nature of my full-blown, Out Of [or In] The Closet, Dick-Hungry gayness (perhaps not her words, exactly, but mine, translated thus).

While I contemplate my incipient homosexuality, momentarily baffled as to why I crave pussy yet feel nothing for wanting to 'suck shank' *in vulgarus*, or experience anal-bailiwick, or [in the Latin] – and for the sake of etymology - *penetrare, passim* (in the ass-buggering sense) -- and perhaps I could, or my counselor *certainly* would, attribute this to a lack of imagination or in-touch intimacy with my Inner Child Wants -- I concurrently wonder how long this incredibly vapid session of Need To Feel Honestly will continue. The Jack is wearing off, and I am beginning to feel impatient, nay, even intolerant. I glance at my watch, and see that it is close to seven o'clock in the evening. This, I feel, has gone on long enough, yet I do not want to appear rude, and I certainly don't want Dr. Simonhoffer to convey to Captain Zelig that I am resistant to much-needed, (as fate would have it), counseling and on-going therapeutic rehabilitation.

"I think it would be a good idea to focus on your incessant need for pleasuring yourself," Dr. Simonhoffer says in a soft, melodic voice, not even trying to be remotely subtle, but going for the throat, in a kind of Occam Razorblade simplicity that leaves me no wriggle room whatsoever.

"Do we have to?" I ask tentatively.

"You want to heal, do you not, Inspector?"

"Uh, well."

"Good. Now. Talk to me about your practice of self-abuse. What do you think about when you're doing it?"

My mind becomes a massive screen of white – how am I supposed to answer a question like this? Oh, what the fuck, I suddenly think. *Go ahead, answer the woman. Maybe she knows something I don't.* I take a deep breath.

"I – well, I fantasize about my last girlfriend, I suppose."

"The one you broke up with six months ago, right?"

"Correct."

"What was the cause of the breakup?"

"She said that I wasn't 'there' for her enough, that my work kept me from getting 'closer' or 'more intimate'."

"I see," my counselor nods, with a kind of perspicacious air about her which is truly daunting. "But there were no problems sexually?"

"None whatsoever," I offer a dim smile. "Except that we didn't seem to have enough of it, due to my work schedule."

"Or your possible latent homosexuality, yes?"

Ah, so, we were back to that.

"Uh –"

"Let's move on from that and return to my original question," Dr. Simonhoffer waves a dismissive hand, and begins to write on a yellow pad, no doubt something concerning my newfound anxiety and dirty joy in wanting to suck (and certainly more than suck) the ever protean Cock.

I am silent, until she looks up at me, and raises her eyebrow. "I'm listening."

"For what?"

"For an answer to my question. The mechanics of your masturbatory practices."

"I guess I do it in the usual way," I say, cop-wimp in full mode.

"Show me."

"I really don't want to," I say defensively.

"Why not?"

"Because it's very personal and it's embarrassing. I'm sure you can understand that."

"I'm *trying* to embarrass you, Inspector," my counselor says. "I want you to drop that wall around yourself. I want you to find that little boy who is hurting inside."

"You know … look, maybe as I get to know you better … I'll feel more comfortable showing you the mechanics of, er … uh…"

"Jerking off," Dr. Simonhoffer smiles.

"Yes."

She studies me for a moment, considering (or as she would put it, *perpending*), and even musing … then begins writing once more. I am relieved. She's not going to push the Flogging The Perennial Pants-Pigeon issue. For this relief much thanks.

"Now, I would like to talk about your mother, Inspector," my counselor presses on. "Is she still alive?"

I respond that my mother has been dead now close to three years. Dr. Simonhoffer nods sagaciously as if this explained so much ... I am also trying to understand the clear-so-understandable nature of her nod, but fail in all secondary attempts. Perhaps this slowness on my part is due to my understandable surprise at discovering I really do enjoy the taste of penis versus that of the female genitalia [so theorizes my counselor]. My counselor presses for details *vis a vis* my mother's death.

I inform Dr. Simonhoffer that my mother died tragically, that she was in fact, killed by a falling palm tree in Miami Beach, Florida.

"How awful," Dr. Simonhoffer says, clearly aghast. "How did it happen, Dick?"

"Allow me to retort," I say, taking a breath.

I proceed to tell her that my mother's death was due to a confluence of sad, inexorable series of events which discerning experts at the time defined as 'one of those things that could only happen to one person out of three billion.'

My mother had worked with my father in the shop for over thirty years, and she was not disposed to vacations. This did not preclude my father from taking breaks whenever he pleased, but my mother lived by a very strict code – that while one had one's health, one should always work. She never missed a day of work at Dad's shop. It was only at the behest of the family doctor conveying to my mother that she needed to 'slow down' due to indeterminate blood-pressure issues, that she in fact one day did (slow down, that is…). She agreed to accompany me to Miami Beach for three days of doing nothing more than resting by the pool, after which, she promised she would be back in the dress shop, lickity-split, because, you see, she was 'no shirker.'

And so, that first day by the pool, surrounded by beautiful people, fauna, and palm trees, my mother pulled up a lounge chair, donned her Vogue sunglasses at two hundred dollars a pair, and began officially her vacation.

Perhaps no more than two minutes later, as I was soaking in a nearby Jacuzzi with a possibly under-aged teen bikini model, I heard a thunderous crack. I turned to the source of the noise, and saw that a huge palm tree had split at its center. Within half a second, the entire trunk and attending leaves, was in a freefall. Within the span of another second, my mother was crushed by the tree, which stood easily at over forty feet tall, weighing in at just under one thousand pounds.

The gardener who had been attending to the tree – an elderly gentlemen who was simply hacking at what he believed to be some dying bark-fronds with a small machete – was *par chance* also intoxicated [and a recently-converted atheist] minister of the black persuasion, i.e., Negro, or as he 'put it' to the report-driven policeman after the incident, of 'Ethiopian descent'. Because of his tipsiness (his word), he had forgotten about the warning by a reputed expert on palm-tree root disintegration who had visited this particular resort just three days earlier, stating unequivocally that the trees in this particular resort were rife with a kind of decay component known as Ganoderma butt rot, and susceptible to damage in the extreme by anything other than sensitive and professional care and treatment.

Ganoderma butt rot is caused by the fungus *Ganoderma zonatum*.[3] This organism causes a gradual decline in palms.

---

[3]   Ganoderma butt rot is a relatively new and lethal disease of Florida palm trees. The condition was first discovered in Florida in 1994 and in only a few years it has spread to infect palms throughout the state. At this time, it cannot be said with certainty that there are any palm trees resistant to Ganoderma butt rot. The ganoderma zonatum fungus most often invades a palm tree by means of a wound at the base of the tree. The fungus then begins to rapidly work its way through the tree's butt area essentially rotting the wood. Once the fungus has worked its way through the center of the tree to the surface,

Unfortunately, there is no cure for Ganoderma. It is most commonly a result of an injury to the trunk of the palm. After a palm is injured, the Ganoderma fungus gets inside the roots and slowly kills the tree. Such an affected victim of Ganoderma will slowly decline over a period of time. The fronds will be droopy and will eventually hang limp. Ganoderma butt rot can occur in any palm, but it is most commonly seen on areca and queen palms ... the likes of which this resort was, as they say, 'lousy with.'

On this tragic day, the Ganoderma butt rot had eroded the integrity of the palm tree that murdered my mother, right down to the core. Thus, when the recently converted atheist minister (drunk, mind you) of Ethiopian descent, presently employed as a part-time gardener by this resort, hacked at the poor tree riddled with disease, it simply collapsed upon its own cancerous decay and keeled over dead.

---

it forms a fruiting body called a 'conk', a spongy, whitish mushroom-like growth which grows to form a horizontal disc extending out from the bark. Unfortunately, there is currently no effective treatment for Ganoderma butt rot. By the time the conk has appeared on the bark, the tree is effectively dead and must be removed. While the wood above the butt area can be safely mulched, extreme care is needed when disposing of the butt wood in order to avoid spreading the fungus to other palms. The wood should be wrapped in plastic and disposed of by incineration or taken to a landfill. All tools should be sterilized and care should also be given to clothes exposed to this deadly tree fungus. While there is no sure-fire way of preventing Ganoderma butt rot infestation, the danger can be reduced by avoiding injuring the trunks of the palm trees on one's property.

One should be careful when using lawnmowers and other gardening implements. Should one suspect a Ganoderma butt rot infestation on one's property - and should one not be an elderly, drunken, atheist fuckstick of Ethiopian descent who has pickled himself silly with strong drink, thus jeopardizing not only snoozing old ladies but small animals as well - one would be best to consult with one's local forestry official for information and advice.

This was, by way of lengthy explanation, how my mother had passed away some three years ago.

It was, as I refer to it, a death by palm.

My counselor is again creating pyramidal shapes with her hands, nodding, and punctuating every other nod with an 'uh-huh' or 'I see.'

The vagaries of my mother's passing seem of little interest to my counselor, as is evidenced by her next question:

"Did you ever harbor a secret desire to sleep with your mother, Inspector?"

I am [again] momentarily speechless and do not give immediate retort.

"It's perfectly alright to admit that you felt sexually attracted to her," Dr. Simonhoffer assures me with a knowing smile, as if, indeed, *all* of her patients, or perhaps, every man she *knew*, held secret lust in their loins for the women who gave them birth, and that to deny such a basic, fundamental need within oneself was, in the extreme, a full-blown anathema, and even inconsequential when one is to consider the basically animalistic inclinations among the Male of the Species, in general.

"I – really, I don't think I felt this way at all," I shrug helplessly, and something in Dr. Simonhoffer's demeanor changes just a little bit – a conveyance of disappointment, I think. "And I'm just wondering how all this talk of sex is enabling me to better deal with my grief for both brother and partner."

"If you're going to get adversarial with me, Inspector, the healing process will simply be thwarted, or damaged, arrested before it can even begin."

"I'm not trying to be adversarial –"

"I think I hear an underlying tone of combativeness, Inspector."

"No, really, I'm –"

"I don't have to sit here and be repudiated by you, or questioned, like I was some kind of murder suspect, Dick."

"Maybe you misunderstand –"

"I'm the trained fucking professional in this room, Inspector. Don't tell me how I've misunderstood *any* thing you've said to me thus far."

"I would never presume to do that –"

"We start out from a mutual position of trust and now you've made a one-hundred and eighty degree shift out of healthy communication to one fueled by resentment and subliminal fury, at me, your counselor, no less. It's mortifying."

I am chagrined into silence, recognizing the futility in further discussion with my out-of-her-mind counselor. I shrug helplessly – wondering how much longer this unendurable session with last.

"Will you at least consider the obvious -- that you have a deep-rooted need to share physically with a same-gender significant other?" my counselor suddenly asks, shifts 'gears', as these things go, [with what can only be described as complete objective caring] and [even love] – of the greater, big-picture sense.

I say that I will indeed consider this possibility (*anything, for the love of Jaysus, just to get the hell out of here*) -- that I am indeed glad that I have come here today to share in a completely objective (yet deeply subjective, from a personal point of view) analysis of my multi-faceted issues afflicting my quotidian, or day to day functions as a valuable, giving, useful, albeit highly homicidal (or monster-cidal) individual who has suffered, of late, great personal loss (and that further), I asked my counselor to forgive my just-moments-ago 'rudeness' and 'ill-targeted' rage, and that any seeming offense I may have given was no doubt predicated on, or predicated by, those same above-mentioned losses.

"This is a very good beginning, Inspector," my counselor tells me, now apparently fully recovered from my ostensible abuses against her.

"Can I expect a favorable report to my captain?" I ask in abject humility, tinctured, I believe, with a certain amount of revelatory astonishment which causes me to whisper, versus speak fully aloud. As if sensing my newfound orientation to be something akin to realizing that there is indeed life after death, space aliens live among us, or that I truly am a being of spiritual light whose complexities are so unified as a whole that they cannot be described merely as sums of their respective parts, my counselor nods and speaks softly.

"I will pass on to Captain Zelig that you and I have embarked on a great journey together, to be continued on a weekly basis."

I sniff, wipe a non-existent tear from my eye, nod gratefully, then stand. I turn, and exit the office, doing my very best not to break out in hysterical laughter.

I am successful, until I reach my car.

At which point, I break down, and do not recover for at least five minutes.

I think to myself: I love therapy.

Until next week.

I see that the sun has dipped over the horizon. Nightfall has arrived.

And the Grand Master awaits.

CHAPTER TEN

▼

I arrived home half an hour later, my headache having returned and my disposition generally about as friendly as the Joy Trail of a week-dead hooker. The sun was doing a gentle melt-down over the horizon, turning the sky an orange blue, reminding me of days long gone when I used to vacation in Mexico, down Cabo San Lucas way. I wished I was in Mexico today, and especially tonight, versus where I would inevitably end up with my two new partners, facing an unholy obscenity hell-bent on our collective destruction.

Curadal and Sam were leaning against my door, in the shadows, looking terribly rested and relaxed.

"Are you alright, Dick?" Curadal asks, seeing me shake despite my feeble attempts at trying to hide my alcoholic infirmity.

"Actually, no, thank you for asking."

Sam watches me like a cat about to pounce a mouse, but says nothing.

Curadal glances at his watch. "It's early yet." He looks up at me. "Why don't we go inside and get you freshened up, Dick."

I sigh the sigh of the eternally hung, then nod. "Probably a good idea," I reply. I take out my key and open the door to my apartment building.

In front of my apartment, Mirabelle hovers just a few feet away. She smiles at me, her vaporous form murky and intermittently transparent. I am momentarily concerned that Mirabelle's ghostly presence might startle Curadal and Sam, but I have no need to worry. I glance at them, and they regard my phantom mistress without expression. I suppose it is silly to assume they might be freaked by a ghost – these people had successfully put down a Lycker in record time, and barely batted an eye. Benign little hobgoblins like Mirabelle probably didn't even merit an extra breath.

"Friend of yours?" Sam asked neutrally.

"Yes," I said. "Her name is Mirabelle."

Mirabelle floats near me as I try to control the shakes long enough to put my key into the lock.

"How are you today, Dick?" she asks me in a low, sexy voice.

"Been better, Mirabelle," I say, opening the door. "Got a busy night ahead of me, though."

Mirabelle takes the hint, a small, disappointed expression crossing her face.

"But don't worry," I say quickly. "I'm going to the orphanage tomorrow. I promise."

This instantly causes Mirabelle to smile and she then evaporates without another word. I indicate to Curadal and Sam to enter.

Little Prick hisses from beneath the sofa, and does not even come out to bitch-mewl about his once-again late dinner. I find that odd, but am immediately distracted by my partner. Curadal suddenly produces a bottle from his long jacket, of what appears to be a 12 year old scotch.

"I thought this might help," he says to me, grinning.

I want to hug and kiss Curadal on the spot, but I restrain myself. The inebriated look of gratitude on my face must be something truly comical to behold because Sam starts to chuckle. I take the bottle, nod a non-verbal thanks, then unscrew the cap and take a swig. The burning sensation in my throat and belly is almost instantaneously revitalizing.

"Oh, boy," I hiss, and drink again. I then gesture to my guests to sit down, which they do. I sink into my favorite lounge-chair, opposite my laptop sitting on a small fold-out table. I lift the bottle toward Curadal.

"Want a hit?"

"Thank you, I don't drink spirits," Curadal says smiling. "Or, I should say, not my drink of choice."

I look to Sam. She merely nods no.

For a moment, we regard one another in silence.

"This could be a very hairy night," I said to them at last. "I mean, I've only run into a Master twice before, and barely came out alive on both occasions."

"Yes, you're a historical icon within the vaulted walls of Monster Vice on every coast." I think Curadal is jesting with me, but the look on his face is dead serious. In fact, he's right. I am the only Monster Vice agent, *anywhere*, to have survived multiple Master encounters.

"It is going to be dangerous," Curadal continues matter-of-factly. "And he knows we're gunning for him, which stacks the odds further against us. But we must start somewhere."

The sun continues to creep over the edge of the world, and the light outside my apartment window gradually dissipates. We sit there for awhile, none of us saying a word. Sam never seems to stop staring at me ... and I don't mind one little bit. Like some bench-worn pathetic drunk, I sit there nursing my scotch, as Curadal and Sam remain fairly motionless – watching me. I know that I should feel something akin to embarrassment – my fellow warriors watching one of their own get smashed. Yet I don't feel remotely self-conscious or guilty. Nor do I believe that my two guests for a moment want me to feel as such.

"Mirabelle seems nice," Sam finally says something.

"Yes," I mumble. "Very nice. For a ghost."

"I can tell she's in love with you."

I stare at Sam point blank. I sum up that Sam is remarkably perceptive.

"You can tell that?" I say tonelessly.

Sam nods.

"How is sex with a ghost, Dick?"

Now how would she know that, I wonder through a miasma of boozy curiosity.   But I am emboldened by the scotch, and shrug, almost arrogantly.

"It's not bad, Sam," I say.   "Very comforting really.   And surreal.   Because, mind you, she's dead, and the illusion of warmth and flesh is just that – illusion."

"Doesn't take away from the come-factor, though, right?" Sam asks matter-of-factly.

I suddenly imagine that Sam in bed must be an incredible experience.   She recognizes no boundaries, and asks intimate questions on a coolly casual and clinical level.   I am intrigued, and feel an erection coming hard upon, as 'twere.

"No, that factor is not affected, Sam."

Sam smiles warmly at me, as if sensing I'm boasting half a stalk even as we speak.   I cross my legs and take another jolt of 12 year old comfort in a bottle.

I am also more than a little convinced that Curadal and Sam are truly only professional associates.   I cannot put my finger on it, but what they have is completely nonsexual.   As I become gradually drunker I again entertain notions of a romp with Sam at some point down the line.   Something in her eyes tells me she might be receptive to this, though where and when, I cannot say. I begin to drift from the effects of the alcohol.   Perhaps to say I'm merely drifting is a misrepresentation because it seems as if I've closed my eyes for only a few minutes and in fact several hours have passed.   Curadal is now standing over me with Sam at his side.

"Good nap, Dick?" he asks, again in that tone of voice that suggests he is perpetually amused with me.

"I – what time is it?"

"It's close to ten," Sam says.

I glance at my own watch. Indeed, nearly five hours have come and gone. And from all indications, it looks as though Curadal and Sam were simply content to sit silently on the sofa, watching me doze.

"You've been here the entire time?" I ask, dismayed.

They both nod in unison.

"Ready to go out and collar a Master, Dick?" Curadal grins.

I do not find the proposition remotely humorous. I stand, with Curadal's help, and I have a fleeting moment of terror that I am less than one hundred percent.

But I realize it is too late to back out now.

I screw my courage to that invisible post within my soul and say a private prayer that I do not end up dead when the night sees its end.

CHAPTER ELEVEN

▼

The Crazy Pole Pony is a smarmy, smoke-laden dungeon about five minutes from my apartment. I have been there several times, mainly because the girls are very pretty and though the environment is barf-friendly to only hopeless chimney-smoking alcoholics, there is a certain charm-filled gormlessness to it that lures one again and again to its murky interior. We arrive in my car, though Curadal drives. Samantha rides shotgun, occasionally throwing my way a disarming smile.

I have the shakes, but have sworn off any more booze for tonight. Too much to do, too much at stake - no pun intended.

There is a rather large gentleman of indeterminate race and sexual orientation guarding the front entrance tonight. He is bald, though a tattoo runs across the side of his face that reads "Dog Dirty Dude". I don't bother even wondering what the fuck that means – the pictures are too painful, too ugly to contemplate in tandem with alcoholic delirium. Oh, and he's wearing high heel Fuck Me Pumps, and chain-mail panties. I had to mention that … just as an aside.

While I stare rudely, Curadal and Samantha merely size him up as if he were the milkman.

"Help you, babies?" the Dog Dirty Dude asks, and bubbles of saliva form at the corner of his mouth. I'm actually not sure if it's saliva … or sperm. It has a milky quality to it that … oh, well, you get the picture.

Before I can reply to the query with a newfound sense of professionalism, Curadal speaks in my stead.

"No. And save your breath – our names are not important and don't ask us for our reasons in being here," he says matter of factly.

"You're coming down my rabbit-hole, friend," Dirty Dude says, his smile disappearing. "And I need to know why all visitors are here bunny-hopping."

Curadal, in one swift motion, shoves his hand under bald boy's neck, and throws him into the darkness. I hear the clatter of trash cans and refuse spilling – and I daresay – bones breaking. I wait for Dirty Dude to reappear from the darkness of the nearby alley, but he does not. Down for the count, I assume.

Curadal looks to Samantha and myself, and extends his hand to the door. "Shall we?"

I should protest Curadal's use of excessive force. Dirty Dude looked like an evil, panty-wearing goat-fucker of the first order, and he was clearly threatening, but still. There was protocol, and we were officers of the law. He deserved better.

As if reading my mind, Samantha grins at me.

"He's an apostate of the Master. Don't feel sorry for him."

I look back into the alley, but there is still nothing moving. Samantha gently steers me inside the Crazy Pole Pony.

It would be safe to say that I am familiar with the cozy interior of the CPP. A long, semi-circular bar occupies one wall, while a stage and two poles stand opposite the bar, with the space in between belonging to a disparate set of chairs and tables. Beyond the stage, there is an adjoining room with velvet sofas attached to the walls. Here is where private lap dances transpire, under the watchful eye of a large bouncer named Jules. Jules always seems to be in the Crazy Pole Pony. Jules seems to have no other life. I personally believe that Jules lives here 24/7, and is in truth, an android from the planet Zartha.

Tonight, the Crazy Pole Pony is in full force and effect. Two lovelies entwine themselves around the two available poles, topless only, of course, due to the liquor license regulation of No All-Nude booze-serving establishments. One of the dancers has blonde hair and perfectly fake tits that seem not to move as she performs her various contortions around the pole. The other performance artist is well over six feet tall, with a nearly perfectly flat chest and a thong shoved so far up her ass, one would assume she would need microsurgery to extract it without permanent damage being done to contiguous areas of the anatomy.

The clientele is varied and enthusiastic. More than two dozen girls walk the floor, predatory in their search for eager males willing to scrounge for twenty dollars or more for a muff-grind in the back room. I see some regulars, but don't bother to nod. Only one table remains open in the place, and it is in a dark corner of the room, adjacent to the puss-grinding Room of Frictional Love.

"I got a bad feeling," I mumble mainly to myself, not expecting anyone to really hear me.

"Yes, I agree," Curadal says, though how he heard what I said walking four feet ahead, while Old Time Rock n' Roll blares at eardrum-shattering decibels is beyond me.

I do a three-sixty of the place, feeling as if I'm being watched. Fuck that. *Knowing* I'm being watched. Yet all I see are drunks and strippers, along with the occasional hostess dispensing fun-filled beverages to patrons.

I pull out a chair from the table for Samantha, who looks at me with genuine surprise and gratitude. She gives me a quaint little nod, and Curadel smiles ... indulgently. He also sits, and then finally, I do, though I am now suddenly filled with so much terror that my little pee-pee has curled up in my sack and is calling to me from my groin to run and get the hell out of here, ASAP.

"You think the Master is here?" I whisper to Curadal.

"Seated right behind you, Dick," Curadal says easily.

"What!" I hiss.

"He's looking at you, too. Arrogant son of a bitch."

I'm not sure at this point if I just shart myself, but everything seems to let loose at once … mainly my sense of hope. I turn slowly, and indeed, see what appears to be a very handsome gentleman, surrounded by three enthusiastic strippers, staring right at me. Or *through* me, feels more like.

He smiles. And lifts his glass, as if in toast.

I slowly turn back to Curadal. "Okay. Are you sure?"

"Quite sure," Samantha says. She is watching the Master, and for the first time, I do not see a sense of surety in either Curadal or Samantha.

My rational mind compels me to relax. Relax because … no way, no how, would any Master worth his blood-sucking oats just be hanging out in broad view for all to see. Not like this. It was unheard of. Then again, I hadn't run into that many Grand Masters in my day.

"Alright, what's the plan," I say, leaning forward, eyeballing my two partners. "Rush and stake?"

"You'd be dead before you left the chair, Dick," Curadal says calmly. "And there's no need for that."

"Why is that?"

"Because," a voice says directly behind me, "I am here. At your service."

I turn, and look up at the Grand Master, who stands a few inches from where I sit. He is smiling. Just folks, really.

"Officer Dick Pitts," the Master says. "It is an honor at last to make your acquaintance."

"Please, don't get up on my account," the Grand Master says warmly. "I'll join you."

And with one deft move, he pulls a chair from the other table, and seems to be sitting in it at a speed faster than thought. The three nubiles huddle around him, kissing his ear, playing with his hair, rubbing his shoulder.

"My friends," he indicates to the friendly strippers, who are not immediately predisposed to speech.

The Grand Master looks from me to Curadal, and then to Samantha. Then back to me.

"So. How is it that you are working with vampires?"

My mind is filled with little twinkles of synaptic overload. I cannot first believe that I am farting distance from a Grand Master, and then cannot further mentally digest the content of his seemingly absurd question. So, with a customary alacrity of communication of late, I simply grunt.

"What?"

"Vampires," the Grand Master says the word slowly. "Your friends. They – are – vampires."

I chance a glance toward Curadal and Samantha, who remain silent, their eyes fixed on the Master.

"I dunno what you're talking about," I mewl. Though there is a fleeting memory of a certain talking werewolf not so long ago who likewise made absurd allegations about my two new partners.

I force a chuckle of disdain.

But the Grand Master is now concentrating on my companions. When he speaks, it is with a low growl.

"Foolish. You are no match for me," he says. "I am part of a new evolution, a superior evolution. You may be more ancient, but as they say in the television series, I'm better, stronger, faster."

I recognize those lines from the Six Million Dollar Man. I feel momentary elation – that my memory has not failed me as yet. And then I consider the circumstances I find myself in ... sitting next to arguably the most powerful vampire on the planet. I wonder if moving my chair a few inches further away from the Master might help.

"You're a freak," Curadal says. "A mutation. Nothing more."

I am abruptly reminded of the Master's amazing statements. That I am working with vampires. It still does not register.

And then it suddenly does.

I turn to Curadal, then to Samantha.

Ah. So many questions are suddenly answered for me, so much seems crystalline clear, all in one galvanizing moment of mental acuity.

My friends – my partners ... *are* vampires. Bloodsuckers. Killers. Enemies to the human race. There werewolf wasn't lying and neither is the Grand Master now.

I feel like a kid suddenly needing to go poo-poo.

I need air. I cannot breathe. I'm surrounded by alien life forms whose sole purpose on the planet is to feed on me like a piece of pork loin.

The Master again regards me coolly. "You've been most troublesome, Inspector Pitts. One of my subordinates suffered at your hand a few nights ago, along with his harem. I was vexed. Vexed to the point of mild annoyance."

I say nothing. I can say nothing.

The Master waves his hand casually into the air, as if to indicate 'well, these things happen.' He sighs. "No matter. My family continues to grow, and you will never imagine where it grows most."

"Children," Curadal says, and his eyes, I can tell, are filled with subdued fury.

The Master smiles. "Yes. Good guess, Old One." The Master looks to me, and leans forward in what is a fairly game imitation of one trying to courteously explain something of vast complication to a dribbling idiot. "I am communicating my powers, my gifts, to children. As many as possible, Officer Pitts. I am perfectly capable of procreation, as any human, but in addition, I am able to transform children into powerful allies." He pauses and winks at me. "As I could do for you, my once-bitten friend."

My affliction, I adduce, must be obvious to the Master. Fear is being slowly replaced by anger.

"You're biting children?" I ask, and my voice sounds like a feeble, puerile whimper of offense that comes off more like a pout.

"Biting, I like that," the Master chuckles, his eyes never leaving those of Curadal and Samantha. "Biting. How well you phrase it."

The Master sits back and seems to revel in the moment. My hand instinctively finds its way down to my Magnum, tucked in my front holster, but one glance from Curadal makes me freeze.

"My advice to all of you is simply go home, and allow things to unfold as they will," the Master says magnanimously. "In this way, you ensure your immediate survival, and save myself and my associates undue exertion in having to destroy you, at least for tonight."

With that, the Master glances around at three individuals who approach the table where I am seated with the vampires (all the vampires, that is). One of them, to my astonishment and child-like sense of disappointment, is Jules. Though I have no idea how this present scenario will unfold, I am momentarily depressed that I may soon have to Stake Jules into oblivion.

"What is it you want?" I suddenly find myself asking.

"I beg your pardon," the Master says.

"What do you want? What do you hope to achieve? Earth is still populated by the dominant race. Hemans, that is. We outnumber you by a million to one. In the end, we'll stamp you out of existence."

"That is like saying a room full of cockroaches outnumber yourself, Mr. Pitts. This does not guarantee that the cockroaches will emerge victorious in the food-chain scheme of things once all out war would to be waged between you and them. They are inferior in mind and body. You would have the advantage by virtue of your intellect, size, strength and resourcefulness, notwithstanding their numbers. So shall we all – monsters, as you call us – one day enjoy dominance over the pathetically weak and venal human race."

"Because you're smarter and stronger, right?" I say.

"I believe I just said that," the Master smiles engagingly.

Curadal and Samantha, meanwhile, have remained curiously silent. Their attention seems more focused on the Master's entourage of female strippers and the likes of Jules and his tag-team companions. Weighing options, I surmise, calculating risks, etc.

"But let's get back to your vampire partners, Mr. Pitts," the Master says, shifting tone.

"You seem pretty sure that they're vampires," I offer a weak verbal parry.

"I think you are, too," the Master says.

I say nothing, though glance at Samantha, and I know she can see my annoyance. She gives me an apologetic look, but it is brief. I turn my attention back to the Master.

"You see, Mr. Pitts, they believe that they are no worse than myself. That they are actually helping humanity by hunting down their own kind. They deny their thirst, and their hunger, and latch on to some kind of moral ambiguity – a silly belief that Man and Vampire could live in peaceful co-existence. Why do they do this, you ask?"

"I didn't ask," I reply with a false sense of courage.

"But of course you're curious," the Master says in that damnable voice of sanctimonious certainty. "Then allow me to enlighten you. They're creatures that feed on your life essence. They are predators. Inhuman. They are no less monstrous than myself, no less terrifying. So why the disparity between them ... and me?"

"Okay, I'll bite," I say (no pun intended). "Why?"

The Master now stops smiling. "Because they are weak. Because they have been contaminated by human hypocrisy and human vulnerability. They feel too much. They fret, like you do. They doubt themselves. They fear they are indeed evil. And that there is ultimately punishment from some nameless and omniscient god for such evil, and they wish to avoid that damnation. Further, they have deluded themselves into believing that they are practically human themselves, based on their civilized and humane approach to life. They are drunk with delusions of morality."

I look to Curadal and Samantha. Curadel speaks very softly: "You're nothing. Just another freak."

"A freak that can crush you, Old One."

"Oh, please," Curadal says.

And then things happen very fast.

I am suddenly on my ass, against the wall, I think having just been slapped out of the way by my old friend Curadal. He has lunged toward the Master, and tackled the latter, to the effect that both he and the Master have flown half-way across the room from the attack. Samantha, meanwhile, is out of her chair, and seemingly levitating, as she slashes at Jules, whose head neatly separates from his body, leaving the trunk on two legs, standing there for a moment frozen, before finally keeling over. The strippers are screaming – and I now see they have fangs.

I move at a sluggish, human pace, dragging my .357 out of my holster, firing at one of the Master's male bodyguards. I am dead on with two shots, taking out both eyes of the now-screaming companion to Jules – who I note, also, has fangs. I glance around the Crazy Pole, and see that most of the non-vampiric population are all screaming, and fleeing the place in droves. Some remain frozen at their tables, even the two strippers on stage stare dumbly into the dark.

"Get the fuck out of here!" I howl, my voice shrill and scared.

I turn, and see that the Curadal and the Master are slashing at one another near the bar, with the Master getting in some rather impressive blows. He is clearly the stronger of the two, yet Curadal does not appear worn down – even remotely weakened. He delivers slashes and blows as effectively as the Master, and while the Master appears enraged, Curadal seems oddly calm.

Samantha screams to my left, pulling out the still-beating heart of the third body guard, and shoving it into the creature's open mouth.

Jules' head, rolling on the floor, still looks like it's alive. His eyes roll around, and his tongue hangs out nearly six inches. It is too absurd to describe. The head stares at me, and I see impotent rage in either eyeball.

From someplace out of the fucking blue, another fanged stripper throws herself at me, and barring the fangs, on any other occasion, I would be aroused by the frontal assault. However, considering that she has the breath of a rotting carcass, and a gleam in her eye that clearly denotes a lack of interest in my continued well being, I shove the muzzle of the .357 into her face, and pull the trigger.

I am showered with gore, goo, brains and fuck-all knows what else, some of the shit getting into my mouth. I resist the urge to rolff, and really don't have time for the luxury, anyway, as Samantha yanks me beside her.

"Stay close, Dick. This could get hairy," she whispers.

"This isn't hairy already?" I stammer.

She does not respond, as she releases me, and flies across the room, decking a poor escaping stripper to the floor, as she lunges on the back of the Master.

I run over, and lift the stripper up, and shove her toward the exit. Somewhere a fire has started, in the back room, and at the end of the bar. Smoke begins to fill the rooms, and my line of sight is becoming murky and occluded. I try to find an opening by which to take a shot at the Master, but he moves so fucking fast, like film in a shutter accelerated to thirty times the speed of normal.

I am really almost an observer in this battle of the vampires. An afterthought to all participants, when it comes right down to it. I spin on my own personal axis, but see that there are no other vampires ready to attack. It is now just the Master, Curadal and Samantha, in one big free-for-all slug fest, which moves from the bar counter, to against the wall, and then up to the ceiling. I stare, open-mouthed. Gravity is defied on a moment by moment basis, and the sounds that come from the mouths of the embattled bloodsuckers freezes every other fluid freezable in my body.

I feel a stab of agony at my ankle, and look down. Jules' head, disembodied as it may be, has now latched its considerable jaws into my Achilles tendon.

I scream, kicking at the chomping-head, but unable to detach the grotesque thing from my leg. I fire into it at last, blowing brains, bone and gristle into the air, once more filling the smoke-filled atmosphere with a fun-combo of inhuman detritus.

Suddenly, two other strongmen, as I call them loosely at this point, appear from behind the stage. They are both black, hissing, fangs barred.

The Master yells from the ceiling, dodging a thrust and slash by Curadal. "Leave. Now. We're finished here!"

Samantha detaches herself from the ceiling, and drops to the floor beside me, where I am spread-eagle, covered with blood and slime, my .357 aimed at the two Master lieutenants.

The two lieutenants hiss, and then move into the shadows and out of sight.

The Master descends to the floor, a nose hair close to me, his eyes red and piercing … for a moment, I do nothing, can in fact, do nothing but stare into those pits from hell.

"We'll speak again, Officer Pitts," he hisses.

And then he is gone, in literally, a puff of smoke. The departure seems almost corny. Seen a vampire today, Dick? Yep, sure did. He almost turned into a bat, but decided to just poof and disappear. Like in one of those Hammer films with Peter Cushing or Christopher Lee. Vampire exit strategies – turning into a wolf, or bat, or smoke. Got it.

Curadal puts a hand on my shoulder.

"Dick, are you alright?"

I freeze momentarily – and then jolt backwards, my gun up, pointed at both Samantha and Curadal.

"What in the name of fuck is this all about?"

My gun shakes, my hands tremble, my mouth tastes like I've been sucking the dick of a juvenile alpaca, and everything hurts.

Oh, and my partners, lest anyone forgot, are vampires.

"Dick, please," Samantha coos. "There's an explanation."

"I'm listening," I snap back, ready to blow the shit out of anything standing in front of me.

"Can we at least go someplace where it is less smoky and less rife with the trappings of death?" Curadal asks. Somewhere, still blaring, is that Ol' Time Rocking Roll.

I discern the sense of Curadal's request, and though I am seething underneath with adrenalin and fury at my two 'partners' – I nod.

"We'll go to my place," I say tonelessly. I do not lower my .357.

"Dick," Samantha says, "you can put the gun down. If we would have wanted you dead, it would have happened ages ago."

I again consider the immutable logic of Samantha's words. I take a breath of acrid air, and reholster my weapon. I'm not feeling good right now.

"I could almost use a scotch myself," Curadal says. "You, too, Dick?

"Yeah. I'm ready. But I mean, shit, Curadal ... I better be pretty fucking happy with your explanation ... you being a ... a ..."

"Vampire, and all," he finishes for me.

"Yeah. That."

"It will be a tale that you have heard before – but which you will not believe, as this time there is a different and tragic spin to it which is true and heart-rending."

What is it about these fucking vampires that they sound like they're out of a Nathaniel Hawthorne novel? Even the Master sounded like he had practiced speech with iambic pentameter in mind.

"Alright, Curadal," I say. "I suppose you've saved my life enough times in the past 24 hours. I'll give you the benefit of the doubt. Not that I have a choice."

"Thank you," Samantha smiles at me.

The fire and smoke have scorched much of the stage, and I hear sirens blaring in the background.

"Let's get the hell out of here," I say, and head for the nearest exit.

CHAPTER TWELVE

▼

Mirabelle is waiting for me, and I see the look of disappointment on her face, as she notices I still am occupied with company. She hovers over my doormat, as I approach, feeling dog-tired and irritable. She notices my general demeanor, the one wherein I am still covered in gore and drying body parts.

"Hard day at the office, dear?" she says, trying to lighten my clearly unpleasant mood.

"A doozy, darlin'," I mutter, and insert my key into the door, and open it.

"Do you mind if I stay awhile, Dick?" Mirabelle asks. I look to her, then to my companions. They seem to have no objections, and beside that, even if they did, I would have told them to get fucked. Mirabelle looks sad tonight, and sometimes ghosts get like that, because, you know ... they're dead, and Mirabelle is my friend, so that's that.

"Sure, honey. Make yourself at home," I say, and Mirabelle smiles and floats in ahead of me.

Little Prick lies on the sofa, giving me an angry meow. No reason to really be angry with me, but cats are like that, I've found. They occupy their central universe of self-importance, and if you don't acknowledge their godliness, they get pissy.

I head for my bottle of scotch, half-empty, provided I remember, by Curadal earlier that evening. Another mental footnote that my vampire partner, and his extremely hot vampire companion, once more had pulled me through a rough patch.

I plop down on the sofa, and attempt to pet Little Prick, who will have none of it, racing off under the table and away from my loving touch. Mirabelle, however, simulates 'sitting' at the other end of the sofa. I still hold the bottle of scotch in my hand, then notice that my manners are slightly remiss, as I stare at Curadal and Samantha.

"Drink?"

Curadal smiles, and reaches for the bottle. "Scotch, yes. But I never drink wine."

Curadal's attempt at humor is not lost on me, as I recognize the famous line delivered by Bela Legosi's vampire. I smile ... just a little.

Samantha wastes no time, and sits down at my kitchen table, crossing her legs, holding my gaze. Curadal walks over to the window, and stares out into the night.

"The Grand Master is out there still. He's waiting for the right time to strike at us."

"Tonight wasn't an opportune time?" I ask, a trace of sarcasm in my voice.

"No. He'll want to torture us first. You will be the first he'll deal with – probably something standard like slow disembowelment with a blunt instrument of some kind."

"How refreshing," I reply, again feeling the need to hurl.

"As for Samantha and myself ... he will choose something more ... protracted in nature."

"Curadal, please," Samantha says.

Curadal offers an apologetic smile. "I'm sorry, my dear."

"What about these children he's been feeding on?" I suddenly remember.

"Yes, they're out there, and hidden," Curadal nods. "He's keeping them someplace where you – we – can't get at them. Some have no doubt already turned, and there's nothing more monstrous, more single-minded, than a vampire juvenile."

"How do you know this?"

"Call it general information in the vampire collective."

"Why didn't you tell me earlier?" I ask.

"Obviously I chose not to tell you quite a bit, Dick. Which is now why we are here, to clear the air, yes?"

I listen to this, glance at Mirabelle, who is listening intently as well. I then get down to the purpose of our talk.

"Alright, Curadal. Let's hear it. From the beginning. If you don't mind."

Curadal turns to me.

"No, Dick. I don't mind at all. Let me first start by telling you that my name is not Curadal."

"Okay, fine, what is it?"

Curadal sighs, looks to Samantha, and then back to me.

"The letters in the name have been transposed."

"Curadal," I say, "or whatever your name is, get on with it."

Curadal steps forward, and hands back the bottle of scotch. I take it, and take a swallow, my eyes riveted on the vampire.

"My real name is Dracula."

*   *   *   *

It is safe to assume that after that declaration, had you gone on a guess (and you would have been right) - the air was suddenly filled with spit-spray and scotch, as I damn near choke. It could just be me, of course, but there is something about a bad night at a strip joint, filled with vampires and disembodied heads munching on one's leg, and then finding out that one's partners are bloodsucking abominations that can put one on edge. Again, maybe I'm being a bit girlie about the whole thing, but what takes the proverbial cake is when my vampire partner reveals to me he is really Dracula.

Thus, needless to say, I am peeved.

"That isn't funny," I say, wiping my lips and trying to clear my throat filled with bile and scotch-saturated saliva.

"There is no humor in my admission," Curadel – or rather, excuse the fuck out of me – Dracula says.

I then abruptly laugh. It's been a long night. I look to Samantha, Dracula and Mirabelle, who is floating over my sofa, and I realize suddenly that my world is a dream within a dream of multiple unrealities that I cannot begin to fathom on any level whatsoever. I am sitting and drinking scotch with vampires and a ghost in my living room, not to mention a neurotic cat that hates my guts. The laughter passes, and I consider sobbing like a schoolgirl.

"I realize this is all a bit much for you," Dracula sighs. "And I again apologize that I deceived you earlier, Dick. I will start from the very beginning."

I am now reduced to simply staring, waiting, trembling. There is, I feel, a distinct possibility that I have become mentally unhinged, like someone who might suddenly be exposed to a vacuum or a depressurized aircraft five miles above the earth, and whose brain begins to boil like oil in a scalding vat.

"I was born in the year 1438. My father was known as Dracul or Vlad the Second. My country was Romania Wallachia, and it was a time of the Ottoman expansion."

I sit there frozen, trying to stay focused.

"You're really … you're not shitting me … you're really Dracula?" I whisper.

Curadel looks at me and smiles sadly. "Yes, I am he. But I am not the Dracula you think you know."

"Not the Dracula I think I know," I repeat stupidly. "What, you're the kinder, gentler version of the famous vampire?"

Dracula looks at me with an expression of genuine admiration. "Why, yes, I am. Because, you see, I am not that Dracula at all."

I stare with a blank expression. "I don't understand."

"I shall press on. You see, born to my father Vlad the Second, were four sons. Myself, the youngest of the Dracul, was named at the time, Radu Dracul, the Handsome. My eldest brother was Vlad the Third. More famously known as Vlad the Impaler."

I nod, but say nothing.

"In Turkish, he was known as the Impaler Prince or *Kazikli Bey*. The Transylvanian Saxon texts referred to him as *Jan Dlugosz*. He was my brother and he was guilty of countless atrocities against humanity. He is now the stuff of myth and even then, he was thought of as an inhuman monster, a creature that drank blood. Hence the source of so many legends."

"So he was a vampire, too," I say, getting into the story somewhat.

"No," Dracula replied. "He was a human being. As were my brothers. I, Radu the Handsome, was the only vampire in my family."

"But ... I've never heard of Radu the Handsome. Everyone, on the other hand, has heard of Vlad the Impaler, and assume he's the bloodsucking Dracula of historical fame," I say, and am surprised at how articulate I sound.

"The vagaries and distortions of history, perpetrated even more by my old friend Bram Stoker," Dracula shrugs. "It is the way of things."

"You ... you were friends with Bram Stoker?"

"Yes, for awhile, when I lived in Dublin from 1889 to 1894. I told Bram what I am about to tell you now. He wanted to memorialize it as an autobiography, but I suggested instead that he tell the story as a fable. It turned out to be a most lucrative decision."

"You knew Bram Stoker?" I ask again in wonder.

"Yes, well. A very bright fellow, though his wife was a bitch. But I don't like to speak ill of the dead," Dracula smiled. "In any event, I supplied the narrative of fact, and Bram embellished and dramatized my character as he saw fit."

"Wow. So the stories about vampires and crosses and garlic – all that is true?"

"Of course. Along with stakes in the heart, transmogrification, mirrors, metamorphosis, the power of hypnosis, the dread of holy ground and churches, and immortality. But you know this already, Dick."

"I do?"

"Is it not stakes that kill present-day vampires? Do not crosses offend their sensibilities? Can not garlic serve as an effective deterrent to vampire attack?" Dracula smiles just a bit. "Prick us, do we not bleed, harm us, and do we not revenge?"

I stare blankly.

"Shakespeare," Dracula sighs. "Merchant of Venice."

"Oh," I say, not giving a shit. I want to get back to my immediate dilemma – having a conversation with the most famous vampire that ever lived, pardon the poor choice of words.

"So ... your brother wasn't a vampire. Just an insane sadist," I say.

There is a moment of silence, as Dracula gathers his thoughts. I glance at Mirabelle, who like myself, appears curious and astonished by Dracula's familial revelation.

"That is correct. After many political misfortunes, my famous brother finally achieved absolute power of Wallachia. His early reign was marked by the elimination of all possible threats to his sovereignty. This was done mainly by impalement. Thus, the name, The Impaler Prince."

"Right," I say. "I get that."

"My brother faced many threats to his leadership, not the least of which was the rivalry in southeastern Europe between the Ottoman Empire and the Hungarian Kingdom. Vlad decided to side with the latter, and that is when the killing began in earnest. Those who opposed him were butchered. 10,000 were impaled in the Transylvanian city of Sibiu. The year before, another 30,000 were impaled. There is a famous woodcut of the period that shows Vlad feasting amongst a forest of stakes and screaming victims writhing in agony."

"Christ," I mutter in bemused fascination.

"His victims included women and children, peasants and great lords, ambassadors of foreign powers, and the list goes on. No one was immune to his cruelty. History has sometimes portrayed my brother as insane, but nothing could be further from the truth. He simply enjoyed killing and torture."

I nod. "Well, we all have our itsy bitsy quirks, don't we?"

The humor is not appreciated, as Dracula stares at me with cold, unsympathetic eyes.

"Death by impalement was slow and painful, Dick," Dracula shifts gears. "May I elaborate?"

Before I can respond – or protest – Dracula is again speaking.

"Victims sometimes endured for hours or days. My brother often had the stakes arranged in various geometric patterns. The most common pattern was a ring of concentric circles in the outskirts of a city that constituted itself as an enemy-state. The method of torture he most enjoyed – a horse attached to each of the victim's legs as a sharpened stake was gradually forced into the body. The end of the stake was usually oiled, and care was taken – great care – that the stake not be too sharp, lest the victim might die too rapidly from shock."

Dracula pauses as I choke back an impulse to bitch-puke.

"Normally, the stake was inserted into the body through the anus and was often forced through the entire system until it emerged from the mouth. There were, however, many instances where victims were impaled through other bodily orifices or through the abdomen or chest. Infants were sometimes impaled on the stake forced through their mother's chests."

"How awful," Mirabelle squeaks next to me.

"Yes. Oh, there were other modes of torture, to be sure: nails in heads, cutting off of limbs, blinding, strangulation, burning, cutting off of noses and ears, mutilation of sexual organs, scalping, skinning, exposure to the elements or to animals, boiling alive – but I won't list them here, not now. To do so would only sicken you more."

"Thanks," I say neutrally. "Uh, but Dracula, just a minute. This is all very fascinating anecdotal information on your fun-filled brother, but can we get back to you for a moment? Like, when did you become a vampire? Or were you *always* a vampire?"

"I have prefaced my personal journey with my brother's life because it is part and parcel with my own misfortune. You see, during my brother's reign, I was appointed to various small governorships around Wallachia. History has called Radu the Handsome a minor character in Vlad's life – and history, in this instance, is not wrong. I deliberately avoided the limelight. I was disgusted with my brother, and those who served him. I was a solitary young man, and I loved my books and quiet walks, and had even considered a career switch from magistrate to -"

"To what?" I asked, now thoroughly roped in to the story.

"I thought seriously of becoming a priest. I was torn between the Franciscans and the Jesuits, and I was days away from making this decision when the vampire came into my life and changed my destiny forever."

I glanced over to Samantha, who remained as still as a statue, eyes glued on Dracula.

"The vampire," I repeated. "Who was he?"

"He told me that he was the original vampire – the first vampire - an offshoot of human evolution that came into being 2,000 years ago. He was in fact a person history has come to hate and abhor for two millennium."

Dracula paused for a few seconds in what I am convinced is an arbitrary bump of drama.

"His name was Pontius Pilate. The man who sentenced Jesus Christ to die."

CHAPTER THIRTEEN

▼

I am poleaxed, or as my three-year old niece would probably say, 'malaffoo-ka-kalished.'

"No," I say in disbelief. "You're shitting me."

"I wouldn't do that, Dick, not at this stage of our relationship. I have deceived you enough as it is," Dracula responded.

"Pontius Fucking Pilate. Unbelievable."

"History of course is fairly certain how Pilate died, but because he had become a vampire, and was thus consigned to roam the Earth forever, he was able to arrange things where he simply disappeared. It's not difficult to do – eliminate one's own identity, create a new one as needed. In fact, it is a practical imperative to surviving through the ages in the world of Men."

"How … how did Pilate become a vampire?"

"It was a reward from Satan," Dracula sighs. "Or more accurately – a curse."

"I'm sure you're going to elaborate."

"Certainly. Pontius Pilate was turned into a vampire by way of a bite from that species now come to be known as *Desmodus rotundus*. It was Lucifer who sent the beast on its deadly mission. Pilate told me he was attacked by the bat the day after Christ was crucified."

"So he started drinking peoples' blood from that point on," I surmised in horror.

"On the contrary. Pilate was basically a humane man. You will recall how reluctant he was to execute Christ, and was forced into this decision by political pressures at the time. He did not understand initially what had happened to him. He did not, for instance, understand his craving for blood. He sated himself with the blood of animals, and told no one of his affliction."

"But he did bite people, right?" Mirabelle suddenly peeped next to me. "That's why vampires are thought of as so evil. They bite people and turn them into other vampires."

Dracula sighs and smiles sadly at Mirabelle. "Alas, that physical mechanism that causes our hunger, could indeed be construed – and I believe is – evil. But like the nature of men in general, evil can be controlled, even suppressed. With considerable concerted effort, it can even be eradicated."

"You're saying that vampires aren't bad news, really, they're just misunderstood bloodsuckers?" I say neutrally, not really sure if I believe this argument for vampiric compassion.

"I am saying that the nature that compels us *is* evil. It is a curse from the devil. But it need not <u>rule</u> us. And in fact, I believe, within both Samantha and myself, that evil has been successfully quashed."

"Uh-huh," I say.

"Not so with the new super vampires of the here and now," Dracula says. "They have given themselves over to their natures completely, and perhaps because of the biochemical complexities triggered in them by the Popov Phenomenon, they have little choice in the matter. But I digress. Mirabelle, you question the vampire's reputation specifically."

"Yeah, I guess," Mirabelle shrugs, and offers me a small smile.

"It is true, that once we inflict our bite, our victims are then subject to vampiric transformation, or death, depending on the severity of the attack. If our hunger drives us to feed without abandon, transformation for the victim is one hundred percent. The results of resurrection are hideous – as you well know, Dick."

"No shit."

"On the other hand, with control and disciplined feeding, a vampire can create a companion vampire, one that retains complete function of mind, body and soul, and is not turned into an insane piece of unholy flesh, blindly and madly searching for a way to sate its insatiable hunger."

"Dracula," I say slowly. "You have killed human beings over the centuries, correct?"

Dracula looks at me without blinking. "Correct. I have done so, and each and every time I was possessed of the Hunger."

"The Hunger?"

"It is a term applied to a vampire that has no control over its hunger. It is a time that manifests itself rarely, and cannot be contained – but it is during those times, that a vampire is at its most dangerous. It was at those times that I lost all sense of rational perspective, and occasionally killed and fed on human blood."

Mirabelle and I say nothing.

Dracula lowers his head. "It has happened to me less than a dozen times, but it shames me greatly to recollect those moments of animal abandon. And it is, I fear, how the vampire myth, in part, became so famous in my home country of Romania Wallachia."

"I think I get it. When the Hunger hit you – you went out and started putting the fangs to the general population."

"Something like that," Dracula nodded.

I am fascinated, my revulsion on the details of vampire behavior-management momentarily quelled.

Dracula puts down the glass of scotch he has been holding, and sits next to Samantha. He stares at me with eyes that are tinctured with tears.

"It was during a period of the Hunger that Pilate fed on me, though his strength of will was such that he could control that demonic urge to feed completely and with lethal finality. Thus, I became the thing I am today – a vampire, to be sure – but a thinking, feeling, cognizant being, able to differentiate between good and evil."

"But you still kill people for their blood," I say with what I recognize to be a tone of contempt and disgust.

"No."

Dracula's response surprises me. "No?"

"I do not feed on humans anymore. Nor does Samantha. You might call us addicts who maintain a kind of twelve step program, the end result being, we simply do not kill people."

"But how do you survive?" Mirabelle asks in her soft lilt?

"Animals. Specifically, pigeons."

I cannot believe what I'm hearing. "Pigeons?"

"There are enough of them around, wouldn't you agree?"

"Pigeons?"

Dracula nods.

"You're shitting me."

"You keep saying that, Dick. No, I'm not shitting you. Ask yourself why you see so many pigeons in the city – but so few *dead* pigeons. Have you ever noticed the lack of pigeon corpses on the street?"

I put on my dead-pigeon-deficit thinking cap and ponder Dracula's question. In fact, I have rarely seen a dead pigeon in Los Angeles. Once in a blue moon, maybe, one that is squashed by a car, once I found one torn apart by a cat – but aside from that…

"Pigeons," I repeat again.

Dracula looks to Samantha, and takes her hand.

"Pigeons – and coconuts. Coconut milk has many constituents similar to pure blood plasma.[4] That … and we can feed on one another," he says, smiling.

---

[4]   During World War II when blood supplies were running low it was discovered that the liquid inside young coconuts could be used to substitute for blood plasma. It is considered a viable substitute for blood plasma because it is sterile, cool, easily absorbed by the body, and does not destroy red blood

"What?" I say, the coconut statistic obliterated by the more astounding news of vampire co-parasitic survival practices.

"We vampires are able to sustain our daily existence by also feeding off one another. Incremental portions, of course, but the blood that flows in our respective bodies is sufficient to do the trick."

"You suck each other?" Mirabelle asks. And the way she phrases it makes me inadvertently chuckle.

"Charmingly put," Dracula says. "Yes ... we do indeed suck one another. So, in addition to the pigeon dynamic, we are quite happy with not murdering helpless human beings to live. In fact, aside from the vicious and insane mutations that we've seen develop due to the Popov Phenomenon, most vampires live in this way."

I stand, feeling a little drunk, staring at Dracula incredulously. All my senses are assaulted, my understanding of the vampire myth shorn to the bone (again, sorry for the mixed metaphor).

"Most vampires?"

"Well, Dick, I may possibly be the oldest vampires on the planet, but I'm not the only one. Samantha is only a century younger than myself, for example. There was an unofficial census taken in the vampire community about 50 years ago, and it is estimated that we number over a million worldwide."

"There was – a census taken?"

---

cells. It is a natural isotonic beverage with an excellent level of electrolytic balance, similar to what we have in human blood.

On another note, it has been said that there is a better chance of being killed by a falling coconut then being killed by a shark. This is not some bogus, bullshit allegation. The noted director of the Florida Museum of Natural History, George Burgess, in his International Shark Attack File was quoted "Falling coconuts kill 150 people worldwide each year, 15 times the number of fatalities attributable to sharks." It is not clear how Mr. Burgess obtained these statistics, but such a study on palm-tree-falling related deaths, compared to say, oh, coconuts or shark attacks, might be a bloody interesting laboratory study.

"Yes."

"But ... a million vampires? This was way before the Popov thing, right?"

"Of course."

"My god. A million blood drinkers," I say, momentarily forgetting myself.

"We're not that bad once you get to know us. We're not a whole lot of fun at Sunday mass, but –"

"I don't mean that. I mean ... I mean that vampires are famous for killing and drinking human blood. That's what they do. That's the job description. Vampire. Fangs. Blood. Living Death. People killers."

"A lot of myth mixed with fact, true," Dracula says softly. "Vampires are a different form of life in this world, a different species. But to say that we are all homicidal is like saying all human beings are serial killers. It's simply inaccurate, and in fact, aside from the Starving issue in our lives, we're quite peaceful."

I stare, flummoxed.

"Furthermore, we are able to function on a limited basis during the day, though it is uncomfortable. The mutations, like the Grand Master tonight, however, can only operate at night. Sunlight would kill them. But again – they are pure evil, no doubt about it, while we are ... something less than that." Samantha finally chimes in, silent up to now.

"Then why do so many cultures throughout the world, down through the centuries, portray vampires as evil, bloodsucking monsters that live in coffins and exist to prey off of humans?" I ask, trying to find a way to expose Dracula in some way ... though I'm not sure how ... or why.

"Are there not myths and legends of space aliens? Flying saucers? Twirling wheels of fire that fly? Big Foot? The Abominable Snowman? Ghosts?"

"But ghosts are real, Mr. Dracula," Mirabelle counters.

"They were not real until the Popov event. In fact, the Popov scenario changed the planetary dynamic completely," Dracula says with a cool clinical detachment. "In other words, young lady, you should not exist. You should have passed on at death."

I am pacing now, thinking, shaking my head in wonder.

"Peaceful vampires," I repeat. "I'll be goddamned."

I turn to Samantha. "I suppose your story is equally sentimental." My sarcasm is ill-concealed.

She smiles - that smile that tells me one day she would have no objection to a frenzied tussle in the old coffin velvet with me.

"Actually, my story is not sentimental whatsoever, if that's how you choose to characterize Dracula's background."

"Okay, sorry. How did you become a vampire? Someone famous like Marie Antoinette fanged you?"

She smiles again, and something inside me melts. I want Samantha, I realize, bad, and dirty, and … now.

"No. When I was bitten, I was eighteen years old, as I appear now."

"You do look very young," I admitted.

"For someone close to six hundred years old, I consider that a compliment. Thank you, Dick."

"Okay, go on."

"It was Dracula who fed on me during the Hunger. I was eighteen years old, and ensconced in Our Lady of The Holy Trinity, about 70 miles outside of Venice, Italy. I was a young nun, happy in my service to God, incapable of error or regret, untouched by grief, and still a stranger to despair."

"Very touching," I say, and I mean it.

"I was a virgin."

I wait, and my mouth drops open as Samantha speaks again.

"I was a virgin back in 1552, and I am still one today."

✳   ✳   ✳   ✳

I smile, and find this genuinely amusing.

"Okay, now you're putting me on."

"No, Dick. I am still a virgin. I have never known a man. At least, sexually."

I am mystified. "But ... the Master Vampire said he could reproduce like human beings. Is that a lie?"

"No, it is the truth. Vampires, contrary to the dark ramblings of myth, and Hollywood, are wholly capable of biological reproduction," Dracula speaks up again. "And many of us are quite fond of sex. And there are those who have no use for it any longer, like myself."

I have no interest in Dracula's sexual ambivalence. My focus again shifts to Samantha, an amazingly beautiful woman who continues to exponentially captivate my heart and loins simultaneously.

I realize I am sputtering again. "But ... you don't look ... I mean, you don't seem like ... it's just that –"

"Are you implying I look like a little slut, Dick? Is there an absence of virtue in my demeanor, or manner of speech? Do I look like a whore?"

I shut up, and then realize she's messing with me. She laughs softly, and it is a beautiful laugh. I smile, and fuck me gently with a blunt power-tool, but I believe I'm blushing.

"No," I stammer in my best wussy. "I'm sorry. It's just that you seem so ... worldly."

"I *am* worldly," Samantha says, still smiling. "Worldly, but not prone to frequent acts of fornication."

"By choice, I assume."

"Completely. I have yet to meet anyone who I would want to do the Nasty with. I believe that's how, among other phrases, screwing is referred to these days, yes?"

"Uh, yep. That's certainly one way of putting it." I believe I am falling in love with Samantha, and I turn to Mirabelle, who stares at me with what I swear is a touch of jealousy and hurt.

Samantha continues with her saga of how Dracula found her in a field one twilight, near her church, and consumed with that strange and horrific affliction to all vampires known as the

Hunger, took her mortal life by feeding on her. He had used restraint, and thus, she became a full-fledged, ass-kicking, red-hot smoking, vampire-babe who, by the way, could also fuck *but* chose not to for the most fundamental and touchingly romantic of reasons, that being ….

… she had yet to fall in love.

Samantha went on to say that she and Dracula had become friends, and she thus was invited to be his traveling companion through the ages. He taught her how to feed on animals only, how to instill terror in the hearts of pigeons everywhere, and how best to disappear from the world of men during those periods of the Hunger stranglehold. She was versed in no less than twenty languages, but that she would need to brush up on her Eskimo Inuit, if push came to shove. She had disciplined herself to learn every Martial Arts technique in existence, as well becoming proficient in any number of weapons warfare and personal combat.

She could also play the piano, she said, as well as Mozart, and her violin virtuosity was right up there with Itzhak Perlman and Isaac Stern, yet could not surpass her cello accomplishments, which she stated (modestly) were on par with those talents of Yo-Yo Ma.

I was, of course, wondering, pig that I am, if she believed herself to be a super-charged fuck-bunny in the making, given the fact that she'd never, as she put it, Done The Nasty, and that she must certainly be the horniest virgin on the planet. Or so I dared hope, so I dared dream.

She smiles at me again.

"Dracula also taught me how to read minds," she said.

My own libidinous smile evaporates.

"Oh."

"It's a vampire talent," Samantha says.

"Uh-huh."

"But I try not to invade an individual's privacy."

"Is that a fact."

"But I do find the term fuck-bunny amusing," she says, and her smile broadens.

Shit. Busted like a Tai hooker trying to fake a blowjob.

"I do, in fact, have … urges, Dick. I simply have not as yet acted upon them. My vows with my church were very specific about the rules of chastity – and celibacy. It is difficult to disengage myself from that early discipline. You do understand, don't you?"

"Oh … sure. Of course," I nod. I suddenly ask myself what my therapist Dr. Simonhoffer would make of my discussion with Samantha, and my base desire for her, concomitant thereto.

Then, for just a moment, another thought strikes me, more germane to the whole vampire thing in general.

"Dracula. Samantha. I want to back up a bit, and ask you about the crosses, and garlic. You mentioned that you two fear those, as do the Popov vampires and werewolves?"

"Yes, Dick. As I said before, we cannot stand to be near these things. They are an anathema to all vampires, and werewolves."

"But you're *good* vampires," I say. "I'm puzzled, you see."

"The question of our moral rectitude being somewhat unequivocal in terms of the power of these things over us."

"Yes … I guess so," I say. "It just seems that if you are people who deliberately eschew murder, why would you thus be affected adversely by icons associated with goodness? I'm having trouble with that."

"You almost wonder if God is playing fair with us, right, Dick?"

"You could say that, yes."

"It's a good question, Dick. Remember, the genesis of the vampire began with Pontius Pilate. It is a curse from the Dark One, and of course, he is enemies with the power of light, and the Christ. Thus, we are all subject to, by our very evil origins, the terrors inherent to crucifixes, garlic, mirrors, running water and holy ground – all things affixed to vampiric existence that are deadly and intolerable to us on every level."

"So even if, you like believed and loved Jesus, it wouldn't matter, the cross would still freak you out?"

"Yes, dear," Samantha says. "That's just about it."

Mirabelle sighs. "That doesn't seem fair. I like you guys," she says, and I say to myself, you gotta love the ghost of a whore with a heart of gold.

Samantha smiles warmly at my little Mirabelle. "Thank you, honey. That's very sweet of you. And I like you."

"As do I," Dracula says.

And for a moment, there is silence.

Well, shit on a stick, I think to myself. Friendly vampires. Fangs with Fuzzy Feelings. Nice Folk Nosferatus, just hanging out, drinking scotch with old Dick and his squeeze, the phantom Mirabelle.

I consider this, then take another moment to just stare at both Dracula and Samantha. I finally nod, weary to the bone, the events of the day fully caught up to me ... along with the scotch.

"Tell me," I say wearily, "why both of you are cops."

"One has to do something to make a living, Dick," Dracula replies. "And being a cop in Monster Vice allows Samantha and myself to maximize our talents for destroying the evil opposition."

I nod and sigh.

"Okay. Thanks. What a story." I then walk over to the window. I glance at my watch, and see that the sun is beginning to rise. I realize my companions and I have been talking for hours. I look to them now. "So now what? Where do we go from here?"

"The big question, Dick, is do you want to go *anywhere* from here with us as your partners?"

A good question, and the answer flies unhesitatingly from my lips, catching me off guard. "Of course. I'd be a fool not to work with you. You're assets. That, and you're not trying to fang me on a moment to moment basis."

"Excellent," Dracula says. "Then our work lies before us. And it will be daunting work at that. I give ourselves one out of ten chances of survival against the Master and his minions, based on the sheer preponderance of numbers in his favor."

"I was sooo afraid you'd say that."

"The Grand Master, like ourselves, is close to shutting down for the day to come. But by tonight, he will surely come searching for us, Dick. You – and Samantha and myself. He will never forgive our intrusiveness from a few hours ago."

"I figured as much."

"If it's alright with you, we'll return here tomorrow at sunset, then strategize."

"There must be something I can do today, something to give us an edge," I say.

"Yes, there is," Dracula says.

"What?"

"Stay alive."

I'm about to respond quickly that this is not a problem ... but I see Dracula's point. Every day in Monster Vice lowers the statistical probability of continued survival. I nod, then look to Mirabelle. "Alright, I'll work on that one.

Dracula and Samantha rise, and head for my front door.

"It must be a helluva life," I say to them.

They regard one another, and Samantha nods. "It is. I wish I could say it is a happy life. But you probably know that's not true."

"Join the club," I say.

"See you tomorrow, Dick. And thank you for your understanding."

They turn in unison, and are about to exit my apartment.

"Dracula. What happened to Pontius Pilate?"

He turns and looks at me and smiles. "I don't know, Dick. He disappeared one day. We were traveling companions for a time ... but then he just wasn't there one day."

"What do you think happened to him?"

Dracula sighs. "I believe in every vampire's existence, there is a time to evaporate into the fog of time. If not to die, then simply to hide. He may be dead, he may not be. Or he may be waiting."

"Waiting for what?"

"Again, I don't know. This is all theory for me, conjecture."

I nod and think about what Dracula has said. I shake my head and whisper: "I think I would kill myself after a time. To live so long, to be the vanguard of so much purported evil – the poster boy for villainy."

Dracula seems to consider this with true thoughtfulness. "Yes. You may be right."

He then turns, and with Samantha, exits through my door, closing it behind them.

I stare at my door for a moment, shaking my head.

"Jesus H. Christ," I say.

"Dick?"

I turn, and see Mirabelle staring at me from the sofa.

"Yes, Mirabelle?"

"Can I stay with you for awhile?"

She didn't even need to ask.

"I was hoping you would, sweetheart."

She smiles.

"And I'm going to check up on your daughter today. I promise."

Mirabelle floats over to me, and kisses me.

"Thank you."

She then begins to cry.

CHAPTER FOURTEEN

▼

The sun is fairly low in the sky when I awake, and for a moment, I think it is a little past dawn. But in fact, I've slept away most of the day, and it is already late-afternoon.

I remember that Mirabelle had left me almost immediately after we had sex hours earlier. One moment she was there, and in the next second, she was gone. She does not say good-bye. Like a thought, fleeting and insubstantial, she evaporates into the ether. I sigh, suddenly feeling very empty. I ache all over, and my leg still hurts from the chewing Jules gave me earlier at the Pole Pony. Since I am already Bit, a vampire attack short of one involving decapitation or disembowelment, has little other effect on me, aside from causing annoying pain and discomfort.

I jot down a to-do list mentally of today's activities. I will report my findings on the Grand Master to HQ. Of course, I will edit that report accordingly, not mentioning that, by the way, two of Monster Vice's Finest are vampire police officers. I did not need to ask Dracula or Samantha if their anonymity was something that needed to be protected. Duh. A no-brainer.

After a much needed shave and shower, I feed Little Prick, who has decided for reasons unfathomable, to allow me to pet him (perhaps, though, it is because I provide an extra large helping of breakfast in the cat bowl). Zelig from Monster Vice has emailed me, but it is simply a query as to my well-being, not a demand to know what the fuck-all I've been doing for the day. I reply that I'm fine, laying low, then enter my report into the computer, and send it off, not yet wanting to put in an appearance downtown. I have things to do, and promises to keep.

It's around 4pm, and there's still stuff on my agenda. I take a hurried piss, throw on some cologne, then jump in to the car and head for the first chore of the day.

$$* \quad * \quad * \quad *$$

The first orphanage in Los Angeles was established in 1856 by the Daughters of Charity of St. Vincent de Paul at the corner of Alameda and Macy, where Union Station now stands. The hospital that grew out of the orphanage was the first in Los Angeles as well, officially opening in 1858 in the Aguilar Adobe on Upper Main Street. St Vincent Medical Center even has a museum and archive at Third and Alvarado. It is home to many ghosts and spirits – a place festooned with the floating undead. These wandering souls are mainly children of crack-addict mothers or suicides – perennial victims of the streets of Los Angeles, and worsened by the Popov Incident and murder rate that has risen a hundred percent from vampires and werewolf attacks.

I will keep my word to Mirabelle and visit her daughter at the orphanage. Afterwards, I will check in on my sister-in-law, and my nephews. I cannot quell a constant sense of anxiety within myself as I head south on the Hollywood Freeway for St. Vincent de Paul. The source of my uneasiness is not hard to discern: For it is an official and unequivocal fact that werewolves now walk on holy ground and that the Grand Master is alive and well (sorta), and presumably looking to draft as many children as possible into the ranks of the mean and blood-hungry. Further, if vampires like Dracula and Samantha can move about with relative impunity during the day, if only for the briefest of durations, it is logical to assume that other vampires have figured out a way to do likewise – and if not now, then sometime down the line.

I am, my fellow *malchiks*, with these gentle thoughts rambling, tempted to begin drinking right about now. But I am determined to exert some measure of self control – a measure of self-resolve that I will levy upon myself for at least another half an hour.

I turn off the Alvarado exit and notice a bevy of pigeons tearing at some stale bread along the sidewalk. Vampire food, I say to myself. Mommy, look: Little feathered finger-sandwiches, waiting to be scarfed down by a hungwy wampire. Yum, yum. Make sure you chew the beak, honey. Isn't that special.

I've been awake less than an hour, and I'm already punch-drunk.

My mind rifles itself back to last night, and our encounter with the Grand Master. Dracula has maintained that our chances of prevailing against this Super Vampire are extremely low. And yet, even super creatures are vulnerable ... this much I am sure of. I reviewed, as a kind of mental exercise, what I understood of vampire pathophysiology.

The human body contains six quarts of blood. Your basic bloodsucker can scarf that down inside of a New York Minute, then be ready for an extra helping just seconds later. They're like seagulls, always famished, always possessed of the urge to snack. Yet what drives them to feed? So far, science had yet to find a reason – the mystics were way ahead of us on this one – vampires, quite simply, were intrinsically evil.

Monster Vice actually collared a Tuti last year and dissected it; we fed it some pretty choice hemoglobin, laced in about a pound of Vicadin. The Tuti never really fell asleep, but it sure didn't put up a hassle once we cut into it. The collar was historically significant because a Tuti had never been hauled in before — either here in L.A. or across the world - and our Med Techs wanted to see what made the monsters tick. Correction, until Dracula had informed me that he had collared a Master himself.

And yes, in case you're wondering, I was the cop who made the collar and lived to tell about it here on the West Coast.

As it turned out, the vampire simply doesn't possess a normal set of internal organs. Well, a normal set of internal organs that *function* on a human level, anyway. This is not, however, an impediment to the bloodsucker's talent for locomotion and flying, or transformation to animal or winged beast. So, logically, one must assume that a vampire does not exist according to the laws of existing biology. It operates under its own rules and order. Forget about trying to attach a subset of logical protocols to their lives ... such as could be characterized. Couldn't be done.

Fine.

Wonderful piece of deductive reasoning, I think. Nothing new. The guys at a thousand laboratories all over the world would say as much. Vampire. Evil. Supernatural. End of story, and just deal with it.

I pull up to the orphanage, find a parking place, and turn the car off. I still feel anxious.

Fucking vampires, they really get under your skin.

And now, according to the Grand Master, we have kid vampires to deal with. I've never had to stake a kid before. I don't know if I could, in all honesty. The freeze reflex could kick in, and that would be a bad thing indeed. Somehow, I would have to inure myself to that potential scenario.

The foyer to the orphanage feels more like the anteroom to a morgue, versus a caretaking hospice for parentless juveniles. There is a dreadful stillness to the place, and I see no one in the halls, nor hear the pitter-patter of little children's feet nearby. All I see, seated behind a desk, is a rather large woman who looks at me as if perhaps I was the most dangerous pedophile in the world. Maybe I'm just feeling vulnerable, perhaps that is only a look of intense professionalism she offers me. Yeah, probably. Then again...

"Excuse me," I say, "I'm looking for a little girl."

Already, I know that I have chosen the wrong words.

I try to be amusing, or at least charming. I chuckle, shake my head, and wave my *mot mauvais* to the four winds. "I mean, I'm looking for a particular little ... a child of around eight."

I stop. This is going from bad to worse.

The woman says nothing, but continues to stare coldly at me. I wonder if she has a loaded shotgun pointed at me from beneath the desk. Probably.

I then notice her eye-line as she continues to rudely stare without comment.

She is eyeballing my crotch.

The *old lecherous cow*, I think, realizing it is an unfair thought – that perhaps this poor woman has not been with a man for some time, and that my presence here – a robust example of middle-aged pulchritude – causes her to stare at my nethers with unabashed fascination.

I sigh. I guess I still have some kind of magic, I think. I am mildly flattered.

But she continues staring. It is almost too much. I sigh, and look down at my pants, wondering for a moment if I spilled something on them, and that indeed this gazing lady behind the desk is simply fascinated by my sloppy food spots rather than the concealed, tempestuous promise hidden within.

The urge to melt into something liquid is immediate.

For I see that my fly is open.

The urination process, clearly a hurried act of ten minutes earlier, ended with me forgetting to zip up the old Pecker Bat Cave. I remember that I have just recently asked, as of seconds ago, for a little girl, and a child ... with my fly open.

Not a good first impression.

I moan in suppressed mortification, and quickly fumble with my pants.

"Sorry," I whisper through a grunt. "These things happen."

"Yes, I'm sure they do," the receptionist replies without even trying to crack a sympathetic smile.

I catch my breath, regrouping, and take out my wallet and badge, and open it.

"I'd like to see Jennifer Wilson."

The *uber*-receptionist glances at my badge, then looks back to me.

"May I ask why, Officer Pitts? Is she under arrest?"

No," I offer a smile. "I just need to see her."

"It's very late for visitors. Visiting hours really end around four."

"I know. But this is important."

"I'm sure it is. Perhaps you could come by another time. The children have just finished their afternoon nap, and they're preparing for their last classes of the day."

Why does it feel like the whole world is fucking with me?

I hold back a rising surf of annoyance, and smile again.

"Another time would be inconvenient. And I won't be long. Could you arrange for me to see her? Now, please?"

Godzilla-woman stares at me silently.

"Before the next ice age?" I smile again. I feel like my face is aching from all this forced friendliness.

The *uber*-receptionist stares at me for a moment longer, then rises, turns, and trundles out of sight.

I am alone, and I begin to have a strange feeling.

There is something wrong.

Terribly wrong.

CHAPTER FIFTEEN

▼

My gun is withdrawn from my holster, and in my hand within one second, at most.

I move around the receptionist desk, and head into the main hallway where Strong-Like-Bull Receptionist-Lady disappeared to. There are doors on either side of me. I open one. A classroom within, I note, empty desks, a blackboard, a few bookcases. Onward.

Somewhere down the hall I can hear hissing. My heart begins to sink. And then from around the corner, I see it.

A kid. Around eight years old.

With fangs.

Blood dripping from his mouth.

His eyes staring at me with blind, voracious hate.

A vampire.

"Oh, shit," I whisper so softly, I can barely hear the expletive that has escaped my lips.

The kid moves toward me very quickly, and I get off a shot that slams the little vampire against and through a pane window twenty feet away. I turn a corner, and find the uber-receptionist lying dead, her throat torn apart.

More hisses.

I come across another adult, a young woman of thirty, disemboweled. I almost slip on strewn intestines and pancreatic goo. The vampires, the little darlings, come into full view, unafraid. There are around six of them now, boys and girls who just wanna have some bloody fun. I realize what has happened in one galvanizing moment.

The Grand Master has been this way, and has fed.

More accurately, he has fed with intent to convert. The conversion has clearly been successful. I don't know how I know this, but I do.

Suddenly, there is a scream – a child, I can tell – who is terrified and I shall presume, unbitten. The screams, shrill and desperate, emanate to my right in an adjoining hallway. I back up, not turning away from the vampire children, but back-pedaling quickly. Finally, I spin on my heel and run.

The screaming continues. A half open door looms ahead of me, and I crash through it. There, still screaming, and using a pillow as a kind of weapon, is a little girl, trying to fend off two other children, both girls – both now of the vampire persuasion. She looks at me, pleading and horror in her eyes.

The two little bloodsuckers turn to address my presence, and I put a bullet in each of their sweet little hearts. They drop to the ground quickly, but I know they will not stay down for long. I rush forward, and grab the child's hand, as she begins to sob.

"It's alright, honey. We're getting out of here," I say.

"They were my best friends," she sobs.

"Are you hurt? Were you bitten?"

She shakes her head adamantly. "I hid in the closet when he came. When the big man came."

The Grand Master.

"Sweety, you stay right behind me. Do not let go of my hand. Alright?"

She nods emphatically, her tears evaporating, as if something inside of her had suddenly kicked in – a survival instinct that defied a child's sense of pain and heartbreak.

"What's your name?"

"Jennifer," she says softly, and I hear hisses down the hall once again.

"Jennifer Wilson?"

"Uh-huh."

"Your mommy sent me, honey."

"Mommy's dead, mister."

Now was not the time to argue the finer points of Mirabelle's discorporate existence. I hold onto the child's hand, and move toward another door at the opposite end of the room.

I marvel momentarily at the coincidence of my being here just as this orphanage has been attacked and transformed into a playpen for toddler toothiness of the most unholy sort. I do not try to sort through rational explanations, because one ghastly thought leaps to mind: The Grand Master is operating in the daytime!

But Dracula said that was not possible. Any outside, daytime exposure –

Wait a minute.

He could have come up through the drainage system, or the sewers. Within these walls, protected from the sunlight, he could still do damage. And I realize this is exactly what has happened, as I come to an open warehouse platform, Jennifer in tow behind me, and see a huge grate in the floor. The grating has been removed, and a gigantic, gaping maw of a trap-door can now be clearly seen.

I had to get to my car. Fine time to leave the Walkie on the seat. Shit on a stick.

Jennifer was silent, as I did a full 360 of the loading platform. Nothing moved, nothing hissed. The vampire kiddies must not have cared much for the pursuit, or they were simply getting adjusted to the "changeover."

There is an exit, a half-open cargo door directly to my right.

"Let's go," I whisper to Jennifer.

We slip through the exit, Jennifer easily, me, older and fatter, with some difficulty, as the door seems locked into this marginalized position for comfy exiting.

Outside, there is no movement whatsoever.

I grab Jennifer's hand and bee-line for my car. As I open the passenger side of the vehicle for Jennifer, I look up and stare at the parking area near the front entrance. I can see a figure — a huge hulking creature. He stands, motionless, and his face is indistinct to me for a few moments. Small children exit from the orphanage, and huddle around the creature like a retinue of weaving planets.

And then the face comes into focus.

Along with those eyes.

I look at the Grand Master, who smiles at me. And then he taunts me with a small wave, as to say "Hi, jerk-off. Surprise, surprise."

I am almost about to panic uncontrollably, remembering that it is still daylight out, and that if this is the case and the Grand Master is happily traipsing about non-nocturnally, then we're all fucked from here to Botswana. But then I come to my senses and note the sky. The sun has dipped over the Hollywood Hills, north and west from my position. There is no direct sunlight, polarized light only … and thus the Grand Master suffers no direct exposure. Further, he is in the shadows, reinforcing his position of safety.

I almost do something stupid – like rush madly for the Grand Master, attacking him in a frontal tackle. But little Jennifer, seated in the car already, tilts her head and looks out to me, tears in her eyes.

"That's him, mister. Can we go, please? Please, can we go?"

I glance at Jennifer, and more than pity, I feel that Jennifer has more sense in her than in the dumb goose of a police officer now contemplating a direct assault on a Grand Master, alone, without backup, and by the way, supported by over a dozen little vampires all hungry and ready to feed.

"Yeah, good idea, honey," I nod to her, and force a comforting smile. Jennifer even smiles back, wiping away a tear. The child has something about her that melts my heart. Her eyes, perhaps. Eyes like her mother, I think distantly.

I get into my car, and start the engine.

The Grand Master remains where he is standing, merely watching me from his comfortable distance.

I punch in a few buttons on my dashboard."

"Monster Vice, this is Pitts, 340, on station. I have multiple fangs in my vicinity. Location, Daughters of Charity of St. Vincent de Paul at the corner of Alameda and Macy. I count a Master, and a dozen plus children, all turnovers. Request back-up and full tactical."

A momentary hiss, and Zelig is on the line. "Dick, what the hell are you doing down there?"

I look to Jennifer.

"I'm doing a favor for a friend, Zelig. And I can't stick around for the party."

"I have units heading your way now," Zelig replies. "What do you have that's more important than Fang Detail at an orphanage?"

"I'll tell you later."

"Alright, I know you had a helluva stink last night. When are you back full time?"

"Tonight."

"Doing what?"

"Killing the greatest threat ever to Mankind and trying to stay alive in the process," I say easily.

There is silence for a moment, then Zelig clears his throat.

"Okay, sounds good. Fill me in later."

"That's a 10-4, boss," I say, then disengage my com-link to Monster Vice.

As I pull out of the orphanage parking lot, I see MV helicopters move in formation above, and I hear sirens from all directions. I sigh, realizing that the Grand Master and his new brood of baby fangs will have disappeared from here by the time Monster Vice arrives in force.

It is clear to me that the Grand Master wants to choose his own battlefield, and with his own combatants. Those combatants being Dracula, Samantha ... and yours truly.

It is still only late afternoon, but the sky seems much darker to me, ominous, foreboding and filled with the promise of bleak things to come.

I look to Jennifer, who stares at me with large, brown, weepy eyes.

"You're okay now, Jennifer," I say. "You're safe."

"You're wrong," she says softly. "Where are we going?"

"A place where no one can hurt you."

Jennifer considers this in silence for a moment, then looks to me, an eerie wisdom in her expression.

"Do you really believe that?"

I don't, and decide to simply shut the fuck up and drive.

CHAPTER SIXTEEN

▼

I arrive at my brother's house in twenty minutes. I have called ahead, and Mindy is home, though the twins are out with friends. Mindy meets me at the door, as Jennifer stands beside me. We hug, and hold each other for a long moment.

"You okay?" I ask.

"As okay as possible under the circumstances," she says, and her lower lip begins to tremble. "Come inside, Dick. You, too, sweetheart."

Mindy excuses herself for a moment, moving into a nearby bathroom for some Kleenex. I look around the house, and feel myself instantly wilt, the adrenalin of the past half an hour neutralized into nothingness.

"And who is this?" Mindy returns and blows her nose in a tissue, looking at Jennifer.

"This is my new, best friend," I say. "Jennifer, this is Mindy. Mindy, Jennifer."

Mindy smiles, holds out her hand to Jennifer, who takes it and shakes. Mindy then looks to me.

"And who is Jennifer?"

"She's … someone who needs a home, Mindy," I say. "Her mother is … she's not around these parts lately, and I was hoping that she could stay with you for awhile."

"Here? With me and the boys?"

"If you don't mind."

"Dick, really," she says, clearly annoyed. She then looks to Jennifer, as she takes my arm and leads me out of the foyer. "Honey, Jennifer, why don't you help yourself to something in the kitchen while I talk to your new best friend in private, okay?"

Jennifer is easy. "Okay," she says, and heads into the kitchen off and to the right.

Mindy backs me against a wall, smiling, shrugging. "Dick, who is she?"

"She's an orphan. She's the daughter of someone I knew – someone who recently died. I'm trying to help the family out by –"

"By bringing her here to live with us?"

"Well … I mean, she can't live with me," I say, and feel this is a fairly obvious statement.

"Why not? Little Prick would feel jealous?"

"Now don't pick on my cat."

"Why can't she stay with you, if you want to help out so badly?"

"Because I'm in the middle of a few things, Mindy. I'm investigating Bill's death, I'm kind of focused on this very special and very dangerous project, and I'm not really what one would consider to be a strong, healthy father figure."

Mindy stares at me uncompromisingly. "I'm sorry, Dick. I'm not up for this."

"Mindy, please."

"No. The boys and I are barely hanging on, and can I remind you that Bill has only been dead for a few days?"

I suddenly realize how unfair I'm being with my sister-in-law. To inflict a stranger on her, another child, to infringe on her grief, the boys …

"I'm sorry," I say, feeling like a piece of navel lint. "I'm not thinking too straight."

Mindy puts a hand on my shoulder. "None of us are."

I look to Jennifer, chewing on a cookie, seated on a high seat up against a counter-bar.

"Why don't you take her to a friend?"

"All my friends are dead, Mindy," I say, withering.

"Well, there are child-care facilities –"

"I don't want to subject her to that," I say. "Something happened today, something pretty traumatic."

"What, Dick? You mean, to the child?"

"To both of us."

She waits for an explanation. I do not want to get into a discussion over this.

"Jennifer," I call out, "we're leaving, okay?"

"Okay," Jennifer says, still munching the cookie.

I look back to Mindy. "I didn't just stop by to burden a strange child on you. I wanted to check in, see if you needed anything."

"I need Bill back," Mindy says. "But you can't help me with that, can you, Dick?"

I clam up, feeling tears in my eyes, and fighting back the urge to drop to the ground, curl up in a ball and sob. I turn quickly, and walk into the little kitchen area where Jennifer sits. I take her hand, and we walk to the door. Mindy follows until both Jennifer and I are standing on the stoop.

"I'll check up on you," Mindy says. "Keep your cell handy, alright?"

"Sure. You do the same. I'll keep you up to date on things," I say.

We hug again, and Mindy touches my cheek. "Maybe if I was feeling stronger, Dick, I could … you know." She looks to Jennifer, then to me.

I nod. "Of course. I'm going to go home and stab myself to death for my insensitivity."

"Don't do that. It would scare your cat and your new best friend."

I look around the doorway, at the garlic hanging from ropes, not only around the door-frame, but on the patio perimeter and the gates, and of course, nearby, the church. At least I know that Bill's family is as safe as can be from vampires and werewolves.

"And the boys will be back home by dark," Mindy says, as if anticipating my next question.

I nod again. "Doors locked, crosses handy, and my cell. Deal?"

"Deal, silly," she says and kisses me again. She looks to Jennifer, smiles. "Bye, sweety. You're going to like living with Dick."

"Stop it," I mutter.

I then turn and head back to the car with Jennifer.

"She's nice," Jennifer says. "But real sad, right?"

"Right."

"Sadder than you?"

I can't answer that.

I really can't.

CHAPTER SEVENTEEN

▼

Okay, so I guess you can all call me Pappy.

I check my watch as I open the door to my apartment. Now close to seven o'clock. I expect that Dracula and Samantha will be dropping by shortly.

Jennifer sees Little Prick, and jogs over to the sofa where the lazy old fatty-cat lounges, blinking sleepily.

"Kitty!" Jennifer whispers.

She sits down and begins to pet my cat. I am stunned fuckless. Little Prick doesn't let *anyone* pet him. He barely gives me the time of day, and half the time only that when I'm opening a can of Purina. Now he sits there and let's little Jennifer paw at him without complaint, without a hiss, without even a warning nip.

"He's nice," Jennifer says.

"He's faking it," I say, closing the door behind me and already wondering on the Big Question Of The Day: How am I going to keep a child here for any length of time? I realize I'm crazy. What am I doing? I can simply take this kid down to Child Services, and drop her off there. There are records down at the orphanage, I'm sure there is due process to be followed, some kind of child protocol to address.

I had forgotten about the orphanage. I wonder how that went this afternoon.

I check in with Monster Vice. Zelig is out in the field, but I am told that when my backup arrived at the orphanage … all that was found were the corpses of every employee in the facility. However, many of the children were listed as missing. The investigation was still ongoing. I disengage my phone, staring out the window. Exactly as I surmised. The Grand Master has other plans, ones that don't involve a tail-tangle with Monster Vice Tactical.

I turn to look at Jennifer, and see that Mirabelle is hovering above her, close to the ceiling. She is staring down at her daughter, and she is crying. Jennifer is oblivious to her dead mother's ghost. She continues to pet Little Prick who continues to amaze and annoy me by purring loudly.

Mirabelle catches my eye, and points to my front door. She then floats quickly toward and through it. She wishes to speak to me in private.

"Jennifer, I'll be right back," I say.

"Okay," she says, as she begins to tackle the scratching of my cat's receptive ears.

I head into the hall, closing the door behind me.

Mirabelle stands there, smiling at me.

"She's so beautiful," Mirabelle says.

I smile. "Cute as a bug."

She nods.

"I know what happened at the orphanage today," Mirabelle said. "I was able to get some help to protect Jennifer long enough for you to get to her."

"Help?" I ask, shocked.

"Other ghosts. And a few other things floating around that I've made friends with. Enough helping hands to distract the child vampires from hurting Jennifer."

I don't pursue this line of questioning. And the main reason for this is what Mirabelle says to me next.

"I won't be seeing you anymore, Dick."

"What do you mean?"

"It's time for me to leave here."

"Just like that?"

"No," she says, and approaches me. "Because you've set me free, Dick. Jennifer is here, safe with you now. That's all I really needed to know – that she was taken care of."

"Mirabelle – I don't know how long I can keep her. I'm not a parent, there are laws, I'm sure there must be rules of guardianship and –"

"You'll make it all work," Mirabelle says, and leans in to kiss me.

"But –"

"Good bye, my friend," Mirabelle says. "Remember, I really do love you. Take care of yourself."

I try to find the energy to protest, to say something further – perhaps even to beg her *not* to leave just yet. I have grown accustomed to her company. I've grown fond of my little ghost.

But it is too late.

She dematerializes instantly.

"Mirabelle," I whisper, reaching out to where she was standing seconds ago. "I love you, too," I say softly, and then open the door to my apartment and return to the land of the living.

I lean against the door, and stare at Jennifer, who is now finished petting Little Prick and taking in the surroundings of my apartment. I stare for a moment, then am mindful that I have a tear running down my cheek.

Mirabelle is gone.

I shall see her no more.

There is a pain in my chest which is unmistakable in terms of identification.

I am somewhat heartbroken.

I take a breath, blow out with a weariness not even Methuselah would be able to match. I nod to myself and say that magic word – that word that keeps me going.

Onward.

I have a new responsibility.

"Want something to drink?" I ask Jennifer.

"No."

"Eat?"

"No."

I've run out of hospitable things to offer. "Look, kid —"

"You can call me Jennifer," she says and smiles at me.

"Okay. Sure. You can call me ..." I trail off, not having given this whole name thing a lot of thought.

I'm suddenly irritated. What in the name of sweet, bleeding baby ducklings am I doing with a kid in my house?

I grumble. "Well, I'm not daddy. And you don't need to call me Mr. Pitts. How about just Dick?"

"Okay, Dick," Jennifer says.

I look at my watch, then out the window.

"Wanna play a game?" Jennifer asks with typical child-like perkiness.

"I'd rather eat glass," I mutter.

It's dark out. Later than I thought.

And that's when the phone rings.

I flip out my cell, and speak.

"Pitts here."

The voice is low, clear, hurried — and one I do not recognize.

"Get out of the house."

"What?"

"You have Fangs coming through some drainpipes. The sun is over the horizon. Get out of the house. Now!"

I rush to the window, and indeed ... the sun has set.

"Shit."

The voice speaks again.

"Hurry."

I hang up the phone, and grab Jennifer's wrist. I notice Little Prick has already scurried for his favorite hole in my kitchen wall, sensing the worst, and determined to survive. I'm not worried about my cat. If I were dead in the house, he wouldn't hesitate to eat me within a few hours. Little fucker.

"Come on, kid. Don't ask questions."

Jennifer is a great kid. She holds on to my hand as I race to the front door.

*   *   *   *

I open the front door in time to see one vampire, huge, tear through the floorboards of my hall. I take out my .357 and fire. I miss high, wide and handy, though if I were aiming for something in Phoenix, I would be golden.

I run with Jennifer, away from the vampire. The hallway floor in front of me shatters, as an enormous claw reaches upwards. I step on the claw, and fire five shots into the hole. Howls of hurt answer back, but I take no comfort in this. The vampire is in pain, but far from fucking dead.

"Move, Jennifer!" I yell, though no need for this instruction. Jennifer is practically leading the charge out of my apartment, myself being the one in tow.

We exit the front door, just as a black car, a Cadillac Esplanade screeches to the side of the street. The door opens.

I see no one. Only darkness within.

I don't question providence at the moment.

I shove Jennifer into the car, then leap in myself.

The Esplanade screeches off, as I still have one leg hanging out of the doorway.

I don't mind.

The vampires exit the front of my apartment, three of them. They snarl in fury, as the car accelerates, and turns a corner, leaving the bloodsuckers in the dust.

"Close," a voice says on the other side of Jennifer, who sits in the middle of myself and the stranger.

"Yeah," I mutter. "And who are you?"

The owner of the voice leans forward, out of the shadows, and extends his hand. I notice that he is a priest, around fifty-five, balding, with a beard that still has the remains of what looks like lunch (chicken soup) peppered in the rangy mange.

"Father Mel Gastroni, at your service, mate."

I shake the hand of Father Gastroni, who I gather with a fair degree of certainty is Australian, then look to the driver, who's head does not turn around.

"Our chauffeur is Colonel Jason Kellog, United States Marines," Gastroni nods to the driver.

I glance in the rear view mirror and size up Kellog's face. A face carved out of stone, as marine military as you can get.

"Pleasure, colonel," I say quickly, then look to Gastroni. "Was that you who just called me?"

"It was," Gastroni grins, then looks to Jennifer. "We were monitoring your house for some time. And what's your name, lassie?"

"Jennifer," Jennifer says.

"Well, it's nice to meet you, Jennifer. I'm very happy the vampires didn't get you."

"Me, too."

Gastroni pinches Jennifer's cheek, and she giggles.

"How did you know about the Fang attack?" I ask.

"Good intel, Officer Pitts. I am working with a mutual friend of ours."

"Who?"

"Dracula. And Samantha, too, I might add. Good people," Gastroni says.

"Yeah, both vampires. I guess you knew that already."

"Of course, mate."

I turn, glance through the rear window. Night is falling fast. Gastroni presses on.

"Dracula discovered that the Grand Master had sent the fangs after you and the child, to capture and torture accordingly."

I glance at Jennifer – a father's protective aside to his child and the use of the word 'torture'. But Jennifer is made of sterner stuff than I can even suspect. She digests the information soberly, I can see, and gives a brief nod.

"Hate vampires," she whispers.

"Me, too," Gastroni laughs, then looks to me again. "Dracula and Samantha are able to, on a somewhat limited basis, throw their consciousness into the vampire ether and assess what moves the Grand Master is making. They conveyed to me the plan of attack on your apartment, and so we took prophylactic action to insure your safety. The vampire Remote Viewing technique is only effective some of the time, but in this case – just minutes ago – their efforts were clearly rewarded. "

"Clearly," I nod. "Where are we going now?"

"To our place. The colonel and I occupy a kind of safe house. We'll strategize from there on a sensible course of action."

"You mean beyond staying alive and escaping the Grand Master's efforts at killing us," I say neutrally.

"Yes, that is what I meant," Gastroni nods, then looks to our driver. "Colonel, home, please."

"Yes, sir," Kellog replies, a snap in his voice.

I have the sudden feeling that in addition to what has just happened with the vampires, the evening was going to get stranger still.

CHAPTER EIGHTEEN

▼

Though it is still daylight, it is a murky kind of daylight. Early evening fog seems to have come out of nowhere and as I look eastward toward the San Bernardino Mountains, I see dark clouds churning, cumulous formations that will guarantee snow for Arrowhead Lake and Big Bear. I find myself wishing that I were in the mountains now – fishing, kicking back in front of a warm fire, sipping mold wine, or absinthe. I find myself longing for escape, a different life, maybe even reincarnation.

The car turns left on Gower, which is a few miles short of what will soon become Los Feliz. Colonel Kellog drives silently up the winding hills of what is known as Old Hollywood. I look down, and am surprised. I find that Jennifer has somehow crept her hand into mine and she is holding it. I am not sure if she is holding me to comfort herself – or to provide comfort to me. I sense, somehow, it is the latter.

I take out my cell, and make a quick call to Monster Vice, instructing a Clean Detail to head for my apartment and deal with the vampire residue. I am confident the Tutis are gone, but I want to verify that the rest of the tenants are safe and unbit. I somehow sense that they are – the vampire contingent Jennifer and I encountered wanted me, and were not on a general Feed Hunt.

I glance out my side window, and see a few discorporates – ghosts – floating in and out of trees near a house. They are harmless – apparitions like Mirabelle who for one reason or another, are earthbound. There is a soft glow to the phantoms at this time of day, as the sun has set, as the light begins its inevitable translation to dark and night. Like preternatural fireflies, the ghosts wisp in and around the trees, into and around the houses, twirling and loop-de-looping through telephone lines. If the ghosts were the *only* result of the Popov Phenomena, things would be great for both the deceased and undead. Peaceful coexistence would be the rule. Live and let die - yet remain dead and friendly, if you're forced to stay close to home and hearth.

Such is not the case.

The Esplanade pulls into a driveway and I stare up at a house, easily a hundred years old, Victorian in appearance. A young priest awaits our arrival. He opens the back door, and I step out, Jennifer's little hand still in mine.

"Good afternoon, Officer Pitts. I am Father Ivory."

"Yeah, hi."

Father Gastroni and Colonel Kellog round the corner of the car.

And this is when I notice that Colonel Kellog is wearing a kilt.

Jennifer tugs my hand and whispers softly to me. "He's wearing a dress, Dick."

I say nothing, and don't need to, as Colonel Kellog speaks in a low voice, the annoyance in his tone undeniable.

"It's a kilt, young lady. Not a dress. A kilt. There's a difference."

"What's the difference?" Jennifer asks.

"Men wear kilts. Women wear dresses."

This seems to satisfy Jennifer's momentary curiosity – but not mine.

"Is the kilt the new battle fatigue for fighting the undead, Colonel?" I ask, trying to interject some good humor into the mix.

But Colonel Kellog merely eyeballs me, then turns and enters the house silently. I turn to Father Gastroni.

"Sorry. I didn't mean to offend."

"Don't worry about it. Colonel Kellog has endured much at the hands of the vampires, Officer Pitts."

"Please. Dick."

"Yes, Dick. The colonel is suffering from a mild case of post-traumatic stress syndrome. But don't let that scare you. He's a top soldier, a professional, and a very effective vampire killer."

"I think he looks nice in the dress," Jennifer says.

Gastroni laughs, a robust laugh that even makes me smile in spite of myself. "He'd be happy to hear that, young lady. Please, come in, both of you. The night is upon us."

True enough. Darkness crept up quickly, and I cannot help but shudder at the thought that the Grand Master is out there, somewhere, plotting.

Father Ivory has followed alongside us, and now turns to the older priest.

"Father Gastroni, Dracula has called and said he will be here within the hour."

"Thank you, Phillip," Gastroni says to young Father Ivory, then turns to me. "I always feel a sense of great relief when Dracula and Samantha are around. Don't you, Dick?"

"Yes, I always feel much better when in the presence of the plasma-drinking undead."

Gastroni smiles. "You're being facetious, mate."

"Sorry, I'm still trying to get used to the friendly vampire thing. Takes a bit."

"Yes, yes, jolly right."

Tut, tut, how you go on, Dick. Getting your undies in a twist over a few vampires who you now call friends.

I am led into a large room just beyond the foyer, Jennifer's little paw in mine, and regard a fireplace about the size of the Oval Office, and an interior that I would guess is Pope-approved in terms of crucifixes everywhere, red velvet walls, and iconic statues of the Apostle and Jesus Christ nearly everywhere you look. This is all fine by me ... 'cause I take comfort in this kind of ambience, being that I'm the kind of guy that fights Satan and evil and monsters and vampires and other god-awful things that wish to wipe out humanity on a day to day basis.

Father Ivory pats Jennifer on the head. "Want some cookies, dear?"

"Chocolate chip?" she brightens.

"And Sugar. And Cinnamon."

"Wow."

"Excuse us," Father Ivory looks to both Gastroni and myself. "Looks like I'm on cookie detail."

Jennifer pads off with her New Best Friend – Father Amos Ivory.

I sink into a nearby couch before Father Gastroni offers me a seat. He seems to care not a shit that I'm making myself at home. I'm tired ... my only excuse. Tired beyond words. Gastroni watches Jennifer disappear with Father Ivory.

"She's a cute little girl," he says.

"Yes, she is."

"I prefer cute little boys."

I say nothing.

Gastroni grins. "Kidding, mate. Little priest humor."

"Oh. Ha, ha, ha, ha."

"Drink, Dick?"

"No."

"You're worried about tonight with the Grand Master?"

"A tad."

"Sure you won't have a scotch?"

"Thanks, no."

"McCallan. Fifty years old."

"No."

"One small one?"

"No. Okay, maybe one."

Gastroni (conveniently) has the bottle of 50 year old gold in his hand, and he pours me a hefty little pick-me-up in a glass that is somehow suddenly, mystically in my hand – as if perhaps I was on an episode of the old series comedy *Bewitched* and my every need was catered to at the wriggle of a nose.

Gastroni reaches for two odd looking jars on the table.

"You don't mind, mate?" he asks.

"Mind what?"

"That I partake?"

I don't have a goddamn clue what he's talking about.

"I indulge myself in cocaine and PCP now and then. Just to fortify myself in the spiritual sense. You're welcome to join me."

I look at the jars, as Father Gastroni begins to pour powder from both – one white, in consistency, and the other, close to jet-black.

"No, thanks," I say. "Scotch will do it for me."

Mind you, I judge no man on what he needs to do in this crazy, nutty world we now occupy. More so, when he is a man dealing with battling super-Vampires and other nightmares that threaten Mankind routinely. Father Gastroni is clearly a brave fellow, so I cast no aspersions, or even consider any doubt as to his effectiveness once in the fray. But I will confess momentary surprise that a priest would so casually offer me an opportunity to get fucked up royal on some fine white and what amounts to powdered elephant tranquilizer. Surprise, mind you, that is all I have to pass … not a moral judgment whatsoever.

Father Gastroni produces a small 'snort pipe', which also possesses a small razor blade attached. He begins cutting the odd mixture of white and black powder. As he does so he prattles on with me.

"Tonight, when Dracula and Samantha return, we will be a force of five. Them, myself and the colonel, and you. We shall soon know with Dracula's return, where the Grand Master is headquartered, along with his demonic little minion."

"You mean, the children at the orphanage?"

"And those that came before them, yes. You know he is conscripting children at large to be part of his army."

"Yes," I say, chilled again to the bone. "He told me the other night. Bastard."

"Dracula has doubts that we can overcome the Grand Master. Do you?"

"I don't know. I've only faced Masters – and they're pretty tough to defeat. As for the Grand Master ..." I shrug. "It was a helluva fight when I was with Dracula and Samantha. It seemed that it was a pretty even contest."

"You're wise to be so pragmatic. Not one for rash declarations, are you, Dick?"

"Father ... no. Hell no. And you'll have to excuse my French."

"Yes, yes, not a problem."

He begins to snort the black and white powder. He coughs, shakes his head, hacks up what my cat would call a major meow-furball, and closes his eyes, savoring the high. He opens his eyes a moment later, his lids heavy with contentment, his eyes distinctly bloodshot. Gastroni smiles, and winks at me.

"Nice."

I nod and sip my scotch.

"You know, my cat died recently. Do you like cats, Dick?"

"I'm not sure. I own a cat. Or he owns me. We live together. I guess we tolerate one another," I say, and it's the truth.

"See, I loved my cat," Father Gastroni says, already cutting more black and white. "Loved her beyond belief. Portia, that was her name. A lovely feline."

I continue drinking scotch, and am cognizant of the fact that I'm entertaining a buzz. A welcome one.

"We were like peas and carrots together, Portia and me."

"Portia? Your cat's name was Portia?"

"Yep. Lived to be 18. Kidneys got her in the end. Happens with cats a lot."

I nod and sip.

Gastroni goes in for a second snort.

"Oh, yeah, sweet Jesus," he winces, shaking his head and clearing his throat.

I glance around the room. I have no idea where Colonel Kellog has disappeared to. Perhaps to change into a more casual kilt? I just don't know.

"So when Portia died, I thought, in a way, a piece of me died, too. I was crushed. This was about, oh, four months ago. Seems longer when I think about it. Then again, these days, most everything before the vampires and the werewolves ... it all seems so long ago."

"Yes," I say, watching Gastroni meticulously cut more of the black and white powder on the table, and then mix it together.

"Find yourself using that term a lot, Dick?"

"What term is that, Father?"

"These days. These days, we're doing that ... these days, things are different. These days ..."

"Ah. Yes. Yes, I suppose I do."

Gastroni nods, glances at his watch, then continues cutting white and black powder.

"Love is rare, mate. When you find it, try to hold on to it. It's a treasure the Lord gives us, and it is not one we should treat with triviality. I learned this with my Portia."

"Your cat."

"Yes. My kitty."

I like Father Gastroni. But ... I'm aware of the passing of time, the darkness outside ... and I'm wondering where Dracula and Samantha are. And what the game plan for tonight will be. So I am only dimly attentive to Father Gastroni's dissertation on love and dead pets.

"So, keeping that in mind – that love is truly a gift, a present from the Almighty – I swore I would always treat such a blessing with reverence. In my own particular way, demonstrative of my own personal soul desire. Does that make sense?"

"Hm? Oh, yes. Yes, quite."

"I had Portia cremated, but I didn't bury her. I didn't want to be that far from her. I didn't want to be that alienated. I didn't want her to be alone, separated from the person who loved her most of all. I guess that sounds a bit odd... she was just a cat."

"No, I ... I mean, animals ... they can become like family for us. My own cat, the little fu-- ... the little darling ... he's become something very special in my life. Words fail to really describe it, but it is a kind of kinship, I reckon."

"Yes," Gastroni brightens, and nods vigorously. "A kinship. A bond."

Gastroni leans in and snorts the odd amalgam of white and black powder.

"Father, I'm curious. What is that black stuff? I know the coke and PCP are the white ... but that black powder. I'm in the dark."

"Ah, I was coming to that," Father Gastroni says, and pours a shot of scotch for himself as well. "You see, because I couldn't bury my cat – because Portia somehow conveyed to me spiritually that this was simply not acceptable – like I said, I had her cremated. I kept her ashes. Here."

Father Gastroni picks up one of the jars. The one with the black powder in it. "In this vessel."

I stare at the jar, and swallow hard. I'm trying to make the mean, nasty pictures in my mind go bye-bye, but I can't.

"The black powder. That's your cat's ashes?" I whisper.

"Yes. My love, my Portia."

"Her ashes."

"Yes."

"You snort your cat's ashes," I say, probably sounding like I've just been ravaged anally with a blunt party spoon.

"Yes. Well. I inhale her essence, let's put it that way," Father Gastroni says.

I suddenly feel ill, and the scotch, so lovely and so friendly of moments ago, begins to do a little tidal wave of protest in my tummy-wummy.

"You snort coke, PCP and dead cat," I say.

"I guess that's the bottom line, yes," Father Gastroni says, but then he holds up his hand. "Now I know that sounds strange."

"You're kidding."

"No, no, I know how that sounds. But for me, it's more like a kind of spiritual transubstantiation which comforts me. I feel that while Portia's flesh has dissolved from this world, has been transformed from flesh to ash, that to assimilate her in my body … well, I believe there's a kind of spiritual symbiosis there which is unique."

"Very unique," I croak. I kinda want to run and get Jennifer and move to Bali right about now.

"You're not just patronizing me, Dick, are you?" Gastroni grins.

"What? No. It's just … well, like you said. It's … you really … is that really your cat's ashes?"

"Grade A Portia." and Gastroni snorts again. He winces, shakes his head, and screams out once again: "Oh, yeah, Jesus!"

He opens his eyes, smiles at me.

"You think I'm crazy."

"No. No. I mean … well."

"You think that because I utilize my cat's ashes to get high on a nightly basis, you think I'm nuts. Buzzo. One can minus a six-pack. Admit it."

"Father –"

"Admit it. Say it. You think I'm insane."

"I'm really not one to judge –"

"Say it, Dick," Father Gastroni says softly.

"Alright. It sounds pretty fucking weird. What happens once your cat's ashes run out? She's still gone? She's still…" My god, I was entertaining what sounded like a rational discussion about the nuances of snorting a cat's decomposed and roasted remains with industrial narcotics.

"Thank you for your honesty. Yes, it sounds pretty, as you say, fucking weird. I'll give you that. As to your other question, Portia's ashes will always survive to one degree or another – even through various devolutions of ashen integrity. The old theory on the indestructibility of matter, and all."

I really, reaalllly don't want to ask what that means. But –

"Uh … what does that mean?"

"Well, once I have chemicalized myself with Portia's essence, naturally, the body from a digestive standpoint, must purge itself of waste. Fecal matter, specifically, the contents of which most certainly contain some residue of Portia, since my bloodstream has absorbed her and dispersed it accordingly. You still with me?"

"Oh, yes. Very much so."

"So, with every bowel movement, I take that residue, and in turn have it cremated. Those ashes of that residue can then be recycled."

I look at the jar filled with black powder.

"So … you not only snort your cat … you snort your own ashen shit – a composite of both shit and cat ash?"

"Well. Yes. But before you think I'm completely wigged out, let me explain further."

"I'd prefer you spare me the details."

"But as a forensic professional, I think you'll find this interesting."

"No, really. I have no dream to know more. Please."

I really do believe I would have politely gotten up and left the house in the next few seconds, had it not been for the timely return of Jennifer, with Father Ivory and Colonel Kellog right behind her.

Kellog looks to Father Gastroni, and then to me.

"We just received word from Dracula."

"Yes?" Gastroni says.

"He found the Grand Master."

"Where?"

"The old Santa Monica Airport."

Gastroni sighs, then looks to me.

"So. It begins. Nice night for it, right?"

I'm not sure nice is the word I would have chosen.

Fucked up, perhaps ... but nice?

Nah.

"One thing more," Kellog says.

"What's that?" I ask.

"Dracula says that the Grand Master knows we're coming. And he has a message for you, Officer Pitts."

"Yeah? Tell me the message."

Kellog looks down at a piece of paper.

"The Grand Master is going to make you his personal blood-bitch." Kellog offers a shrug. "Rough translation, according to Dracula."

Kellog looks up at me. It is Jennifer who asks the question of innocence, as she regards me curiously.

"Does that mean you're gonna be his girlfriend, Dick?"

No one says anything, no one chuckles ... and I am grateful for the silence.

CHAPTER NINETEEN

▼

"Looks like you're very much on the Grand Master's radar," Father Gastroni says to me, as we walk down a long hall.

"How does Dracula know so much about what the Grand Master is doing?"

"I told you, he and Samantha have this talent of tapping into the vampire collective. It's a technique very much like Remote Viewing. Or something akin to it."

"Remote Viewing. Never heard of it."

"Remote viewing was actually experimented with and utilized by the Defense Intelligence Agency back in the 70s, 80s, and 90s. It was essentially psychics working with the government to utilize their clairvoyant powers by throwing their conscious eye into any part of the world, and then report back anything of any worth."

I nod, interested. "This is news to me. It sounds kind of fringe and fascinating."

"Eventually, it was abandoned as a full-worthy practice for espionage and other things dealing with spying. Not enough empirical evidence to convince anyone that the psychics were accurate enough of the time. Lack of funding soon gave way to lack of interest in pursuing the technique for purposes linked to national defense."

"But Dracula and Samantha can do this, with pretty much reliable accuracy," I say.

"They can, because vampires are *truly* psychic," Gastroni replies.[5] "Not like human beings where psychic capability is willy-nilly at best."

---

[5]   In the field of parapsychology, *remote viewing* is a neutral term for extra-sensory perception, usually performed during experiments in which the percipient tries to describe a distant location or the environs of a distant agent. Remote viewing allows a "viewer" to use his or her intuitive abilities to gather information on a target consisting of an object, place, or person, etc., which is hidden from the physical perception of the viewer and typically separated from the viewer in space by some distance.

Stargate Project (no relation to the popular television series) was one of a number of code names used to cover "remote viewing programs". Others included Sun Streak, Grill Flame, Center Lane by DIA and INSCOM, and SCANATE by CIA, from the 1970s, through to 1995. It was an offshoot of research done at Stanford Research Institute (SRI). The research program was launched partly because some intelligence officers believed a 'psi-gap' had emerged between America and the Soviet Union, for example the reputed abilities of Nina Kulagina.**

In 1995 the project was transferred to the CIA and a retrospective evaluation of the results were to be done. The CIA contracted the American Institutes for Research for this evaluation. An analysis conducted by Professor Jessica Utts showed a statistically significant effect, gifted subjects scored 5%-15% above chance, whereas the noted long time CSICOP psychic debunker Ray Hyman concluded a null result. Based upon their collected findings, the CIA followed the recommendation to terminate the 20 million dollar project.

The "viewers" themselves were from varied backgrounds, with what some described at the time as possessed of traumatized mental and emotional psyches. Arguably, when you're a psychic, you're probably out on a limb in terms of your sense of rational thinking and behavior. To go further, it might be fair to say that most self-proclaimed psychics are either frauds or just out of their-fucking-minds-delusional. Perhaps a small percentage actually possess genuine psychic capability, but to wander through the morass of human flotsam that proclaim they are gifted with these clairvoyant talents is not unlike experiencing the unimaginable enduring red-hot probing agony

We turn a corner, and then enter a large room, filled with an array of weaponry that would challenge anything that Monster Vice could offer in its armory.

I am suddenly aware again that Jennifer is holding my hand, and I marvel how accustomed I am to enjoying a kind of mystical bond with my new child-friend.

"Wow," Jennifer whispers and I wow-tend to agree.

---

of mercury-tipped enemas. That being said, the effort is probably best left unexpended. Still, it should be noted that professing a talent for psychic ability in, say, a crowded bar filled with beautiful and gullible women who are either drunk or drug-challenged by hallucinogenic assets such as Ecstasy or GBH, such a declaration of psychic enhancement, is practically a certifiable guarantee that one has an excellent chance of getting laid.

**Nina Kulagina, Ninel Sergeyevna Kulagina (Russian: Нине́ль Серге́евна Кула́гина) (1926 - 1990) was a Russian woman who reportedly had great psychic powers, particularly in psychokinesis. Academic research of her phenomenon was conducted in the USSR for the last twenty years of her life. During the Cold War, silent black-and-white films of her moving objects on a table in front of her without touching them, demonstrating her abilities under controlled conditions for Soviet authorities, caused excitement to many psychic researchers around the world, some of whom believed that they represented clear evidence for the existence of psychic phenomena.

Nina claimed that in order to manifest the effect, she required a period of meditation to clear her mind of all thoughts. When she had obtained the focus required, she reported a sharp pain in her spine and the blurring of her eyesight. One of Nina's most celebrated experiments took place in a Leningrad laboratory on March 10, 1970. Having initially studied the ability to move inanimate objects, scientists were curious to see if Nina's abilities extended to cells, tissues, and organs. Sergeyev was one of many scientists present when Nina attempted to use her energy to stop the beating of a frog's heart floating in solution. He claims she focused intently on the heart and apparently made it beat faster, then slower, and using extreme intent of thought, stopped it. It goes without saying that this was a tremendous day for scientific observation – but a shit-kicker if you were a certain, unnamed frog in the cross-hairs of a large, surly Russian woman whose sole purpose for thirty minutes was to see how quickly she could consign you to Xenopus tropicalis chordata oblivion.

Facing us were four open cabinets, easily ten feet tall, nearly touching the ceiling of this particular chamber. Hanging within was every conceivable piece of firepower known to modern gunnery. Then there was the one cabinet, occupying the center of the room with custom-designed cross and long bows, of varying length, width and breath. Arrows hung neatly near the bows, all metal tipped.

"What's your flavor, Officer Pitts?"

"Beg your pardon?" I stare dully at Father Gastroni.

Gastroni smiles, and nods to Kellog, who steps forward, and points to the first cabinet, filled with what appears to be semi-automatic rifles. He reaches for one which I recognize immediately to be a M16A2 – the standard service rifle for both the United States Army and Marine Corps.

"I call this my nipple-twister," Colonel Kellog smiles. "Caliber, 5.56 millimeter, gas-operated action, with rotating bolt. Rate of fire between 750 and 900 rounds per minute. Nice muzzle velocity, feed system of 20 or 30 round detachable box magazines and an effective range of 600 yards."

I am, in a kind of esoteric sense, concerned that Colonel Kellog might just well ejaculate right there on the spot, what with the way he holds the 'nipple twister' and how he is now petting the muzzle with clear love and affection. He suddenly tosses it to me. I catch it without even a flinch. I must admit – holding the damned thing is downright comforting as images of the Grand Master subjugating me into blood-bitchery invades my pummeled imagination.

"Good balance," I say.

"Can I hold it, Dick?" Jennifer asks.

"Over my dead body, sweetheart."

Colonel Kellog then wanders over to the cabinet filled with an array of hand-pistols. He reaches for the closest weapon, weighing it professionally.

"I'm sure you recognize this little darling, Officer Pitts. And you look like a Beretta kinda guy."

I give back the M16, and take the pistol he now offers and nod.

"M9 9 millimeter Beretta. Replaced the M1911A1 pistol in .45 caliber. Semiautomatic, double-action. Length, roughly 8.54 inches, barrel length, 4.92 inches, if memory serves, and a magazine capacity of 15 rounds. Am I forgetting something?"

"Muzzle velocity," Colonel Kellog grins, clearly enjoying my articulate expertise.

"1200 feet. Let's not forget the convenient redundant automatic safety feature to help prevent unintentional discharges."

"I'm impressed," Father Gastroni says. "You know your weapons, Dick."

With my free hand, I reach into my shoulder holster and pull out my own M9. "Never leave home without it. I'm also partial to the .357 Magnum."

"Yes, agreed," Colonel Kellog nods approvingly.

Father Gastroni casually lifts up a Kalashnikov semi-automatic rifle, and I can tell he is well-versed in its intended application.

"A man of the cloth bearing instruments of death?" I needle Gastroni, just for the fuck-all fun of it.

"My sheep must be protected, mate," Gastroni replies, without losing a beat.

"You can see we're well armed," Colonel Kellog says. "I prefer the BERSA Thunder 380." He reaches for a small, handsome pistol, holding it up to the light. "Introduced in the late 1990s by an Argentinean firearms manufacturer, the 380 is light, and has a reputation for reliability that pretty much meets or outmatches the Beretta."

And on and on. Jennifer and I continue to be "toured" of the arsenal. Need a silencer? Look no further. Scorpion police-specials, with very convenient interfacing features to the Glock 26 and the Kahr K9, replete with elastomer wipes. Don't like Scorpions? Fine, the Spider thread mounting silencers are equally fun-filled and eliminates the muzzle flash signature and bothersome first round pop.

There was, quite simply, just a ton of good shit in this room. RPGs, 40 mm and M79 grenade launchers, NVPG140 night vision binoculars, and high explosive (HE) smoke, flare and CS gas grenades. I reach for one of these.

"What good are poppers against vampires?"

"Detonation of those puppies produces Holy Water vapor," Colonel Kellog says. "And laced with just a touch of garlic powder. Just so the bastards go down screaming."

There is something that scares me about Colonel Kellog, and it's not the kilt ... though that is goddamned scary unto itself. He reminds me distantly of Hanson in terms of his sheer delight for vampire torture and extermination.

Colonel Kellog now stands in front of the center cabinet.

"And last, we have our stake-arrow munitions," Kellog says, and when he says this, he says it with clear ecstasy in his voice. "The *perfect* weapons for the Vampire Problem.[6]

---

[6]   The cross-bow dates back to ancient Greek and Chinese times. It was more famously influential in European theater warfare from 800 to roughly 1500 A.D. The arrow-like projectiles of a crossbow are called "bolts." These are much shorter than arrows but can be several times heavier. There is an optimum weight for bolts to achieve maximum kinetic energy, which varies depending on the strength and characteristics of the crossbow. Modern bolts are stamped with a proof mark to ensure their consistent weight. In order to accommodate the groove that the bolt rests in, bolts typically have only two fletches, rather than the three fletches commonly seen on arrows. Crossbow bolts can be fitted with a variety of heads, some with sickle-shaped heads to cut rope or rigging; but the most common is a four-sided point called a quarrel.

In the case of completely ass-buggering your basic vampire, turning its day or night into bad, bad picnic of pain and suffering, the cross-bows presently being displayed by Colonel Kellog could more than sufficiently do the job with any number of fangs ... provided you had the time to reload, fire and reload. Cross-bows could be more quickly and efficiently reloaded, then say, a long-bow – which was also available in this Vampire Room of Impalement and Death. None of these weapons in the opinion of certain law enforcement officers, however, could be more demoralizing to Mr. Cocksucker Nosferatu than a blessed .357 Magnum and a Bishop-blessed stake, preferably of

Jennifer releases my hand and wanders back over to the hand-pistol cabinet. I glance at her. "Don't touch those, Jennifer. They're dangerous."

"I know, Dick," she says to me softly. "I'm little, not dumb."

Well, fuck me gently with a chain saw, excuse me.

Colonel Kellog, Father Gastroni and Father Ivory form a semi-circle around the cabinet.

"These were personally blessed by His Holiness," Gastroni says in whispered awe. "As a matter of fact, every bullet, every round, every arrow is blessed."

"The Pope?" I say, surprised beyond measure. "You have access to the Vatican?"

"The Vatican funds this entire operation, mate," Father Gastroni says. "They have worked with Dracula now for almost two years. They provide the money, and Dracula deals with the military defense contractors."

"Dracula cuts deals with the military?"

"He's had several lifetimes of negotiating experience, Dick," Gastroni says. "And he's had decades in developing and nurturing relationships with top people in the Department of Defense, and various other entities specializing in national defense and civil law enforcement."

"I'll be damned," I whisper, marveling at Dracula's vast resources and resourcefulness in general.

Father Gastroni now turns to me.

"I recommend we arm up and prepare ourselves for departure. Dick, you're welcome to anything in this room."

I glance at the RPG. I reach for it, and sling it over my shoulder. I then grab a few of the .44 Holy Water grenades. "Thanks. This should do me."

---

mahogany composition, and sharp as shit on a stick. This is a subjective opinion only, and it could be hazarded in terms of guessing that certain kilt-wearing USMC colonels would argue otherwise – or for that matter, coke n' shit snortin' priests with chicken-flavored beards.

"Father, if you don't mind, as we may have a long night ahead of us, I should probably off-load now," Colonel Kellog says.

"Right, mate. Good thinking."

"I'll see you in my bedroom, say in five minutes?"

"Yes. I'll pick up the grease, and we'll get down to it."

Colonel Kellog nods to me, then turns, and exits the gun chamber.

"Father Ivory, could you see if we have any more of that KY Jelly in the kitchen?" Father Gastroni says.

"Yes, I'll check now, Father."

"Bring it to me in front of the colonel's room."

"Yes, father," the young priest says, and exits the armory.

Now ... I again feel little chills of confusion pitter-pattering up and down my spine. I'm hearing that there is going to be some presumed activity in the colonel's bedroom that includes something called 'off-loading' and KY Jelly, and last, but not least, Father Gastroni's participation in such activity. I suddenly crave more scotch.

"Father ... I don't mean to pry," I start out slowly, "but –"

"Walk with me, Dick."

I turn, and Jennifer still seems fascinated with the weapons, though heeding my behest to her not to touch anything.

"Jennifer, let's go," I say.

"I'll be right there, Dick."

Father Gastroni leads me gently by the arm. "She'll catch up to us, mate. Seems like a very resilient little lass."

So I allow myself to be guided by the coke-snorting padre, out of the room, and into the hallway.

"You're curious as to what 'off-loading' means. And how the whole KY thing is pertinent thereto," Father Gastroni says.

"A tad curious, maybe," I say, trying to sound casual, but still having a case of the willies ... almost terrified as to what the explanation might be.

"You see, Dick, both Colonel Kellog and myself have been bit."

I stop, and regard Father Gastroni in shock.

"Bit? You?"

"Yes, Dick. Like you, too, I believe."

I say nothing.

"Dracula told us you were infected. Like you, the Colonel and myself must also go through the daily regimen incumbent to the Tungsten mandate."

"I'll be dog-gone," is all I can say.

"So, that being said, we must induce ejaculation."

"I'm with you so far. I'm a little fuzzy on your needing KY Jelly and meeting Colonel Kellog at his bedroom. That part eludes me."

Father Gastroni nods, as if he were about to give some bit of trivial accounting information to a secretary or some other lowly functionary. "It's really very simple, though I warn you ... it is unorthodox."

"I'm all ears."

"Colonel Kellog's encounter with the vampire that assaulted him was traumatic beyond what he could rationally come to grips with. The vampire was an actor who was performing in one of the local theater's production of Macbeth. The actor had been bitten a few hours before, and had pounced on Colonel Kellog not far from where he worked, at a recruiting station for the Marine Corps in downtown Los Angeles."

"Ooo-kay. I'm still with you. I was pounced outside of a grocery store."

"And I was taken just a block away from my church in Palm Desert," Father Gastroni says. "Bad luck, mate, right?"

"Damn straight."

"The attack on Colonel Kellog produced in him a fantasy-need to wear a kilt – a reminder, perhaps, that the vampire who fanged him was part of something Scotland – the play Macbeth – and that if he wore something particular to the Scottish peoples in general ... then perhaps he would always be protected from future vampire attacks."

"That's nuts," I say.

"Yes, it's odd. I look at it as more of a post-traumatic superstition-induced phobia. Whatever, he wears a kilt, it makes him feel better, and that's that."

"I'm waiting for the KY part," I say, shuddering.

"Inclusive with that piece of post-traumatic sartorial fetish, Colonel Kellog discovered that he suddenly had an inexplicable case of self-hatred. That hatred was also transferred to women."

"Why women?"

"Don't know, mate. Neither does he. Perhaps it has something to do with his sense of self-loathing. Perhaps he feels so violated, so filthy after exposure to the vampire attack – anything associated with self, or another human being vis a vis a traditional love/sex relationship became an anathema to him. Anyway, that's what the therapist who we obtained for Colonel Kellog suggested. Sounds reasonable."

"Okay. He hates himself, hates women, and hates Scots, except for the kilts," I say, check-marking off the very weird points of Colonel Kellog's affliction.

"Because of his self-hatred, he maintains that he simply can't touch himself in any kind of self-auto erotic sense. In other words –"

"He can't jerk off," I adduce quickly and am proud of myself that I translated Father Gastroni's verbage so rapidly.

"Right, mate. He is unable to masturbate. And since he hates women, the problem is two-fold. If he were homosexual, that might have even been helpful, but thus is not the case."

"Uh … but back to you … and the Ky?" I press.

"So, keeping all this in mind, Colonel Kellog, in order to survive the bite-factor, as you know, must still utilize the Tungsten Maneuver every 24 hours. As you know, you miss your deadline and it's Changeover time."

"Right, get it."

Father Ivory approaches Father Gastroni, holding a bottle of olive oil.

"We're out of the gel, Father. Will this do for tonight? I'm sorry, I got so busy today, I forgot to stop at the Toy Shop."

"This'll do, Father. Thank you, mate," Gastroni takes the olive oil and then stares off momentarily. Father Ivory turns and leaves. Gastroni clicks his tongue.

"Where was I?"

"Kellog's inability to jack-off and how he gets by," I say.

"Yes, there we go, mate. So, to make a long story short, Colonel Kellog needs daily assistance in this matter. Since he refuses to touch himself, and since he abhors women, and since he is not gay, I ensure that our friend is serviced accordingly."

I stare at the olive oil in Father Gastroni's hands and make the linear deduction of one plus one equals two. "Please don't tell me that —"

"Yes, I am able to precipitate the necessary 'off-loading' as we term it these days for Colonel Kellog. I have, in essence, become a kind of nurse. Instead of providing a bedpan – I offer lubrication and coaching."

I back up a little. I want to both laugh and cry. I again wonder what my life has become. I ask myself, no, I scream to myself: why am I meeting the strangest fucking people on the planet of late? What evil deed, what foul piece of debauchery did I indulge in, what unpardonable sins did I commit in the last life, or lives before this one? What did I do to deserve this kind of surreal madness in my existence?

"You jerk off the colonel with olive oil," I say dully.

"Or KY. Or Crisco, when all else fails. Even hand lotion, properly warmed, can achieve the same effect."

"You masturbate the colonel ... but you say he's not homosexual."

"He is not. Nor am I. By the way, I need no assistance in the masturbation department, thank you very much. I subscribe monthly to Playboy and Farm Teen Tigress. The shaved Asian edition last week was particularly fulfilling."

"And what do you suppose Colonel Kellog thinks of as you're stroking his cock?" I have now surrendered to the madness and sound very cool ... or perhaps more accurately ... completely resigned to living in the Fifth Ring of Hell.

"I asked him that once. He told me that he fantasizes about God," Gastroni says, then smiles. "That's nice, don't you think?"

I have no words. I have no immediate feeling in my body. I have, as Bruce Lee once put it, 'become like water.'

"Now you'll have to excuse me," Gastroni says. "I'm on dick detail." He laughs, clearly finding this terribly amusing. "Oh, good lord, that's funny. I surprise myself at times."

He then turns, opens the bedroom door where presumably Colonel Kellog is preparing himself for a priestly prick-session, and then disappears within.

I do not move.

I cannot move.

I wonder if this is perhaps my lowest moment.

Yes, I decide at last. This is it. No doubts.

How much lower can it get?[7]

---

[7]   Really, a point must be made for the sake of setting the record straight and for general edification. For anyone remotely confused, autoeroticism is the practice of stimulating oneself sexually. The term was popularised toward the end of the 19th century by British sexologist Havelock Ellis, who defined autoeroticism as "the phenomena of spontaneous sexual emotion generated in the absence of an external stimulus proceeding, directly or indirectly, from another person." The most common autoerotic practice is masturbation, and the two terms are often used as synonyms, although masturbation can also occur with a partner.

Many people use dildos, vibrators, anal beads, Sybian machines, and other sex toys while alone. Autofellatio, the act of sucking one's own penis, occurs in less than 1% of the male population (is anyone surprised?). Autocunnilingus is the act of licking one's own vulva (now there's a stocking-stuffer). Both acts are very rare because performing them requires great physical flexibility. There is a joke that the reason dogs lick themselves is that they _can_. As if this isn't fucking obvious. Ask any dog, if you speak canine, and he'd

＊   ＊   ＊   ＊

tell you that in addition to the can-do dynamic of ball-licking, there's the 'shit, that feels real good' element attendant to such testicular-tongue-teasing. Further, he would no doubt add that since he's a dog, there's really very little else to do with one's time aside from sniff another dog's ass, when opportunity arises, sleep, eat, observe various obsequious behavior-patterns for the Master Human providing the Alpo, and then ultimately – irrevocably - taking a shit. Ball-licking comes under the canine category of recreational distraction in an itinerary otherwise crammed with meaningful activity. In any event, that aside, autoerotic behavior is considered to be a normal part of <u>human</u> development, beginning when children are able to stimulate themselves sexually.

More germane to the current point, some people, for religious or personal reasons, believe autoeroticism to be wrong. For example, masturbation is considered sinful by the Roman Catholic Church because it does away with the procreative and unitive dimensions of the sexual act and only gives one pleasure, and is therefore an offence against chastity.

To ram the proverbial point fully home (perhaps a poor choice of words given the nature of this defining moment in self-abuse), a few autoerotic practices are considered unsafe. These include autoerotic asphyxiation and self-bondage. The potential for injury or even death that exists while engaging in the partnered versions of these fetishes (the choking game and bondage, respectively) becomes drastically increased due to the isolation and lack of assistance in the event of a problem. Well, Christ. Is there confusion on the jeopardy factor regarding this issue? Questions? Thoughts? Feelings?

All things being equal – if you're a vampire-fighting priest who already possesses fetishes of, quite frankly, unfucking believable weirdness (such as snorting the immolated residue of your dead pet, and 'cutting' it with some high-priced narcotic like PCP and/or cocaine – not to mention the crystallized remains of your own fecal matter, well -) – chances are you don't give two corn-dirty ass-nuggets how the Roman Catholic Church feels about whacking off. Further, when such a priest has devoted himself to massage-milking his compadre's Little Friend Freddy daily to ensure his continuance on the planet … well, be damned to orthodoxy and other trivial banalities concomitant to current religious rules and doctrine. Jerk me once, Father, for I have sinned – Jerk me, twice, and cum on you! This could be a correct inference to, as stated, 'a little priest humor'.

As I turn away from the door, I force myself not to imagine the images of Father Gastroni cock-cuddling Colonel Kellog's *UberWeiner*. I am inexorably depressed beyond words. I am inexplicably on some kind of surreal Trail of Tears, from which there is clearly no escape. I must ride with the tide of utter weirdness and simply try to not go batshit out of my gourd. To that end, I now head back to the armory to fetch Jennifer.

She meets me out in the hall, as I am about to enter.

"So when are we going to go out and fight that big vampire that ate all my friends?"

I stare, poleaxed with astonishment, then I laugh – a release I greatly need. I put my hand on her head, and give her an affectionate tussle.

"You, my little lady, are going nowhere except up to bed. I'm sure our guests won't mind us staying here for awhile. Like we have a choice, now that vampires have discovered my apartment."

"But I want to help, Dick. I'm not afraid."

"You're a child," I say. "Try to understand the job description. You do not go out and execute vampires. That's my responsibility. Along with our very strange allies. Is that clear?"

"But I don't want you leave me alone here," Jennifer says plaintively … and I believe that in my life, I have never experienced the feeling I am now having. It is a strange tug in my chest – an ache of caring and need and adoration – perhaps the sensation only a parent can feel. I crouch down so that Jennifer and I are face to face.

"Honey, I won't be gone long."

"You might get killed," Jennifer says.

"Look – I …" I stop, and try to scrounge through my mind for a piece of comfort to refute that terribly accurate statement by my little friend. Finally: "Jenny, I'm not going to lie to you. You know what I do for a living. Yes, I might get killed. But I'm not planning on that."

"If you get killed, who'll take care of me?" Jennifer's little eyes begin to tear.

Aw, shit. I am so screwed.

"I won't get killed this time, okay? Maybe another day."

Jennifer sniffs back the tears, but won't let me get off that easy.

"If you do, I'm not staying here."

"Now what's wrong with this place?"

"The place is okay. It's just that ... I dunno ... the people are a little strange."

A little!!!! Understatement of the millennium.

"They're good people," I say softly.

"I know. But the one guy wears a dress, and, and ... you know what I mean?"

"I thought you liked the man in the dress."

"I do. But, Dick ... it's a dress. Okay?"

I grin again. Jennifer is a smart cookie. And she has an excellent feel for the Weirdometer Reading of this place, and its inhabitants.

"And what about your cat?" Jennifer asks. "He's all alone back at your house. Maybe *they* got him."

I smile, knowingly. I would personally bestow a Nobel Price on any bloodsucker or hobgoblin that would ever be able to corner, capture or kill Little Prick. His favorite hiding place in my kitchen wall is connected to a maze of cat-size tunnels intertwining through my apartment complex. There are literally hundreds of places to hide. I have no doubt that my wily cat has explored every one of them.

"My cat is fine, Jennifer. The police department I work for is there now, probably, and they're cleaning the place top to bottom. They'll be so much garlic hanging off doors and gates, that no vampire will show it's face for a mile around."

Jennifer thinks about this, but doesn't respond.

"But I'll stop in and see how he is tomorrow. If you'd like, I'll bring him here. I still think it's best we stay in this house for awhile."

Jennifer doesn't look happy, but she doesn't seem like she wants to discuss the matter further.

Father Ivory suddenly appears.

From behind me, Father Gastroni and Colonel Kellog appear. The colonel looks vaguely flush-faced.

Don't go there. Just don't go there.

But of course, I fuck up, and put the proverbial foot into the horse's mouth.

"So, how did it go?" I say – and mind you, I'm not trying to be flip or clever – it just came out.

And when I say came out, you know what I mean – and I think you do, and –

Cut it out!!!! Right now!!! Cease and Desist!!!

Father Gastroni and Colonel Kellog say nothing for a moment. I suddenly feel like some kind of rare mucilaginous invertebrate – an agglutinant amphibological and crepuscular jellyfish that oozes an iniquitous aphotic diabolism – a thing that exists thirty thousand feet deep in the Mariana Trench someplace in the remote Pacific, and exists solely to quiver in spineless, tenebrous vagariousness, an entity so vile and so inexorably feculent and mephitic, that words defy any description I could possibly muster to characterize how super-pluperfect-fucking-low I feel at this very moment.

I try to crawl out of the shit-hole I've just verbally dug.

"I mean … oh, Christ … what I meant was –"

"Thank you for asking," Father Gastroni says, as he clenches and unclenches his right hand … no doubt due to some kind of recent exertion. "We're all good to go."

I am determined to move past this incredibly embarrassing moment with alacrity and stealth.

"Father Gastroni, I was wondering if Jennifer could stay here with you while we're gone? With Father Ivory, I mean. Do you have room for her?"

"Mate, we have room for both of you, it's not a problem," Gastroni replies amiably. Colonel Kellog, I notice, stares at me neutrally. As if I was perhaps a percipient witness to his necessary treatment by way of Priest Prick Palpation, and that for even being *only* an inactive participant (akin to possessing forbidden knowledge of the Ancients), I would no doubt have to be eliminated at some point down the line by way of hanging or firing squad.

I am of course reading into all of this quite out of a kind of queasy disbelief that this is my life – and these are the kind of people I now hang out with.

Suddenly, Jennifer turns away from us, and walks out of the room.

"Jennifer, honey," I call out.

But she is gone. I look imploringly at Father Ivory, and he reads my mind. "Don't worry, sir. I'll see that she's comfortable. I think she has a case of the shys."

I nod, then look to Gastroni. "Where is Dracula now? At the airport, waiting for us?"

"Not at all. I'm right here."

I turn, and there is Dracula, with Samantha, already well armed and ready for battle.

"Shall we?" Dracula looks to all of us.

"*Carpe Nosferatus,*" Gastroni nods.

In Latin - Seize the Vampires.

I nod as well.

"I'm for that."

CHAPTER TWENTY

▼

As I walk out of the house, I again turn, searching for Jennifer. But she is nowhere to be seen, clearly undelighted with being left alone with Father Ivory and with me having to go out and face near certain death.

I walk to the Esplanade, my RPG hung over my shoulder. Kellog is staring at me, and I am distinctly uncomfortable. Samantha strides up next to me.

"Mind if I ride with you in the back, Dick?" she asks soothingly.

"I'd like that," I say.

I open the door to the Esplanade and Samantha enters first. As Gastroni has bee-lined directly for the passenger seat, and Dracula to the driver's seat, it is clear that I will share the back seat of the spacious vehicle with Colonel Kellog and Samantha.

We are now seated, and ready to go.

Dracula looks at me in the rear view mirror.

"How are you doing, Dick?" he asks.

"I'm okay, partner," I say, though I feel far from fucking okay, if you please.

"This will be a tough night, you realize that," Dracula continues. "He's waiting for us. He has reinforcements – and he'll use the children against our small contingent."

"Why don't we just request MV back-up?"

"Because if the Grand Master even sniffs a full-on Monster Vice Attack Team, he'll simply evaporate into the landscape. He doesn't want that kind of battle. He wants to finish you, me, Samantha, and throw in our good father, and his very able colonel, as well. It's personal, don't you see?"

I do see, and it pisses me off.

"Yeah, well," I mutter impotently.

"It's our weapon against him. Preying upon his pride is how we must finish him."

I glance at Samantha, and she nods, putting a hand on my knee. "There is no other way, Dick."

I look to Colonel Kellog who says to me: "Did you know that turtles can breath through their asses?"

I stare at Kellog blankly, as Dracula starts up the car and I hear Father Gastroni sigh. "Colonel, please."

I decide not to reply to Kellog's query, as the Esplanade moves down the drive-way and out onto the street leading to the freeway.

But I do not get off that easily.

"It's true, you know," Kellog continues, matter-of-factly, looking out into the night. "See, the turtle has a pair of air sacs called bursae which opens off the combined digestive and urogenital chamber. That's a fancy way of saying that the turtle can absorb oxygen through the sacs by way of it's poop-shute."[8]

---

[8]   This can be viewed as a who-gives-a-shit side note, but in due reverence to *Chelonia,* order of *Testudines,* all turtles have extraordinary anaerobic capacity – they have survived up to 33 hours in a pure nitrogen atmosphere. Most reptiles have a high anaerobic capacity compared to mammals, but even they can't survive much more than 30 minutes without oxygen. Although basically air-breathing, many aquatic species have developed ways to pick up oxygen even when submerged. Of these, the most remarkable, which some turtles share with dragonfly nymphs, sea cucumbers, and certain televangelists, is the ability to breathe through one's butt. We've all heard the expression "blow it our ass." If you're a kind of aquatic atramentous mollycoddle, with an asshole heavily vascularized to facilitate the uptake of oxygen, then this is no mere figure of speech.

"And you feel, Colonel, that I have a burning desire to hoard this kind of knowledge?" I say dully.

It is Samantha who leans over and smiles charmingly, as I scoot a micro-inch away from Colonel Kellog, who I now feel is completely 'out there' and one gonad minus a full prick-pack in the sanity department.

"That's quite interesting, Colonel Kellog," she says, dripping charm. "I'm more intrigued by dragonfly nymphs myself."

"Really, why is that, Samantha?" Kellog says.

"Well, the nymphs, as you know are aquatic. They are able to take water in through the rectum and absorb oxygen through gill-like structures in the hindgut. They can also travel by jet-propulsion by expelling a powerful stream of water from their rear ends."

"I didn't know that," Kellog says, nodding thoughtfully.

Father Gastroni now turns to us from the front seat. "I've got one better, guys. Sea cucumbers."

"What about them?" Kellog asks.

"Sea cucumbers are related to starfish. They have an elaborate respiratory tree system branching from the end of the digestive tract, through which they breathe. Kinda like Mr. Turtle, but slightly different."

I sit there silently, thinking: Mommy… mommy. Make them all go away…

"Continue, Father" Kellog says to Gastroni.

"Sea cucumbers can use the anus in self defense. Some can shoot out sticky threads that can entangle an enemy. Others actually disembowel themselves when disturbed: they eject the digestive tract and respiratory tract from the old bung-hole."

"Wow," Kellog whispers, as if perhaps he's just received benediction from Christ himself.

"Yeah, the innards crawl around by themselves for awhile outside the cucumber, and as they are sticky, they can also entangle an attacker. Then the little bugger just blithely crawls off to regenerate its digestive tract while its victim is being consumed by the self-motivating expelled guts."

Colonel Kellog leans back and sighs, this latest information that has been imparted to him physically taking the emotional wind out of him.

Samantha looks to me, and winks.

It is said of soldiers about to go into battle that the most insipid banalities are exchanged, mainly to alleviate apprehension and fear. I can accept that. This conversation, however, takes on an entirely new dimension in pre-combat byplay.

And for some reason, I cannot momentarily rid myself of the image of some turtle sucking in air through its ass.

We drive in silence the rest of the way, and this is extremely fine by me.

CHAPTER TWENTY-ONE

▼

We arrive at Santa Monica airport just before 9pm. This airport is a general aviation facility located approximately six statute miles north of LAX and one mile east of the Santa Monica Bay. The airport has a control tower and, once, a long time ago, handled 400-500 operations a day. Originally called Clover Field, the airport was the home of the Douglas Aircraft company. The first circumnavigation of the world by air took off from and returned to Clover Field in 1924. Three restaurants are on the airport property – like the airport itself, now all closed. They are The Hump and Typhoon, both having runway views, and the last is the Spitfire Grill across an airport street with no view of the runway. The Museum Of Flying at the airport houses a collection of historic aircraft.

It, too, is now closed.

What remains of this once lovely airport are empty hangers, restaurants, and numerous buildings housing office space – now all no longer operational. Reason for this overall closure was due to the near-constant infestation of monsters that this place seems to magnetize. There is no rational explanation for it. The Tutis, Likkers and everything else foul to Man of a supernatural sort, have overrun the area. Establishment owners and airport and state regulators simply threw up their hands a year ago, and sold out to the overrunning Creatures Of The Night. Now the place belongs to the monsters. Monsters, and a fairly large population of indigents, numbering in the hundreds. But they mainly occupy the alleys close to the various entrances and exits. Even many of the mentally challenged and drug addicted know better than to try and set up house inside the airport boundaries proper. Oddly enough, they are rarely preyed upon by the Tutis or the Lykkers – probably because their general blood and organ composition from a chemical point of view is dreadfully unappetizing, given the pandemic use of drugs and alcohol within that particular community.

So, though relatively safe for your basic toothless drug-riddled and drunken bag man, the airport is still an extremely dangerous haunt, and there are so many areas that are compromising to Monster Vice assault forces, that MV has simply declared it a disaster area and not accessible to the general public. Periodically, MV Clean Details go in and try to flush out what they can find – but the monsters are fairly clever, and have early detection scouts all along the perimeter. By the time a Clean Detail arrives, the bastards have all relocated either underground or into contiguous neighborhoods until the assault party has grown weary and left.

It is into this Monster Militarized Zone that my peers and I are about to enter.

Dracula parks outside of what was once the main entrance, now padlocked. Kellog is out of the car, reaching under the seat for a huge pair of metal-cutters.

Samantha exits, and so does Dracula and Father Marconi. I look to them all.

"So what is the plan, if I might ask?"

"We stay together. We go building to building and hangar to hangar. We kill anything that moves," Colonel Kellog says.

"Yes," Dracula says, and then turns to me in particular. "The children will be particularly dangerous. Many are Fresh Bites, and are starving. Keep that in mind."

Father Gastroni performs the sign of the cross on myself and Colonel Kellog. "God be with you." He then looks to Dracula and Samantha, who take an instinctive step back from the proceedings. "My friends, God be with you as well."

"I hope he is," Dracula says.

"Ditto," Samantha says softly, and I reach out and squeeze her hand for comfort. She looks to me, and I can see she is genuinely touched.

"Be careful, Dick," she says to me, and kisses me on the lips.

In that moment, my fellow fang-killers, I could have faced an army of vampires and simply laughed in the face of certain death.

"Now we're gonna party," I say, feeling right now that nothing could possibly go wrong. I sound bold, and in my voice there is the sound of braggadocio, a grandiloquence of determination and steel-nut courage. I am armed with my gimcrack of death, my fire-worthy habiliments of impending hecatomb and destruction - ready to produce an unholy internecion of blood and carnage. There is no sense of intorsion when I say that I am, right this minute, fearless.

I growl heartily to each and every one of my cohorts.

"Let's kick their ass, shall we?"

The decision to do just that is unanimous.

Which is a pity.

Because yours truly has bad times ahead.

And to give you a hint - before this night is through, I'm going to hate the fact that I was the victory sperm that made it to the Big Egg leading to my birth.

We approached the most logical first target building – the main hanger for what once was reserved for the small jets and puddle-jumpers to Palm Springs. Like some cavernous monolith, defiant and silent, the hanger was rife with portent, and I knew just as sure as crap through a goose that there were fangs waiting within. I glanced at Dracula and the others – I was not the only one with this preternatural sixth sense; my compadres, hardened by many a battle, were equally frosty to this, what could be, our final approach.

And then the thunderous, explosive sounds of wings, coupled with hisses and snarls.

Hell is unleashed swiftly on our group.

We open fire in unison, and the gore-fest commences in earnest.

I am knocked and sent flying from my position at the very entrance of the hanger. I am a human glider, as I smash into a row of hedges some forty feet from the hanger exterior. I am now officially separated from my friendly platoon of fellow fang fighters, as I try to shake free the shocking wave of pain extending from the top of my head to my tip-tip tippy toes. I look to the entrance of the hanger, and see the three little tykes responsible for attacking me in tandem, and swatting my ass silly across the tarmac.

They are children.

And they now charge toward me like miniature rhinoceri.

And while that impending threat looms large ahead, I am suddenly reminded of a terrible, terrible reality.

It is now close to midnight.

Oh, bugger!

I had completely forgotten to spank the old Slack Spaniel.

This was not good, and I now revised my earlier assessment of how low things could get.

I was, needless to say, surrounded within a few moments. My RPG and grenades were a few feet away, thrown off my shoulders as soon as I hit the ground. I glanced furtively toward the hanger, and could hear a panoply of gunshots, but could discern nothing of the current fate of my fellow combatants.

I was utterly alone. Except for the three apostates from hell eyeing me with famishment.

The vampires were small, but they were child-turnovers – fresh 'bites', but taken as kids. Which meant, my fellow boner-batters, that I was in for one mean cluster-fuck of a fight.

The sweet little girl who probably looked like Shirley Temple before the Big Change, charged first. Her fangs found my right wrist, and she began milking me like Elsie the Cow. I screamed, fell, tried to throw the little darling off. No go. She hung on like an Alabama tick.

I put my .357 to her head, and made the air go green with vampire brain stuff. But lest you think I had solved my problems entirely, the two other Little Rascal Bloodsuckers (one even looked a bit like Alfalfa) were on me in a New York Minute.

The first one sunk his incisors into my other wrist, instantly breaking the bone. I screamed so loud I felt like Maria Callas at the Met going for a High C. The second precocious youngster went for my heart – and was happily chewing away at my Kevlar Vest when I politely decided to separate his head from his shoulders.

That left Alfalfa, who was still sucking at my wrist like Monica on Bill. My universe of existence became a gray mat of indescribable pain. I was not presently enjoying the Body Electric.

I was weakening. Blood loss and broken bones, along with systemic shock, sent me crumbling to my knees. The child vampire still alive (and we use the term loosely, kidees) was still latched on to my wrist, an inhuman lichen determined to swarm and spread over the pond of plenty.

I dropped my gun. And took a chance the remaining strength I had within me. I grabbed Blood Boy's neck, in a chokehold, and snapped it hard, hoping that I could sever the spinal cord in one glorious moment of triumph.

The kid's body went limp, and the supernatural jaws of death relaxed against my broken wrist. The vampire looked up at me, pissed to the max at this dirty piece of treachery on my part, and then slipped into unconsciousness.

My troubles were far from over.

One, it was two minutes to midnight, and I had yet to Massage the Mambo King between my legs. Old Willy needed a solid jerk, and my dancing card at the moment was a bit full. Reason being, I had to neutralize this last little bastard of a bloodsucker with either a stake or a bullet to the brain. And two, both my wrists were broken, thus my hands were useless. The blood loss was so severe, dizziness washed over me, along with waves of comforting impulses that urged me to either barf or pass out – either option of which would have me awakening as one of Them.

And then my luck changed. Sort of.

From around the corner, a figure appeared. As it drew near, stumbling, staggering, in fact, I could see it was an old woman, probably drunk (or drug ridden) with a face of such primogenial, dare I say, antediluvian cragginess to it, that carbon-dating to determine age and composition under different circumstances would not have been inappropriate. She stares at me as if indeed I was the Living Dead. Not far from the truth, at the end of the day. I realized she was one of the many indigents who occupied the periphery of the airport, and was relatively immune to monster attack based on pure and simple culinary undesirability.

She stops in front of me, swaying back and forth like a sunflower in a Texas breeze.

"Help me," I moan.

"Sure," she smiles, her lips drawn into a kind of crooked grin. "Whad'ya want, cutie?"

"There," I said, indicating the unconscious vampire boy. "It's a vampire. I need you to pound a stake through its heart. There's a hammer and wood in my vest."

The drunken bagwoman (sans bag, at the moment) stared a moment longer at me, then took a look at the sleeping vampire-kid. She nodded.

"Yep. Sure looks like one of them…"

"It is," I assure her.

She waddles over, and I immediately sniff the delicate, yet putrescent aroma of urine commingled with a few other things I don't care to analyze too closely. In short, she has all the personal body ambience of a decomposing skunk. But hey ... who am I to judge?

I'm one minute from The Boner Of No Return if I don't a) get the vampire staked and b) Shoot A Load from here to Tuesday.

The bag lady, who now suddenly has the nimbleness of a gazelle in the Serengeti, fairly hops over to me, takes out my hammer and stake, then without hesitation, drives the wood into the kid-bloodsucker's chest. There's the usual scream, foaming, spasming ... and then all is quiet once again in Christendom.

"Good job," I say, truly impressed.

"Thanks," shit-for-pants bag lady smiles at me in return. "Need anything else?"

Well, as a matter of fact ...

"There's $20 dollars in my pocket, sister," I say, with the great despair of one about to receive lethal injection for crimes innumerable against humanity. "Take it, and then this is what I want you to do."

I tell her of my "need."

At first she is expressionless. And then she smiles.

I see now that she has no teeth, and that her gums are black with fungus.

I again cry for mommy from someplace deep inside, yet am oddly thankful for the lack of teeth, in this instance.

She takes out my wallet, and the money, and then reaches for my pants. The zipper is drawn. Out comes Mr. Playful.

The warm, wet bastion of salvation takes over, and I repress the urge to privately promise to kill myself at a later date.

For those of you who haven't already guessed ... I have *now* reached my lowest moment.

CHAPTER TWENTY-TWO

▼

Fun Mouth Poo-Poo Pants (as I refer to her now) has come and gone (and so have I). I hear still distantly the sounds of gunfire from within various hangers – my friends no doubt in the heat of battle with a coterie of fangs.

I stand at last, and test my balance. Not to sound remotely crass, but I am in pretty fucked up shape.

"So, Officer Pitts," a voice hisses from somewhere behind me. "We're alone at last."

I turn, my heart sinking.

The Grand Master is leaning casually against a lamp-post not far from me. He's dressed in simple jeans, a shirt and a jacket. About as casual as you can get for a night out of Kill The Cop. That cop, of course, being myself.

"You don't look well," he says … smiling.

"Feel great, fuck-face. How about you?"

He laughs. The prick.

"I couldn't help but catch the love-action with your very mature lady friend," he says, walking toward me. "I was moved. Truly."

"We go way back. Way back behind the haystack," I quip, suddenly wishing I was a nameless rabbit somewhere in Montana. Even faced with imminent death, I am exceedingly embarrassed.

The Grand Master nods. "Very romantic."

I take a few steps back myself. Oh, as if that's going to really fucking help…

"I almost hate to see you die, Pitts. You've done an admirable job of surviving where so many others have not."

I look furtively around. I am alone. I have the depressing notion that this may very well be the end of the line.

"I could, however, make you one of my slaves," the Grand Master shrugs, musing on the possibility. "Would you like that, Dick?"

"I can hardly wait," I say with false bravado.

"Though I suspect with your will – you would find a way to make trouble with me, even subjugated so."

"I'm a troublesome soul," I say wearily.

"Yes, which is why it's better if you just die."

He now stalks toward me.

And then a miracle in our times transpires.

A shot from behind me rings out – and I see the Grand Master's head snap back. He screams in agony and rage. When he looks back in my direction, I see that his left eye is gone, obliterated by the bullet shot by my unseen savior.

He screams again, clawing at his face.

"Holy water! Oh, you will pay dearly for this!"

He howls, and I swear to god, his fangs grow three inches out of his mouth. So do his finger nails. He continues to scream, and then suddenly dematerializes in front of my eyes.

I am stunned, frozen where I stand.

I slowly turn.

From around a hedge, the shooter appears.

It is little Jennifer. And she holds a Glock automatic in both hands, the barrel still smoking from the discharge.

"Sorry I was late, Dick," she says softly.

"Jennifer …" I sputter, and walk over to her on very unsteady legs. I fall to my knees, and hug her. I do not want to let go, and she does not protest. "How the hell did you get here, honey?"

"I didn't want to stay in that house. So I snuck in ahead of you guys in the car trunk. It was easy."

I pull back, and laugh, shaking my head, tears running down my cheek. I believe I am crying not so much because I'm still alive, or because a child just saved my life … no, I believe I'm hysterical because a child – my Jennifer – had the moxy to take such brilliant initiative.

And clearly, she's a born vampire killer.

I try to play parent, and attempt to take the Glock from her hand, but it is apparently I can do nothing with my broken wrists.

"I'm pretty handy with this," Jennifer considers the gun, then looks to my wrists. "And you're hurt bad, Dick."

"I've seen worse," I say … though I can't remember in recent history *how* worse.

Dracula suddenly appears, along with Colonel Kellog and Father Gastroni. They are all bleeding, though Dracula seems the least damaged. Clearly, some biting took place, and everyone took a licking. I confess to being mildly surprised that some of my friends are not dead.

And then I see that Samantha is absent.

"You okay?" Dracula asks, approaching quickly.

"Far from it," I say, my wrists useless stumps at my side. "Where's Sam?"

"She got separated from us," Colonel Kellog responds, and as he speaks, blood flows freely from his mouth. He looks to Jennifer.

"What in the name of sweet Christ on rubber crutches is *she* doing here?"

"She saved my life," I reply tersely.

"She's just a kid," Kellog says.

"No," I respond. "She's one of us."

Jennifer looks up to me and smiles, and I put a useless paw on her head, a benediction as it were from one warrior to another – a knighthood for the little lady.

Dracula offers a little grin. "Ah, I see in my mind what happened. Very courageous, child."

"Thanks," Jennifer said. "Let's find some more of those fuckers and kill them all."

We're all stunned into momentary silence.

"Sorry," Jennifer lowers her eyes. "I'm a big potty mouth."

"You're forgiven," I say quickly, then look to everyone. "We have to find Samantha. I have a bad feeling –"

"Yes, so do I," Dracula nods. "But there is still the Grand Master. He's out there. Waiting."

"Uh, I don't think so," I say.

I then explain to my friends in thirty seconds what Jennifer did to the Grand Fucking Master himself.

I do believe Colonel Kellog may have something akin to an epileptic seizure in front of me – disbelief and chagrin immersing his face into a deep purple. Gastroni and Dracula merely exchange a look of profound astonishment.

"He's hurt. The holy water shell must be agonizing for him," Gastroni whispers.

"Which makes him far more dangerous now," Dracula frowns.

"How could he get *more* dangerous?" I say.

"Don't ask," Dracula says. "Now let's go find Samantha."

We are about to fan out when we hear the scream.

"Help me!"

✳   ✳   ✳   ✳

We turn and run, though Dracula is already in motion so quickly, he essentially evaporates before our eyes.

We follow the weak screams of what we recognize to be Samantha's voice. I lag behind the others in the herd charge, my speed greatly reduced by my injuries. Jennifer stays by my side, though she has the presence of mind to continually hold vigil for any further fang attacks.

We turn the corner of the last hanger on the west end of the airport, and find Samantha propped up against the hangar wall. Her body is oddly twisted, her legs particularly – and her hands are both nailed to the wall by rusted metal spikes.

"Oh, Jesus," Kellog mutters.

I kneel down next to Samantha and touch her face. "You hang on, beautiful," I say.

"Trying," she whispers bravely. "The Master nailed me good. No pun intended."

I smile at her courage. Dracula doesn't waste time with small talk. He pries out the spikes with his bear hands – a feat only a vampire could accomplish with superhuman strength. Dracula makes it look easy.

Samantha flops forward, and I am there to brace her with my arms and useless wrists.

Kellog and Gastroni rotate in full circles, holding vigil for anything that flies and sucks.

Which, as shitty timing would have it, now becomes an immediate problem.

The wings and hisses surround us. We look up and around us.

It's literally going to be raining vampires within seconds.

Dracula lifts Samantha up bodily, and places her in my arms, cradle-position.

"Take cover!" he points to a small utility shed ten feet away.

I don't hesitate, as I yell to Jennifer. "Jenny, with me."

Thank god Jennifer doesn't argue. She also recognizes the need to protect both myself and Samantha, since at the moment, we're unable to effectively defend ourselves. Both 'hand-icapped' … again, no pun intended.

I enter the utility shed, with Jennifer right behind me, though she turns on her heel, gun up to the sky. Samantha is still conscious, and I hear her whisper: "Oh, dear god."

We all see it.

The once moon-lit sky is now suddenly black. For a moment, one would think that the airport is about to be enveloped by a thick smoke, or some rain-filled cloud that has challenged climatic rules of precipitation by descending to near ground-level. Sadly, either scenarios are not viable.

The sky is black with vampires.

The roar of the wings is deafening.

"The Grand Master has summoned every vampire in the city," she whispers.

And it looks to be very true. Like locusts, the vampires begin to descend.

"We're fucked," I mutter under my breath.

Jennifer stares out at the flying death coming our way. Her expression is inscrutable. But her grip on her Glock remains firm and unwavering.

Dracula, I can see, is painfully aware of the dilemma facing us all. He could easily escape now, probably even transporting Samantha quickly into that weird vampiric ether of unending possibilities and metamorphosis. But he will not leave us ... he will not leave his friends.

Gastroni and Colonel Kellog hold their ground, watching the tsunami of fang-pox move ever closer.

I glance absently for a moment around the hangers and the runways. I notice small sprigs of metal that rise out of the asphalt. I do not make an immediate connection, but there is something about those sprigs ... something ...

"Oh, shit!" It finally comes to me.

I yell out to Gastroni.

"Father Gastroni!"

The old priest turns to me.

"The sprinkler system. It should still be operational!" I cry out to him, shouting over the din of wings getting closer and closer.

Dracula and Gastroni scan the system sprigs in the asphalt – a failsafe mechanism to any potential fire hazard on the airfield – and look back to me.

"Bless the system!" I yell to Gastroni.

"Bless it?"

"Yes! Then we'll activate the sprinklers. It'll be Holy Water fallout for a hundred yards in all directions!"

"How do we activate them?" Dracula says.

"We'll need a fire!"

"How the hell do we start a fire?" Colonel Kellog snaps at me. "We're kinda running out of time."

Dracula puts his hand on Kellog's shoulder. "I'll handle that." He nods to Gastroni, who reaches into his jacket, and takes out his cross, and kneels. He puts his hand on one of the sprinklers.

"Holy father, with this cross, I bless your instruments of destruction against these god-awful apostates from an angry and vengeful demon. Allow your water to purify and screw these sons of bitches from here to hell and back. Amen."

Jennifer giggles, and turns to me. "He's a potty-mouth priest. I like that."

At the moment, so do I.

The cloud of fangs are about twenty seconds away from touchdown.

It is at this moment that Dracula turns himself into a ball of flame.

*   *   *   *

Y'know … it's a handy thing being a vampire sometimes. So I believe right this moment. You can turn yourself into neat things like bats or wolves or crows. You can transmogrify into mist.

And on occasion … you can turn into the Human Torch.

Dracula is now a swirling pinwheel of flame, and he wastes no time in hovering over water sprinklers. The response is near instantaneous. Water geysers upward like a pyroclastic cloud from an erupting volcano. Within moments, after triggering some twenty sprinklers, the air is lousy with holy water.

Good for us.

Very, very bad for the descending army of vampires, already too close to retreat back into the sky.

The screams are loud, infernal and ululating, as vampire flesh literally melts and dissolves in mid-air. Gastroni and Kellog run for shelter, lest they are deluged by pounds and pounds of molten fang flesh. The stench is indescribable, the sounds of extinction deafening.

"Smells like poo-poo," Jennifer grimaces, watching the rain of vampire gunk pour from the skies.

Dracula has resumed corporeal form, and he walks casually toward Gastroni and Kellog, now under a protective overhang from the hanger. He is being deluged with flesh and no doubt some attendant holy water – his own flesh steams and blotches, yet he shows no pain, no discomfort. Yet I know that holy water is agonizing for vampires. I marvel at his control, his discipline. The guy fucking amazes me.

The geysers spray upwards of forty feet. I'm guessing at least a hundred fangs are wasted inside of a few seconds. More die in seconds thereafter. Finally, a general retreat seems to be in the offing, as the wing-flap dissipates and all that is heard is the steaming hissing of melted vampire corpse-stuff on the tarmac.

I look to Samantha.

"It's time to go home, Sam."

Samantha studies my hands, and reaches out her own bloody hands, caressing my useless wrists. "Poor Dick."

Dracula approaches us, gives Jennifer's head a rub as she smiles, then looks to both Samantha and myself.

"Kellog, Gastroni and myself are going to do a five minute perimeter check of this airfield. I doubt anything is around that wants to fight. They're in hiding now, licking their wounds."

I nod. "We'll wait here."

Dracula moves off with Gastroni and Kellog.

I move out of the utility shed and look at the landscape around me. It's a sea of molten tissue. Jennifer stands at my side.

"I'm hungry," she says.

Now I'm barely repressing the urge to purge with the stench floating through the air, but my little Jennifer is ready for a snack. I continue to be amazed by Mirabelle's daughter.

"We'll grab some fast-food on the way back to the house," I say.

This seems to satisfy Jennifer as she wanders into the morass of fang felch stretching out to the horizon.

And then I see the shadow.

I turn suddenly. The vampire came out of nowhere, probably got lucky and was hiding out in the hanger. It holds a long pipe with a jagged end. It's interest lies not with me. It is charging now for Samantha, who is at the utility shed's entrance. She has crawled there to look out at the airfield.

I scream.

"Sam, look out!"

The vampire charges, using the pipe as a lance.

I don't think. I dive in the path of the charging vampire.

The pipe rams deep into my chest, and there is a white hot fire that ripples through my entire body.

I simultaneously hear gunshots, see the vampire's head explode, hear Sam screaming, her own screams commingled with those of Jennifer ... and then the world goes dark.

As I fall, I feel oddly peaceful.

I figure very quickly that when I wake up, I'll be dead.

CHAPTER TWENTY-THREE

▼

They say when you die your life flashes before your eyes in the span of a single second. Yet within that second, the memories of years rockets to the fore of your soul and allows you to relive those defining moments of existence, some good, some bad, some happy, some sad – as if they were being relived once again in bright, visceral Technicolor.

That's what they say.

For me, it is slightly different.

The world goes black, but then I am conscious literally four seconds later, my face splattered in steaming vampire death-placenta. Some of the crap is in my mouth. And yes, lest we not forget, the pain in my chest is fucking monstrous.

I am aware of Jennifer pulling at the rusty pipe, which hurts even more. Nevertheless, I see that she is able to extricate it with a good, solid jerk outwards. Samantha is cradling my head with her bloody hands. I look to her, see that she is on her side, as her legs are still broken, but she is still able to angle her body on the ground sufficient to comfort me.

As the world spins, spins, spins, I am suddenly aware of Dracula, Kellog and Gastroni, now around me, all talking at once.

"Let's get the hell out of here –"

"Gotta get him back to the car –"

"I'll carry Samantha, Colonel, you and the Father Gastroni pick up Dick –"

"Don't die, Dick, please, you promised –" (this last plea from Jennifer, who through blurred vision, I see is sobbing).

And then the world mists in and out of darkness, my universe for the moment only catching sounds, and discerning movement – that is to say, my body being lifted roughly up and crated to the Esplanade.

It seems I close my eyes for only a second, but when I open them, I am in a bed. Dracula leans over me, but I am not sure what he is doing; behind him is Father Gastroni. Someone is holding my broken left wrist, and I turn slowly to see that it is Jennifer.

"We're fixing you up," Jennifer smiles. "Dracula says you'll be good to go in a few hours."

A few hours?

I chalk up Jennifer's unrealistic enthusiasm for my survival to childish hope and longing. I feel enormous remorse and pity for her. She does not know that the pipe lacerated my lungs and probably even pierced my heart. One doesn't survive that kind of impaling and live. I know that I am dying and I am not afraid. I am vaguely annoyed that Dracula, or Father Gastroni, has not been more forthright with my little Jennifer. To build a little girl's hopes up for the impossible … no, it's not right.

But I am too weak to protest, and again close my eyes.

CHAPTER TWENTY-FOUR

▼

When I awaken I feel distinct surprise.

More than that ... I feel astonishment. For the pain in my chest has degraded well by half.

"What the fuck?"

No one is around to hear my baffled query.

I look down to my chest, which is wrapped. I then look to my wrists, which are also wrapped in swaddling of sorts.

I do not understand.

I don't feel bad at all ... and I do not understand.

The door to my room opens, and Samantha walks in, using a cane.

My vision is no longer blurred, and my fever has broken. I try to take a breath, expecting an agonized, labored experience of congestion and blood. But my respiration seems normal.

I do not understand.

Samantha walks in and puts her hand on my chest.

"How do you feel, Dick?"

I shrug. "I ... okay, I guess."

She smiles.

And I have to ask. "How come I'm not dead?"

"You were healed, Dick. Simple as that."

"Healed?"

"Fixed up, as Jennifer put it," Samantha pulls over a chair, and sits down.

I stare at her, amazed. A short while ago, Samantha's legs were broken, of this I was sure, and I'm willing to bet my nuts on the probability that her spinal cord had been severed as well. Now she was walking around with the aid of a cane, as if perhaps she had suffered only a mild sprain.

"How long … how long since we got back?" I whisper.

"It's late morning now. We got back to the house at around midnight. So, almost ten hours."

"Ten hours."

She looks to the windows, boarded up. "Sorry about the windows being closed. But it is daylight, you know, and we vampires have this thing about the sun."

I smile and nod. "So I've been told."

She nods. Then rubs my chest gently. "You saved my life, Dick. Thank you."

"Samantha, I –"

"Throughout the centuries, no one has ever tried to save my life. You showed self-sacrifice. You offered yourself to die in my place."

"Well …"

And then Samantha leans in and kisses me. A long, luxurious kiss which is instantly intoxicating. Her lips are soft, her scent is gentle, and her touch is electric to my soul. When she pulls back, she wipes a strand of hair out of my eyes.

"I love you, Dick," she says softly.

I want to reply … but I find myself merely becoming lost in her gaze, in those warm, ancient eyes that seem more like eyes of a winsome teen-ager.

But I realize in that moment that I love Samantha. In fact, I know that I have been in love with her from the very first moment we met. I am about to tell her this, but suddenly Jennifer comes bounding through the door.

"Dick!"

She leans in and splatters kisses on my face and forehead. I find myself laughing.

"Okay, stop, stop. I get the message, you're happy I'm not dead."

Jennifer suddenly swats my shoulder, though not hard. "Almost bit the big one, Dick."

"Who shot the vampire that nailed me?" I am suddenly curious.

"That was Colonel Kellog," Samantha replies. "He made the shot from fifty yards away. He's very full of himself. Can't stop talking about the fifty footer he took with his sniper rifle."

"I'm glad I made his day," I sigh.

I look down at my wrists dejectedly. "Boy, these puppies still hurt."

"It won't last for long. Maybe a few days. The smaller bones take longer to heal. Internal organs, like lungs, hearts, they reconstitute much faster, and –"

She stops as I stare at her with clear confusion.

"Well, never mind that for now," she says, and then winks at Jennifer. Jennifer toodles out of my room, as Samantha again kisses me and whispers. "I am your official nurse, Dick Pitts. Hope you don't mind."

"Nurse away," I smile. But a shadow looms in my mind quite suddenly.

"The Grand Master," I mutter.

"Yes, he's still out there. And in a good deal of pain from what I understand. Thanks to our little Jennifer."

"We have to find him. Destroy him."

"Yes, in time. For now, though … you and I must continue to heal. Or we won't be of use to anyone."

Jennifer returns now, pushing a small cart, with a bowl and sponges on top of a turntable.

"Bath time," Samantha says, smiling.

I smile back, but then I remember something about the word 'reconstitution.'

"Sam, your back was broken. I know your legs were broken as well. And your hands are completely healed. Is this a vampire thing?"

Samantha nods, dipping the sponge into a small bowl, while Jennifer sits in a chair and watches her prepare to bathe the big, dirty cop.

"Yes, vampires heal at an accelerated rate. It is why we are far less susceptible to what are otherwise considered to be mortal wounds to human beings. I'm not that versed in the technical part of it, but our flesh, our DNA, our cellular structure – it's set up so that repairs to tissue damage is nearly instantaneous."

"And is that how you're healing me?" I ask. "Some kind of vampire voodoo medicine trick? Eye of newt, ear of frog, that sort of thing?"

Samantha laughs. "Yeah, that's what we're doing. Murdering defenseless amphibians to save your life. How transparent we vampire types are!"

"Well, c'mon. I should be dead. Instead, I'm feeling flushed with anticipation of you giving me a sponge bath. What's the deal?"

"The deal is that vampires have some power that can help to heal, transform, and utterly reverse disease and injury. For the time being, let's leave it at that, okay?"

I am about to speak again, but Samantha puts one of her lovely fingers on my lips. "Hush. I'm trying to work here."

I look to Jennifer. "Hush," she says.

And Samantha begins to wipe my forehead with the sponge and I am inclined to do nothing more but relax and allow myself to be pampered.

My mind rambles to other matters, and more questions loom. Samantha is nearly finished with her Dick-bath (no pun once again intended) and she is patting down my face and arms, careful not to touch my pain-filled wrists.

"Sam?"

"Yes, Dick."

"Who nailed you to the hanger wall back at the airport? Was it the Grand Master?"

"Yes."

"Why didn't he destroy you?"

Samantha sighs, looks off distantly. "He said he wanted me to suffer. And that one day, he was going to make me his bride."

"He said that?"

"Just before he rammed the stakes into my hand, broke my back, and shattered my arms."

"The twisted fuck. This Grand Master has got to go," I say matter-of-factly.

I glance at Jennifer and mumble. "Sorry. Potty mouth."

Jennifer merely smiles.

I look to Samantha. "I should check in with HQ."

"Dracula already did that for you. He talked to Captain Zelig, said you and he were still under deep investigative cover on your case."

"Ah."

"Remember, you're both on a task force."

"Yes, I remember."

Jennifer stands and looks at me. "I think I'll go help Colonel Kellog clean guns. I'll see you later, Dick."

She comes over and kisses me on the cheek. "See ya' later, gator."

"Right," I say and smile.

Jennifer leaves. And Samantha and I are alone again.

"I think you need to sleep," Samantha says.

"Okay. But don't leave yet," I say. "Just sit here with me. Alright?"

"I was planning on it, darling," she says softly.

I smile happily – perhaps for the first time in a long time, that is what I feel, despite my physical infirmity. I feel happiness. And love. I don't want the feeling to go away.

Sleep descends upon me and I believe I dream.

CHAPTER TWENTY-FIVE

▼

I awaken with a start. Something has forced me from my blessed slumber – some kind of anxiety. But anxious about what?

I shake off the cobwebs of sleep and see that I am alone. Samantha is gone.

I feel worry.

I look at the clock ticking next to my bed.

And now I know why I'm awake and frightened.

I have slept away the day, and it is half an hour before midnight – the witching hour when the Love Lion must be stroked.

I feel panic.

My wrists are still useless, and I feel the pain and immobility running through the bones and the marrow.

How am I going to do this? No old bag woman around to let me swordfight in her mouth. This is bad.

Worse … because I have a nauseating terror that Father Gastroni may wish to help me 'offload'. I think I would rather die. I think I would rather be the Grand Master's blood-bitch for the next thousand years rather than let Gastroni fondle the Killer Kolbasi.

"Shit," I mutter.

My mind races for options. I try to move my wrists again, and wince in pain.

The door suddenly opens, and through the dim light, I see a figure. It approaches the bed slowly.

I see it is Samantha. She is in a nightie, a fetching little nothing that shows off her rather shapely legs and does no disservice either to her considerable bosoms.

"Hi," she whispers.

"Hi," I say.

She moves toward me, and then her hand is on my Nuzzle Nob, stroking. I am immediately aroused.

"You didn't think I'd forget about you, did you, Dick?"

I am at first uncertain what she means ... and then a wave of indescribable relief washes over me.

"Sam ... you ... you don't have to do this. Your virginity – I know it's important to you, and –"

"And it's time I put all that behind me."

She continues to fondle my hardening Pork.

Before I know it, she has hiked up her nightie, and she is now straddling me, pulling at my pajama bottoms. I help her as much as I am able, my old Sin Stiffy in full vertical readiness.

Samantha fairly impales herself on my Staff of Love, and a soft moan escapes her lips.

I close my eyes, feeling her softness, her indescribable interior which washes over me like warm holy water in a velvet glove. I force the first thought from my mind – that I am making love to a vampire – a creature not human, not quite alive, yet not quite dead. Yet the sensation I feel is one of pure humanity, or exquisite closeness and intimacy.

Samantha ruts against me quickly, and I can tell she has not lied to me: this is new for her, and she is moved by pure instinct and sensation, versus restrained by any kind of experienced technique. She rides hard and desperately, fighting for that peak of excitement she has never known.

She screams out softly, at last, and shudders against me, pulsating against my Bucking Bear several times, fighting to catch her breath.

Needless to say, I have joined her in the breathlessness of it all. I have been spared Father Gastroni's rubber-glove approach to protocol masturbation against vampirism. Praise the Lord!

Samantha smiles, and kisses me on the lips.

Somewhere in the house, I hear a clock strike midnight.

Samantha lies down on my chest, breathing regularly now, enjoying the aftermath of her first experience at love-making. I do not mind her weight ... in fact, at this moment, she feels light as a feather.

We say nothing. There is no need. She has saved me in my time of broken-wristed need and I am sublimely grateful.

"I love you, Sam," I whisper into her ear.

"I know, Dick. I love you, too."

She kisses me again, then kisses my nose and looks into my eyes.

I am lost again in those eternal orbs of warmth and understanding. And a moment later, sleep finds me like a warm blanket, submersing me in its protective darkness.

CHAPTER TWENTY-SIX

▼

I am able to walk by early morning, and before the sun yet rises, I take a stroll around the garden with Samantha, who is content to wrap her arm in mind, careful still not to touch my wrists. But the near-dawn has brought increased reparation to my hands, and I am able to find mobility at last with my fingers. Cartilage and bone seem on the mend.

We talk about everything and nothing. I want to hear about her adventures through the centuries, and she wants to know of my past, of loves once had and now long gone, of dreams possessed and lost, of hopes yet to be and realized, of goals yet still to be sought and gained.

We sneak into a rose garden annexed to the garage, and make love inside, giggling at our adolescent risk-taking. It is frenzied, innocent sex, demanding and hurried, yet blessed with the magic of newness and immediacy.

Put another way, we fucked and fucked and fucked and fucked until Mr. Wriggles was sore and sprouting moss heads.

The sun begins to rise above the horizon, and I urge Samantha inside the house; in her eager haste for love and more love, she must be reminded that it is time for her to rest.

"Back to your coffin," I chide her as we enter what has become my new home.

"I don't have a coffin," she laughs. "I use a bed. Sorry if it puts a crimp in your whole vampire mythology. Beds are quite okay by us."

"If I were a vampire, I'd insist on a coffin. It's *de riguer*, really. Anything less, and you're just a kind of faux vampire at best. A girlie vampire."

"I *am* a girlie vampire. Or haven't you noticed."

I shove Samantha into a nearby bathroom, one of about a dozen in this place, and shag her silly. She has no complaints about this impetuous act, and spooges me in return.

✱   ✱   ✱   ✱

We exit ten minutes later, and Samantha stops me, gently pushing me against the wall.

"I want you to have something, Dick."

She produces out of her pocket a small jewelry box, purple, and velvet to the touch. I look at her and grin.

"Is this a proposal?"

"Silly," she swats me, then hands it to me.

She then steps away from me.

"I can't be too near it," she says. "You'll see why."

I open the small box. Inside, is a gold chain attached to a crucifix. It is a splendid item and I look to Samantha for an explanation.

"I was wearing it the night I was almost killed – just before Dracula found me."

I look at he crucifix again.

"Samantha, this is beautiful. But it's too precious. You should keep it."

"No, it's for you. Perhaps one day … it will be useful to you."

"Useful? That's a strange way to put it."

"Sorry. Please keep it. I give it out of love."

I kiss her and touch her cheek. "Okay. Thanks."

Afterwards, I walk her to her bedroom, kiss her good night (or good day) and the meander into the living room, where I find Father Gastroni and Colonel Kellog sipping brandy. Jennifer is also sipping brandy, and I take issue with this immediately.

"Hey, hey, hey, what's this? You're too young to be drinking that stuff."

"Just sipping, Dick," Jennifer says ... and her voice to me suddenly sounds ... old. I think sadly to myself that indeed, my new little child has aged in the past 24 hours, as have we all.

"Still," I protest feebly. "It's early yet."

Jennifer seems to understand my concern, and puts down the brandy, as Father Gastroni and Colonel Kellog watch on. They are both clearly drunk.

"Hey, Dick," Kellog slurs. "Didja' know I blew that fang-fucker's head to melon shit? The one that nailed you?"

I nod. "Yes, I heard. Nice shooting, Colonel, and thank you."

"Fifty yards, baby," Kellog says, smirking, and taking another hit from his brandy snifter. I do not respond to Kellog's solipsistic ecstasy in vampire snuffing. I'm not in the mood to be indulgent.

"I assume Samantha is tucked in?" Father Gastroni asks me.

"Yes. Dracula, too?"

"Out like a light," Gastroni nods.

Kellog again mumbles, grinning like the Cheshire Cat, looking at me as if I were his new best friend.

"I remember when I was in the Anbar Province, back in '003. Iraq. I was on sniper detail. I used to pick the little sand-niggers off at 100 yards, Dick. 100 fuckin' sand-nigger yardage. Watched their brains explode through the sites."

I sigh. "That's fine shooting, Colonel, but there's a child in the room, if you please."

Jenny turns to me. "It's alright, Dick. I can deal with a little fucking bad language, especially after yesterday."

I simply shake my head, and realize I have absolutely no control over anything or anyone – especially my little Jennifer.

"Goat-fucking cocksuckers. Lost a lot of fine boys to that insurgency."

"Kinda became unimportant, mate, especially after Popov."

Kellog nods ... almost sadly. As if he had just lost something intimate, fragile and perhaps indescribably precious. "Yeah, over now. Place is vampire heaven now."

I look to Gastroni. "Any thoughts about what the Grand Master's next move will be?"

Gastroni leans forward, nods, studying his brandy snifter. "Good question, mate. Yes, I believe that our Grand Master pal will return to the airport and regroup his surviving army of bloodsuckers. I think that was his first salvo, his first offense – lure us into the place, and then attack. But did you notice something?"

I think, not sure where the good priest is going. "Notice what?"

"No werewolves," Kellog says.

"That's right," Gastroni nods. "Remember, the Master is now controlling a lot of the likkers. Perhaps any likker he chooses to manipulate is his for the taking. Yet he did not throw them at us, I mean, not a single one. Why?"

"He may have thought he could finish us off with what he had. About a million flying fangs."

"Yes, I believe so. But wherever he chooses to attack us next time – I am sure that he will utilize these monstrous assets. And then, I'm afraid, we're ... " he glances at Jennifer, who nods soberly.

"We're screwed," she whispers, sips her brandy, then guzzles it.

"Jennifer," I mewl softly, shaking my head.

"It's true, Dick," she says. "I'm just a kid, but I know when things look real bad."

And then she says something that breaks my heart.

"Guess that means I'll never get a chance to grow up. Or meet someone to love."

I believe in that moment all three adults in the room are damned near close to tears. Even Kellog sniffs, coughs, and turns his head away. I reach out and touch her shoulder.

"If I have anything to do with it, you'll grow into a little old lady, pissing herself silly."

She looks to me, her eyes filled with doubt.

And that's when there is a knock at the front door.

Kellog reaches for an M-16 off the floor while Gastroni unholsters a handy Colt APG. Jennifer has retained hold on her pistol, bringing it out from under a seat pillow she's been sitting on.

I, on the other hand, have been fucking all morning and am completely unarmed and useless. It's a look I've been boasting lately. Stick Boy. Unarmed. Useless. Whoo-hoo.

We all look to the front door as it slowly opens.

Weapons are locked and loaded, all of them up and readied.

Only think I have that is even remotely hard and packing is my dick. Damn fine to behold, perhaps, but not much use in a fight.

*   *   *   *

For a moment, nothing happens.

We cannot see who is on the other side of the door. We are surrounded by cloves of garlic, and crosses cover nearly every square foot of the premises, all saturated in holy water.

Then we see it.

A large German Shepherd. Black. And a badge around its collar.

I recognize the badge as Monster Vice.

"What the —"

The dog suddenly speaks, a low voice, weary, the accent is distinctly 'Jersey.'

"Pitts. That you?"

The voice coming out of the dog sounds familiar.

"Yeah ... and ... you're a dog. And you're talking," I state dully.

"Dick, it's me. Birney Klaskowsky, out of Vice."

Birney Klaskowsky. The name ... yes, the name!

"Birney? Is that you?" I stammer in disbelief.

Birney the dog trots over to me, and sits, staring up at me, panting ... a clearly happy expression on the mutt's face.

"Yep. In the fur," he barks.

"But how?"

Kellog and Gastroni, along with Jennifer have lowered their weapons. They watch this byplay between man and dog without expression.

"Don't know if you remember, but I was taken out by a succubus about two years ago. Bitch caught me right outside of the house. Doreen had a heart attack when she saw what the demon did to me."

I tried to recall the details of Birney's encounter with a sexual demon known as a succubus. And sure enough, the details are blurry, but retrievable. Birney was decapitated by a flying succubus, then sexually assaulted by her after he was already dead. All this taking place in front of his wife, who is suffering a coronary witnessing all this. It was the talk of the station for about a week. I think I was still in shock from my mother's death in Florida so I was pretty much out of it at the time and didn't tune in for the particulars.

I nod. "Yeah, I remember, Birney. Tough luck. How's Doreen?"

"Recovered completely and now dating a haberdasher from Inglewood. Biddy ba, biddy boo, whatcha gonna do?"

He turns and licks his dog balls for a moment. The act seems to catch him off guard.

"'Scuse me," he mutters. "It's a dog thing."

"Take your time," I clear my throat.

He finishes, licking his chops. "Sorry. Sometimes the urge is too strong. I'm just getting the hang of all this."

"Of ... all what, Birney?"

"Me being a dog, and all."

"Yes, about that. Is this one of those animal possession things I've been reading about in research lately?"

"Yep, pal. That's it. More and more good cops are going down, but those of us who don't want to Pass On, we stay on the beat as dogs. Bomb sniffers, drug-mutts, cadaver-Ds. Me, I chose Monster Vice."

"Good call, Birney. Glad to have you aboard."

"Thanks, Dick. Which, by the way, is why I'm here. Zelig down at HQ is curious as to how you're doing. Your cell is dead, and I had to spend most of last night and this morning sniffing out scent to find you here."

"You're good," I nod to Birney. "I'm charging up my cell now. Oh, by the way, Birney, these are my friends." I turn to Kellog, Gastroni and Jenifer, and make the appropriate introductions.

"Nice meetin' you all," Birney barks, then looks back to me.

"Lots of disturbing talk along the circuit, Dick. Vampire attacks are up nearly one hundred percent, we have a likker riot down at LAX late last night, creeps are coming out of the woodwork more than ever."

I ponder this and wonder if the Grand Master is utilizing his considerable powers to inflame and foment general monster hostility citywide.

I look at Birney and try to forget for the moment that I'm talking to a large German Shepherd. "I'll check in with the good captain, Birney. As you can see, I've gone through a bit of a rough ride of late."

"I noticed, but was tryin' to be polite and not mention it. What the hell happened to you?" Birney barks.

"I'll tell you later."

"Okay, tell me later."

I look at the wall clock and see that it is approaching nine in the morning.

Jenny walks up to Birney and scratches his ear.

"Thanks, kid. Feels good," Birney slobbers just a bit.

"You got nice big ears," Jenny comments.

"Yeah, so I've been told.   Hey, anyone got some raw hamburger?" Birney looks at us all hopefully.

"Come with me to the kitchen," Jenny says. "I'll bet Father Ivory can find something for you."

Birney paws off with Jenny and I stretch in what I feel is healing pain. I look at the brandy bottle that Kellog and Gastroni have opened.

"Drink up while you can, mate," Gastroni says. "The Grand Master is out there and round two is fast approachin'."

I reach for the bottle and nod.

Truer words were never spoke.

CHAPTER TWENTY-SEVEN

▼

A few hours later, I am comfortably tanked. I watch the noon day come and take a moment to reflect. I glance out at the garden, and see Birney lift his leg and take a well calculated piss at Father Ivory's hydrangeas, while Jennifer walks with him – her new best friend. There is a strange peace in the air. Perhaps the calm before the storm, my pessimistic muse nudges me a second later. Kellog and Gastroni continue to drink in the main living room. Don't ask me what the fuck young Father Ivory does in his spare time. I have only been able to deduce that he supplies K-Y Jelly or like viscous necessities for whacking off. Other than that, I am unaware of what his other functions may be. Perhaps providing jerk-jelly *is* his sole function. The thought sends a shiver through my system.

I already miss Sam. I wish she were awake.

Perhaps I will sneak in and lie down next to her. Maybe slip her the Snoopy Sausage.

I sip my brandy and take a deep breath and release it.

I feel my body repairing itself almost hourly. Whatever Dracula and Samantha did to me, it's taken hold. I can actually rotate my wrists both clockwise and counter-clockwise. By dusk, I'll be lifting weights.

My mind returns to Dracula and I ponder the vampire's incredible existence thus far. Fathered by Pontius Pilate – the

First Vampire! It was almost too much to accept. You couldn't make this kind of stuff up, even for a low-budget horror movie. To be consigned to such a cursed affliction, and then to wander the ages, an acknowledged murderer – yet one who is driven by primal imperatives that are completely uncontrollable, i.e., the need to feed once the Hunger took control. I try to imagine the loneliness, the sense of constant isolation, his foreknowledge that he will be forced to wander the Earth without the shadow or promise of death to give him peace. Driven by self-preservation, he is doomed to scour the world until the end of time. Along with Samantha. And so many others, at least a million or so vampiric souls, so I was informed.

Yet it was a *kind* of immortality. I ask myself that if I was presented an offer to never taste the sting of death, to exist eternally, to forever watch a sun set and know that life is mine to treasure for eons once I awaken from unnatural slumber … would I say no to such an offer? My only penance, my only punishment, would in actuality be existing as a serial killer to whole populations of pigeons or other small animals, whose blood I would substitute for that of human fare.

What would I do, I wonder.

What would *you* do?...

*   *   *   *

After another hour, I slip into Samantha's room.

It is nearly completely dark, safe for one light on near her bed – a table lamp, with chimes that sing as the shade turns 'Three Coins In The Fountain.'

Of course, the windows are completely shuttered closed, this being now the height of the day.

I remove my robe and slide into bed with her. She opens her eyes and smiles, and without further ado, we go at it like feral gophers.

This activity proceeds beautifully for an hour or so. After our final bout, leaving us both sweating and out of breath, Samantha begins to cry.

She sits up, and sobs, staring at me.

"What is it?" I ask, suddenly afraid for her. In fact, it is more than that – her pain is now *my* pain – the kind of empathy only lovers deeply in love can understand. "What's wrong?"

"Oh, Dick. I love you so much. You believe that, don't you?

"Of course, darling. Why are you crying?"

"There is something I must tell you."

"Alright, tell me, love."

"It's a terrible secret and it is something I should have told you before … well, before we became involved."

"Let me guess. You have an incurable disease," I try to joke, kissing her on the lips.

"I wish it were that simple," Samantha sobs.

"What could possibly be worse than some dreadful communicable disease?" I ask.

"It's about *me*," she wails.

"What about you? Sam, what the hell is wrong?"

She stares at me, sniffs, then regains some kind of composure.

"Vampires, as you know, have a gift. We can transform ourselves into most anything in the world. It's quite magical, really, but it comes down to a fundamental ability to very quickly manipulate matter on a cellular level, and reshape it by the power of thought."

"Right," I say. "You can turn yourself into bats and shit. Or fire, like Dracula did yesterday at the airport."

"Yes, all this is true," Samantha says quietly.

"I'm past all this," I say, smiling. "Remember, I do this for a living. Fight vampires and such."

She touches my cheek, and looks into my eyes.

"You remember when I told you I was a young novice when Dracula found me in the field outside of my convent. That he had taken me in the stage of his Hunger?"

"Sure, how could I forget?"

Samantha is beginning to cry again.

"He didn't really … take me during the Hunger," Samantha says. "He *healed* me."

I stare at her, completely at a loss.

"What are you saying?"

Samantha takes a breath and speaks very slowly.

"That early evening, I was out walking by myself, deep in thought and meditation. I had been punished by the Brothers at the monastery. One of many times."

Something clicks in my head. "The *monastery*?"

"Yes. It was not a nunnery."

My throat tightens up. I begin to have a bad feeling.

"Dick," Samantha says to me. "I wasn't a young novice when Dracula found me."

Sam pauses.

"I was a young *monk*! And I was dying."

CHAPTER TWENTY-EIGHT

▼

I sit opposite Dr. Simonhoffer and watch her as she leans forward, considering my demeanor. I am wearing sunglasses, pajama bottoms, and a bloodied t-shirt from my encounter with the vampires at the airport just 48 hours ago.

"Looks like we've been having a little drinkie," the good doctor says in what could be easily discerned as both a compassionate and patronizing tone of voice.

I lift up the bottle of Jack Daniels I have liberated from Father Gastroni's bar, and swill it back, not giving a shit what Dr. Simonhoffer might think about this indiscreet behavior on my part. The hot liquid tears through my throat and stomach with merciless abandon ... and I am grateful for the alcoholic agony of it all.

"Sun is over the yard-arm, Doctor," I smile.

I am, it is safe to say, completely ripped out of my gourd.

"I'm not judging you, Inspector," she says to me, and reaches out for one hand that I have placed on her desk. "And I'm delighted that you have, in what is obviously a significant piece of emotional extremis, chosen to seek me out for guidance."

I drink again, staring at her. She continues to prattle on.

"It looks like you've had a hard couple of days. In fact, I know as much because I read Captain Zelig's report on your airport sting the other night. Quite traumatic, I'm sure."

"That was a fuckin' picnic," I say. "Compared to some other shit..."

"I see."

"No, you really don't, and I don't mean that in an insulting way," I sputter drunkenly.

She leans back and considers me for a moment in silence.

"So. How are we dealing with other matters in life?" she asks me, switching gears. "Have you considered your clear desire for same-gender companionship, sexually speaking?"

I think about this for a moment, and nod.

"Yes, I've given it a spot ... a lot of thought," I respond honestly. "And I believe I am a full on faggot of the first cock-sucking order."

Dr. Simonhoffer's benign smile seems to disintegrate on her face.

"Really, Inspector," she says, "that kind of referencing is hardly appropriate."

"No, no, you were right. I'm a dick-smoker. Mr. Pillow Muncher, that's my new nick-name. Yep. Fact, my current lover is a man. Well, *was* a man. Had a dick, once. Oh, and she's also a vampire."

I'm rambling and I realize this.

"*She?*" Dr. Simonhoffer replies, clearly confused.

"Yeah, long story," I say and drink from the bottle once more.

"Isn't that why you dropped in to see me? To talk, to regale me with long, significant, potentially therapeutic experiences by which we may both share and embark upon a mutually constructive or reconstructive endeavor to heal wounded mechanisms with your clearly trouble psyche?"

Well ... she's got a point.

"Okay," I say, the room for me now spinning in earnest. "About an hour ago ..."

CHAPTER TWENTY-NINE

▼

I am up against the far wall of Samantha's room, trembling uncontrollably. All I can do for several seconds, after I have fairly torpedoed myself from Sam's bed across the room, is stare in abject horror.

"You were a ... a *man*?" I finally manage in a ragged, hoarse whisper?

Samantha is crying again, and nods. "Yes."

It try to quell my rising emotions of loathing, fear, anger, betrayal ... and find some calm in this miasma of madness.

"Tell me everything," I say, allowing myself to crumble to my ass against the wall, staring at Sam through what I realize are stinging tears of acrimony.

Samantha wipes her eyes and stares at me with what I can discern is clear emotional agony.

"I was an orphan when I joined the monastery. I had been raised by some local peasants after my parents had died of plague just after I had been born. From a very early age, I realized I was not wholly content with being a little boy. I was filled with impulses and feelings I did not understand – nor could I control. I found, for example, that I was fond of wearing my foster mother's dresses. I later discovered that I was extremely attracted to other boys. I could not share this secret with anyone else, but I knew that it was wrong – or at least wrong in that time and age."

I listen, still trembling. Hoping perhaps that I will wake up and discover that this is all a dream.

"When I turned seventeen, my foster parents gave me over to the charges of the monks. This was a happy environment for me, inasmuch as there was discipline and a way of life which was regimented. There were rules of what I could do and what I couldn't do. In short, there was God."

Samantha is calming now. She leans back in bed, remembering.

"But I was still not comfortable in my own skin. I didn't like being male, that was the simple truth of it. I wanted to be a woman. I felt in time that God had made a terrible mistake by making me a man. A cosmic error in the big cookie grinder, I used to tell myself. Instead of chocolate chip, one cookie came out cinnamon. Do you understand, Dick?"

"No."

Sam sighs. And nods, clearly not surprised.

"In fact, I really *was* a woman, Dick. A woman imprisoned in a man's body. That was my conclusion, anyway. I prayed to God for a way to reverse this terrible thing, to rectify this cruel injustice."

"You being born male instead of female," I say dully.

"Yes. And then one day, it seems God answered that prayer. It was the night that Dracula found me."

I say nothing as she pauses in her story. She stands now, wraps the bed sheet around herself and walks across the room, away from me, toward the shuttered window. Though what she is telling is disturbing, I am not unaware of the perfection of her figure – the *femaleness* of it – the beauty.

I try to shake free the nagging vision that Samantha once had a dangling cock and that she shared a propensity with me at one time for pissing standing up.

"It was one of many nights where I wandered a bit too far from the monastery's protective grounds. Given to whimsy and day-dreaming, I would oftentimes use the twilight hours for my own kind of meditation, far and away from the madding crowd of self-flagellating monks and Gregorian chant."

She turns slowly towards me and sits on the window banister across the room.

"On that night, some local bandits were in the area. They found me, on my own. Believing me to have something of value on my person, they stopped and searched me accordingly. Finding nothing, the leader of the bandit group broke into such a rage, that he beat me for the next ten minutes. When he finally tired of this activity, he ordered me set on fire."

"Jesus God," I whisper.

Samantha closes her eyes.

"As I could smell my own flesh roasting, it was not so much the pain that angered me. It was something more. The brutality of the inhuman act itself – the pure *evil* of the deed ... this was what I was sure would be my dying thought, coupled with the wish that one day, if there were many lives to be lived by us, that in that future incarnation, I could try to save others from my fate. To help the innocents of a future age."

I watch Samantha and nod.

"I'm sorry, Sam," I say softly. "Burned alive. My god."

"Even dying, I found the effort to extinguish the flames that consumed me. But once that was done, there was very little left recognizable as a human being. That I was still alive was astounding. It was at this point that Dracula entered the scene."

Samantha proceeded to then outline most of what I already knew – with the exception that because of his intervention, Dracula was able to restore her flesh to normalcy once again within the span of a week.

"Once I was completely healed, Dracula asked me what I wanted to do. Something in me had changed. I no longer wanted to go back to the monastery. In fact, I did not know what I wanted. Dracula then presented me with his offer."

"To be a vampire," I say.

"Yes. And more than that – to change myself *completely*. I asked if this was possible in vampires – to change sex, to alter my sexual identity completely, physically, right down to every minute corpuscle. He said this could be done, but only by sheer vampiric will."

Sam considers me in silence. "And that's it."

I shake my head for a moment, but say nothing. It is almost too much to digest, to accept. "So ... you transformed yourself from male to female. Just like that."

"It took a few days," Samantha nods. "But the metamorphosis at the end of the day was one hundred percent, right down to the last strand of DNA in each ovary."

I stand slowly. "You're ... you're really a woman?"

"I think you should know that by now, Dick," Sam says softly.

"No tricks?"

"No trick. Simply cellular metamorphosis."

I walk up to her, and look at her in the eyes.

"Can you forgive me?" she whispers.

I stare into those beautiful eyes. And then I close my own. I nod.

"Yes, Sam. I can forgive you. I ... I just ... I'm having some trouble with all of this right now. I need time to process it."

Samantha takes my hand, and I am sorry that I pull it away. But Samantha seems to understand my reticence in acceptance. She nods slowly, though says nothing.

I retrieve my robe, then look to her.

"Whatever may happen, Sam," I say, "I do believe I love you. Male or female ... that will never change."

Samantha's tears run down her cheeks and she nods, whispering back the words 'I love you.'

I exit the room with one objective in mind.

Find the Esplanade and start driving.

CHAPTER THIRTY

▼

My bottle of Jack Daniels is now empty.

Dr. Simonhoffer stares at me with an expression I cannot immediately identify. Gone is the expression of self-satisfied confidence. Gone also is the practiced gaze of bemused compassion and sympathy. There is something else now that travels behind the corneas of my psychotherapist. Something strange. Something that very distantly makes my skin crawl worse than when I first heard the news that Samantha had once been a guy with a schlong.

"Dr. Simonhoffer?" I prod, though I think it sounds like I just said "Schochter Shimonhefter."

The good doctor takes a breath, and stares past me.

"You ... you love this woman, then?" she asks in a weird, weird voice.

"Yeah. I guess I do. I guess talking about this with you helped me realize that. I'm not as freaked as I was about an hour ago."

"Yes ... yes, that's good, Inspector," Dr. Simonhoffer says distantly.

She stands now, and walks toward the window, then looks out at the sun, now beginning its descent toward dusk.

"Funny how things can become so clear suddenly, don't you think?" she asks me from a galaxy far, far away.

"Yeah, guess so," I say, shrugging.

"Funny how you can look at your life – realize you've been sleepwalking through it – then wake up and take it for what it truly is."

I'm not sure where my therapist is going with this, but I nod gamely. "Yep. Funny 'nuff."

"You live an interesting life, Inspector. I don't think it's a life necessarily always happy – perhaps most of the time, it is not. In fact, you probably are abjectly unhappy mostly. Mostly."

I cannot disagree with my therapist. She has indeed hit the proverbial nail on the head. "Never really aimed for happiness, doc. If anything at all ... maybe a little peace now and then."

"And you seem to have found it in this love you have for your vampire girlfriend," Dr. Simonhoffer says, her back still to me ... as she continues to stare out the window.

"I guess so," I nod. And it's true. My love for Samantha transcends all that was ... what matters is all there is now ... and what will be.

"I ... don't believe I've ever had that kind of love before," Dr. Simonhoffer says to me. "I envy you."

Dr. Simonhoffer now turns to me. She has been crying, I now see.

"Doctor –"

"No, don't say anything, Dick. Please."

She sniffs, then walks back to her desk, but does not sit.

"Your story resonates with me particularly because of Samantha."

"Really."

"Yes."

"Why is that?"

"Because, Dick ... I was also a man once," Dr. Simonhoffer says to me.

Believe it or not, this does not instantly take me by surprise. Birney was once a cop for Vice, and now he's a German Shepherd. Since the Popov Incident, transmigration of souls, while rare, is still something that all of us are beginning to accept as something smacking of increasing normalcy.

And so I suspect that Dr. Simonhoffer means to tell me that she was once some lost soul, and that after having died, decided to inhabit the form she presently possesses. Either with the owner's permission, or just after the prior owner's own demise.

So I dare to ascertain in these few seconds.

"Ah, I see."

"I don't think you do, Inspector."

Dr. Simonhoffer reaches behind head, and releases her hairclip. Her hair, where tightly bound before by the clip, spreads out across her shoulders in a kind of rat-tassle haphazardness.

"You see, I was once a man, but have taken matters into my own hands, and had myself surgically reborn."

Oh, but the world's a-spinnin' now.

"You —"

"I am a transgender, yes, Inspector."

I stare at Dr. Simonhoffer. And I remain calm. I guess nothing can really further phase me at this stage of the game. Nothing whatsoever.

"Well ... good for you," I say heartily. And I mean what I say.

Dr. Simonhoffer does not smile.

She opens her desk drawer very slowly.

"I did not have the benefit of your Samantha's change-over powers. I had to grow a pussy quite artificially. And I do believe I resent that most of all about her."

I really don't know what to say about all this. And so I seize upon the wisdom of the moment that to say nothing is the wisest course of action.

Until I see Dr. Simonhoffer pull out a .38 police special from her desk drawer.

"The expense involved – and the pain, Inspector. You cannot imagine it. I don't mean the physical discomfort – the injections, the hormonal supplements, the growing of breasts – no, the pain emotionally, even spiritually … it is daunting at best."

"Uh, doc – what are you doing with the gun?"

Dr. Simonhoffer ignores me, it would seem. She checks the cartridge bay, but continues to speak. "The real pain is in knowing that no one can rescue you from the decision you are about to make. That there is no kind and loving God that can reverse the way things are – my being born male instead of female, that is. Well, unless you're Samantha and your new friend is a vampire."

Dr. Simonhoffer's tone of voice suddenly turns biting and bitter.

"Your Samantha had that chance … that opportunity from God. Why her? Why?"

I watch the gun in her hand. I sense great trouble and heartache is at hand.

"Doctor, perhaps you should give me the gun," I suggest.

She now looks directly at me.

"My life is nothing," she says flatly. "I have done nothing. I have butchered myself, pursuing my dream of womanhood, and I am a walking, breathing mockery of foolishness."

I again say nothing.

"And it's taken a drunken, cynical, foul-mouthed barbarian like yourself to make me realize just how pathetic I really am," Dr. Simonhoffer says quietly. "A sarcastic, warped, insensitive brute who could never understand a pain like mine … you, Inspector, have shoved a fistful of ugly little ticks in my face, forcing me to acknowledge my own feckless insignificance."

I am again watching the gun.

She raises it.

"And for that, you must pay," she says.

And fires.

I dive out of my chair with only half a second to spare, as the .38 discharges its deadly wrath. I am on the floor rolling, reaching for my own .357.

Dr. Simonhoffer fires at me again, but her aim is pretty poor.

"You must die!" she screams at me in a shrill voice that makes my nad-hairs curl.

She continues to fire. Though she is in my sights, I do not want to shoot her. I fight for options, as I crawl behind a nearby sofa. Bullets rip through throw-pillows. Suddenly, the door to Dr. Simonhoffer's opens, and half a dozen Monster Vice officers have weapons pulled, and are firing at my poor, delusional therapist.

Her body twitches horribly, as bullets slam into her chest and stomach, and one even takes off half of her head. Officers converge upon me, inquiring as to my well-being.

I stand, shaken to the core, now sobered up in the worst possible way.

I look at Dr. Simonhoffer's corpse, now a pathetic ruin and feel utterly demoralized. That I had something to do with this poor woman's misery … that I was the catalyst somehow, by way of proxy storytelling of my love affair with a vampire.

I came here looking for solace.

I now leave heartbroken and torn asunder.

I walk out of Dr. Simonhoffer's office without a word and I consider it a blessing that none of my brothers and sisters in Monster Vice intrudes upon my own personal roller-coaster ride into the emotional and spiritual abyss.

*   *   *   *

"She was out of her fucking mind!" Zelig snaps at me over my cell phone.

"He," I correct my captain. "*He* was out of his mind. Well, wait a minute. He already had the surgery, so … I guess you could refer to him as her, or her as him. Not to split hairs."

"Oh, Christ, whatever. I knew there was something about him, or her. Something I couldn't put my finger on."

"Probably his cock, since he had it cut off," I say without a trace of humor.

"Listen, Dick, I'm sorry you had to go through that. You've had the worst week of anyone I know. I'm going to recommend that you take a six month leave, effective immediately."

"No, thanks, Captain. I'd go crazy. Besides, you forget. We have a Grand Master out there, and it's very likely he's mobilizing an army of monsters throughout all of Los Angeles County."

"Yeah. Yeah, reports seem to bear that out. We've had more wolf and fang infestations in the past 24 hours than this old police dog has ever seen."

"Speaking of dogs, Birney found me. He's fine. Do you want me to send him back to HQ?"

"ASAP. We're going to need him. We also have to train him not to piss all over the cars."

"He's kind of new to the whole canine thing, Zelig," I defend Birney. "He's probably also upset about his wife. That ... and dying."

"Yeah, yeah. Where are you off to now?"

"I'm going to pick up my cat. I assume my apartment is clear now?"

"As a whistle. All your neighbors were out, so the fangs did minimal damage. You're dripping holy water and garlic. You think your cat made it?"

"Little Prick will survive the apocalypse," I say, checking my watch. It's now almost nightfall.

"Stay in touch with me, Dick," Zelig says, leaving his gruff voice in the dust for a few seconds. "And let me know if you need that time off."

"Thanks," is all I say, then disengage the cell.

I drive the Esplanade up Melrose, now aware of a numbing headache settling in, probably brought on by a combination of Jack Daniels, Samantha's revelation, and let's see, what else ... oh, yeah. My transgender therapist trying to execute me in her office.

I turn a corner, and park the Esplanade right in front of my apartment complex.

I do not have to wonder about my cat's whereabouts. Little Prick is sitting in the window sill, staring at me, yowling. He's pissed, and he's letting me know up front that I am far from forgiven for abandoning him for the past two days.

I enter the apartment building and then my unit.

Little Prick walks toward me slowly, giving me 'that look.'

"Yeah, I know. You hate my guts," I say.

Suddenly, Little Prick's ears straighten, and he gives out a wild yowl as he looks at me. And just as suddenly, I fall against the door, and sink to my knees, as sound and a flurry of images invade my mind.

The screams are from Samantha.

And from Jennifer.

I stare at Little Prick, who crouches on all fours, frozen in a fixed state.

I close my eyes.

I see werewolves. And vampires.

They are converging on Father Gastroni's house.

I see blood. I see weapons being discharged.

I hear Jennifer screaming again.

And then all is quiet.

I open my eyes.

I realize that my new 'family' is under attack.

I am hyperventilating, trying to calm myself. I look to Little Prick.

"Let's go, cat. Now."

I turn, open the door, and move out of my apartment.

Little Prick follows me without complaint, as I beeline for the Esplanade parked outside.

I realize that I have very little time.

Correction ... my friends have very little time.

The Grand Master has taken the initiative and brought the battlefield to us. I do not know how I know this – or how these images of combat have been transmitted to me, or how I have been able to tap into an ongoing and unfolding scenario of violence.

All this is secondary.

Primary is getting back to the house. To Jennifer, Dracula, and the others.

And to Samantha.

CHAPTER THIRTY-ONE

▼

I do not need to break through the front door.

The door rests on hinges that have been forced.

There is blood everywhere.

First thing I step over is the decapitated corpse of what I recognize to be young Father Ivory. His head hangs from a pull-chain from the chandelier above me.

I scream out.

"Samantha! Jennifer!"

Of course, there is no answer. I didn't expect one.

The place has been torn asunder. Furniture, lights, rugs, all shredded. And the blood ... the place is covered in blood.

Yet the only body I've found thus far is that of Father Ivory. I deduce that the blood belongs to the attackers for the most part – no doubt Colonel Kellog, Father Gastroni, my little Jennifer and Samantha put up an awesome struggle.

My deduction is confirmed as I see pieces of several werewolves dismembered all over the place. Further, I hear hissing of melting vampire.

A door to a closet slowly opens behind me.

I turn, two guns out, one my Baretta, the other the .357. I'm ready to kill.

Birney the German Shepherd barely crawls out of the small closet. His ears are ripped, one is almost completely severed.

His muzzle is bloodied and virtually all of his fur is covered in what appears to be animal tissue – werewolf flesh, would be my guess.

"Hey, Dick. Trick or treat," He barks, and whines, all in one statement.

I move quickly to him, on one knee, and pet his head gently.

"You stay quiet, Birney. I'll have a medi-vac here from MV in five minutes."

"Don't worry ... about me, Dick," Birney barks plaintively. "You don't have the time."

He coughs and wines, and blinks painfully.

"They took all of them. My new little friend, too."

"Jennifer," I nod.

"Yeah. The likkers. And about a thousand vampires. And one huge fang I can't begin to describe."

"The Grand Master."

"Yeah, sounds about right. He just strolled through here while his army went to work. Killed that poor young priest right off."

"I know. Birney –"

"Dodger Stadium," Birney whines. "That's where he's taken them."

"How do you know?"

"He told me to tell you that," Birney barks softly. "Said he's waiting for you."

"I'll alert tactical. We'll bring down the MV army so hard on this bastard --"

"He says come alone, or everyone dies," Birney coughs. "And it will be the females, he said, who will die the most painfully."

I swallow hard. Fucked again by blackmail.

"Birney, I can't leave you like this."

"Dick, my tail is broken, a few ribs, too. I feel pretty busted up inside, but I don't think I'm paws-up yet. I'll make it back to HQ. But you gotta get your cavalry moving, pardner. I got a feeling there isn't much time."

I take a breath, and shake my head.

Birney again barks softly.

"By the way – I know that Curadel is Dracula. He somehow put that in my brain. Don't worry, I'll keep that our secret."

"I can't beat the Grand Master, Birney. If Dracula and Sam couldn't … I can't, either."

"Dracula said you could."

Now what the fuck is that supposed to mean?

"He's crazy."

"He's Dracula," Birney coughs, and spits up some blood. "If he says you can beat this Grand Master, I wouldn't piss that one into the wind."

This is all madness, of course. Tonight I will die trying to save my friends. Ah, well. It's not a bad way to go.

I pet Birney again.

"Okay. If you feel too weak, just stay put. I'll be back."

"I've heard that before."

"I said I'd be back."

Birney looks at me with pained eyes. He licks my hand and stares at me sadly.

"I wish I could believe that, Dick."

"How about barking something comforting," I jest.

"I don't think you have long to live. But, hey. Look at the bright side. If you come back as a dog, we'll go out ass-sniffing the cute poodles in Echo Park."

"Thanks, Birney. I can hardly wait."

"Little canine humor, Dick. Sorry."

"I'll see you in a bit."

"Right. And my new name is Fifi. Good luck, pal."

CHAPTER THIRTY-TWO

▼

Dodger Stadiums is a large outdoor baseball field located adjacent to downtown Los Angeles. It was privately financed at a cost of $23 million dollars back on September 17, 1959. It has a capacity to hold 56,000 fans, with an attendant parking lot that can support 16,000 cars. Some notable events that took place include Pope John Paul II holding a Mass there in 1987, the Three Tensors singing a concert in 1994, and the Rolling Stones and the Beatles performing a few decades earlier.

It was also the site of one of the greatest mass murders ever to take place on American soil.

Nine months after the Popov Meteor Event, during the first baseball game of the season (Los Angeles Dodgers meeting the New York Mets), a swarm of vampires numbering in the several thousands descended on the full stadium and began killing fans. Because the attack was so sudden, and because panic prevented an organized evacuation, the casualties numbered in the thousands. Many more died due to being crushed by a hysterical multitude, and more thereafter were staked due to 'bite contamination.' Since that time, Dodger Stadium has remained abandoned and locked up, never to be used again as a viable playing field for America's Favorite Pass-time. It stands merely as a memorial to tragedy, a great, silent coliseum inhabited only by ghosts.

Monster Vice is aware that it is festooned with supernatural horrors of every like and description, but much like the Santa Monica Airport, and other unfortunate locations long abandoned and unsupervised, the stadium is categorized as a 'no-patrol zone.' There was talk one day of demolishing the structure as a whole, but various zoning complications and city ordinances, coupled with a generally ineffective metropolitan beaurocracy pretty much stymied the whole blow-it-to-fuck factor.

And so, it is into this arena of phantoms and tragic occurrences of times long past that I now find myself about to enter.

I am armed to the teeth.

I enter through right-center field, just near the foul poles and the bullpen. The lights suddenly come on, one at a time. I look to the pitcher's mound and think suddenly that once, so very long ago, great players like Sandy Koufax, Don Drysdale, Don Sutton, Fernando Valenzuela, Orel Hershiser and others graced that small hill. Now, one figure stands upon it. Smug, defiant, and staring at me.

And though far from being a great player, he is nevertheless, arguably, the most powerful vampire the world has ever seen.

The Grand Master.

"Greetings, Inspector Pitts," the Grand Master calls out, his eerie voice echoing through the empty park.

I give a quick 360 gander to the stadium, but see no one else around.

And no sooner do I turn back to the mound than the Grand Master is standing before me.

"Hi."

And then, like so many times before, I am airborne. Easily a good fifty feet, toward the pitcher's mound. Amazingly, I find myself able to land on my feet, and this is completely armed to the tune of 70 pounds of fang-killing shit-hardware. I am, I assume, becoming more spry in the autumn of my years. Or simply accustomed to being thrown around like a rag doll by vampires and werewolves alike, thus kinda getting the hang of landing on my own two stems.

"Very graceful," the Grand Master speaks, though he is not yelling – his voice seems to naturally resonate.

"Where are they, blood-freak?" I taunt the Master with a childish piece of name-calling.

He whistles, long and shrill.

Silence for a moment, and then I see the tragedy of things slowly unfold.

Dozens of children – new turnovers – begin to fall out into the stands of Dodger Stadium. I should not be able to see their eyes, but I do, from this distance. All are possessed of that red, hypnotic fury of the plasma-starved. Dozens turn into several dozens, and as I turn on myself, a complete 360, I see that the stadium is filling up to the tune of hundreds, then thousands. All kids. All baby vampires.

Then through the left-field bullpen area, from within one of the stadium's vehicle entry tunnels, I see a large cart being pulled by several horses. It is followed by yet another cart, likewise being towed by *Los Caballos*.

But most disturbing of all is that within the front cart, tied to huge cross-beams that resemble the cross Jesus Christ died upon – are Dracula and Samantha. They look nearly comatose from here.

In the cart behind my vampire friends, Father Gastroni and Colonel Kellog are likewise bound, though they are alert, albeit covered with blood and the residue of battle.

I turn back to the Grand Master.

And see the most disturbing sight of all.

Suddenly, little Jennifer is at his side. She stares at me. Her eyes are red, feral, vampiric.

"Oh, god, no," I groan to myself. "No, please, Jesus, not *her*."

"She was downright yummy, Inspector," the Grand Master whispers tauntingly, and amazingly, I hear him even some fifty yards away. I'm sure he has made sure of this, utilizing whatever infernal technique he can for communicating to me in hushed tones.

"You bastard," I growl, and my teeth are clenched so hard together my jaw begins to ache.

And then I hear a voice in my head.

Fight them.

I recognize the voice to be that of Dracula.

I turn slowly, and look at Dracula, hanging from the ad hoc cross, eyes half-open. His lips are not moving as I hear the voice again.

You can win.

And then another voice.

Samantha. *Fight them, darling.*

For a moment I think that I have finally done some very serious damage to myself from too much Jack Daniels imbibing. But then I remember what Father Gastroni said about vampires being possessed of very real psychic power.

I shake my head to my friends. "It's impossible. I can't defeat them. There are too many." I look at the six Masters in attendance to my four friends, holding ropes around their respective necks. One Master alone killed my entire platoon just days earlier. How could I defeat six of them? And please ... let's not forget about the Grand Master only fifty yards away, holding my Jennifer in his power.

Come closer.

Hurry, Dick, I hear Samantha's voice as well.

I turn quickly to see the Grand Master walking casually toward me.

Alright, fuck me. I'll listen to my friends.

I move toward the carts and the Masters immediately release their hold on the ropes. I fully expect them to charge me *en masse*.

Yet they hold their positions.

The Grand Master whistles behind me.

"Try this, Inspector," he says, and removes a sword from within his long coat. "I really want to see how your friends are going to be able to help you through this."

He throws the sword into the air, directly for me.

I don't know what compels me to do such a stupid thing, but I reach up – and am able to grab it, by the hilt. As if by fucking magic.

For the first time, I see the Grand Master's smile wither a bit. I find the expression odd … given his seemingly endless power, and obvious advantage over this pathetically ill-equipped officer of Monster Vice.

"Nice catch," he says neutrally.

Jennifer hisses at me. My heart again sinks a bit. She's running out of time. I sense that she has only recently been contaminated by the Grand Master. There is still hope.

Hope, that is, if God decides to deliver a miracle.

Kill the Masters, Dick.

"Oh, sure, sorry, pardner. Right, I knew there was something on my to-do list. Pay the bills, feed the cat, and oh, yeah – kill the Masters." I'm sputtering out of annoyance and disbelief.

Kill them quickly, sweetheart. Jennifer has only a few minutes before it will be too late…

Samantha's message to me – her voice caressing my thoughts with daring and urgency – jars me into offensive action. I do not ponder the impossibility of my next act. I merely act.

I race toward the Masters, screaming my death scream, sword in one hand, a Glok 5 semi-automatic drawn to my other.

I fully expect to taste Death any second.

It is here.

Now.

And I am ready for it.

*   *   *   *

But Death does not come for me.

However, it comes for others.

The world takes on a kind of surreal quality which is difficult to describe.

I watch as the Masters charge me, but they seem to move in slow motion. So slow, in fact, that I find I am able to decapitate the first Master closet to me without effort.

The head flies high into the air, as the Master's body continues to run in a strange circle. It almost looks like a piece of performance art *dance Francaise*, but I have little interest in watching for long. Five Masters remain, their eyes redolent with fury. And they are charging from all points on the compass.

My Glok is up firing repeatedly (its *raison d'etre* for existence in Gun World) and the face of the next Master kinda just disappears in a spray of bone, blood and goo. I finish the job with another round-house slice of my sword, and it's good-bye Mr. Master Head.

This is impossible, I say to myself. I have killed two Masters in the span of seconds, and it has been effortless. How?

And then the answer comes, gently, trippingly on my mental synapses.

Dracula and Samantha are using some of their vampire voodoo that Gastroni told me about. Somehow, they are reshaping time and the unfolding of events, slowing down the Masters in their attack against me.

With this conclusion happily nestled in my unconscious, I proceed with the mop-up chore of four remaining Masters.

My Glok runs clean, and I lose it, holding my sword with both hands, swinging like Mantle on his last day in The Show.

I disembowel two Masters simultaneously, their evil, pulsating hearts cleaved in two and falling onto the Dodger Stadium turf, much neglected by time and ennui. The air is filled with blood and vampire slop-essence.

I'm beginning to enjoy myself, but am immediately reminded of Jennifer's rapidly decaying state from human to Point of No Return Vampire. That, and my friends hanging pitifully on wooden crosses in front of me.

Two Masters remain.

I glance behind myself very quickly. The Grand Master is walking casually toward me, Jennifer at his side. No doubt, to join the festivities.

I turn back and a Master lunges for me.

Amazingly, as I do not have time to swing my sword, I reach out – and grab the Master's neck. I give a mighty pull, and trachea, along with masticated tissue and arteries fly forth like linguini Alfredo.

The Master's hands reach for his throat in agony, as I ram my fist into his chest, and rip out his heart in one painfully simple move. The Master goes down to his knees and remains there, twitching in what I assume is a death rattle of sorts.

The remaining Master has however struck forth with a bit of luck. He has knocked the sword out of my hand, and now faces me, claws up, teeth dripping viscous drool, eyes as purple as the little purple helmet on the tip of my dick.

He, like the others, attacks with lugubrious velocity. He tries to side-swipe me, but I duck easily, ending up behind him, my right arm around his neck. I take my other hand, clasp it to my opposite elbow, and twist hard.

The Master's neck snaps like dry timber. I then tear the head off and toss it behind my shoulder like a used condom.

Real time suddenly returns.

I leap onto the cart where Dracula and Samantha are bound.

"Hold on," I whisper to both of them.

"No time, Dick," Dracula says. "You still have one last battle ahead of you."

I turn, as the Grand Master continues his luxurious stride toward me, a good fifty yards off as yet.

"How did you do that?" I ask. "How did you slow the Masters down like that?"

"I didn't do anything," Dracula breathes heavily.

"It was you," Samantha wheezes.

I don't understand.

"It was *your* power, Dick," Dracula says.

I just shake my head, as I try to unbind the ropes to Samantha's cross.

"You were near death when you suffered the attack at the airport. The only way to save you was to infuse much of my essence – my inherent vampiric power – into your physiology. As a result ... well, you have a bit more advantage in fighting Masters, as you just learned. Unfortunately, it left me terribly weakened, and I did not see the Grand Master's attack on the safe house in time, nor did I have sufficient strength to fight him. Hence, our capture."

I look from Dracula into Samantha's eyes.

"Don't trouble yourself with us, darling," she whispers. Blood oozes out of her mouth, as it does out of Dracula's as well.

"We're dying," she coughs.

I shake my head, denial in full force. "No."

"In a minute, something is going to happen, Dick. Be prepared for it."

I stare, as tears stream down my cheek, and realize I am holding Samantha's hand. I have ceased all efforts in trying to sever the binds that solidly hold my friends. I sense that to even try is an expenditure of unnecessary energy.

"I love you," I whisper to Samantha.

"I love you, too," she says, and she is also crying. "But I'll always be with you. A part of me, anyway."

"We must move on to another plane of existence, my friend," Dracula says. "But we can give you the remaining power we possess. You will carry that power with you forever."

"It will ... it will make you the most powerful vampire in the world," Samantha says.

And then I completely understand everything.

I am a vampire. Or a strange hybrid of vampire. As if reading my mind (and he probably is), Dracula nods wearily.

"Yes, you are a new species, Dick. And with our collective life force surging through you, you will walk in daylight with impunity, you will fear neither Church nor Cross, and you will not suffer the Hunger of vampires throughout history."

"I don't want this," I say slowly.

"You have no choice," Dracula says. "It is already done." He pauses, and gives me is signature grin: "Look at the bright side – no more masturbation before midnight."

And then both Dracula and Samantha take on a strange, iridescent glow.

"Thank you, my angel," Samantha says. "Thank you for loving me. And if it is at all possible ... I will be watching over you. Good-bye."

I have to back up suddenly, and shield my eyes.

I turn, and see that the Grand Master has even covered his eyes, stopping dead in his tracks. Little Jennifer turns away, releasing the Grand Master's hand and backing away from the monster.

Father Gastroni and Colonel Kellog turn their heads down, eyes squinted tightly shut.

Because I'm the biggest klutz God ever created, I take another step back, and fall ass over teacups from the cart onto the grass. I hit the ground painfully, but I cannot take my eyes off what is transpiring on the cart in front of me.

Dracula and Samantha have now become two orbs of brilliant, star-like light. They are spinning rapidly, like tops. The ropes that once bound them in human form disintegrate.

And now the orbs descend over me.

"Be well, Dick," Dracula says, his voice an echo in my mind. "There is much work to be done. Remember us."

"Remember me," Samantha says softly.

And then the orbs that were once my friends envelopes me.

It is as if I have just been immersed in the most perfect bathwater imaginable. Warm tendrils of energy course through every limb, every cell. The feeling is galvanizing – I feel as if my body is experiencing a prolonged orgasm, starting at my toes, and ending at the top of my head. The joy is overwhelming.

I scream a scream of pleasure.

And then I open my eyes ... aware that Dracula and Samantha are now dead. And that portion of them that was able to sustain themselves in this world, has been transferred over to me.

I look around – but now it is with my new vampire eyes, exponentially enhanced to the point where I can see even a fly on the top of the highest banister in the stadium with zero difficulty.

I look to the vampire children, who collectively hiss, creating a nightmarish noise that has no comparison in the human lexicon of vocal range.

The Grand Master stares at me from the pitcher's mound.

"So," he says. "You are one of *us* now."

"Never like you," I say, a new confidence in my voice.

He smiles at that.

I fly toward Gastroni and Kellog's cart. I reach for their ropes and rip them away, again with effortless exertion.

"What the fuck just happened?" Kellog says, looking for the first time since I've known him to be somewhat out of control.

"Dracula and Samantha," I say. "They're gone."

"May God bless them," Father Gastroni says, and crosses himself solemnly.

I am still stricken with grief for the loss of Dracula, but a hundredfold for Samantha ... yet I have no time to wail for the dead. Not here. Not now.

Several thousand little bloodsuckers are responsible for my delayed reaction to irreconcilable personal tragedy.

"This is bad," Kellog states the obvious.

I turn back to the Grand Master. He remains fixed on the mound. Watching me in silence.

I decide I shall oblige him and make my move.

"I'm going to get Jennifer, gentlemen. And then we're going to get the fuck-all out of here."

I don't tarry for a response.

The Grand Master awaits.

CHAPTER THIRTY-THREE

▼

"Very nice performance," the Grand Master says easily. My eyes wander over to Jennifer, who is a good thirty feet away from me, on all fours like a dog, salivating and staring at me with livid fury and famishment.

"How long ago did you take her?" I ask the Grand Master.

He shrugs in what I assume is a kind of magnanimous gesture. "Not that it will matter to you, half-vampire, but the child is 15 minutes away from being forever lost." He smacks his lips. "Tasty little bitch, I'll give her that."

I see that the Grand Master has not bothered to produce a weapon of any kind.

"I almost regret having to kill you, Inspector Pitts. You have been most challenging. Now that the Old Vampire and his whore-bitch are dead, you and I are alone. Alone to finish it all."

I nod slowly. "Get ready for an express elevator ride to hell, plasma-pig."

"You are confident because Dracula and the woman imparted some of their power to you. No matter. I will still break you."

"You think so?"

"I know so. You're still more human than vampire. And that makes you terribly weak. You are still encumbered with fear and doubt. And your conscience —"

"Oh, Christ. You talk too much."

And then I swing the sword.

The Grand Master surprises me and literally evaporates before my eyes.

"I am a chatty Cathy, I'll give you that," he says from behind me.

I turn. The Grand Master slaps the sword out of my hand. I hesitate for a micro-second, but it is enough time for the Grand Master to pick me up bodily and throw me into the air.

And quite a throw it is. This time I am aloft longer than the first airplane ride by the Wright Brothers at Kitty Hawk. Something more than 14 seconds, I can gather --

Suddenly, there is a stab of unequaled agony running through my body.

I look down at my mid-section ... I have been impaled on some kind of construction piping up in the top section of the stadium. I am literally pinned like a fly.

Blood oozes from my body, but I still feel like I have considerable strength – and I realize that because of my newfound transformation, the wound I suffer now will eventually heal. Still ... the Grand Master has me at a disadvantage, as I begin to pull myself along the pipe-beam in an attempt to free myself.

On top of that several little fang-fiends are running from fifty feet away, no doubt anxious to tear me limb from limb.

I can see Gastroni and Kellog even from here being cornered by child-turnovers. I know that they will be devoured within minutes. I have my .357 holstered, but my Glok remains on the grass below in the field – empty of rounds. And my sword is eighty yards away from the priest and good colonel. They are defenseless.

Jennifer looks up at me from below.

The Grand Master, however, decides to levitate up to me.

I free myself painfully from the beam, in time to slap three bloodsucking *kinder* off the balcony. So that once again, the Grand Master and I are alone.

He hovers in the air.

And I decide to join him, holding onto my leaking entrails.

There we are, nearly five hundred feet above Dodger Stadium, facing off against one another – suspended in mid-air.

Again, the Grand Master appears surprised.

"Very intriguing," he says. "The Old One and the bitch gave you a lot to work with."

"That's what friends are for," I smile, as if I didn't have a care in the world. Please pass the Academy Award, if you would ... because I'm terrified. And I hate heights.

"Let's finish this, shall we?"

I nod. "Fine by me, you evil son of a bitch."

The Grand Master releases a howl and lunges toward me. I meet his attack full on. As we tear into one another, we begin to descend. The blows we exchange could kill ten men collectively, but for the Grand Master and myself, they are stunning blows merely at best.

I am already healing myself, my midsection sewing itself up by magic, so I am free to utilize fists and cuffs.

I have only one sure-fire way I believe I can destroy the Grand Master ... and it is only a hunch. If this does not work, we no doubt could go on assaulting one another for all eternity without one victor to surface.

I escape from a clutching hold the Grand Master has on me, and reach into my jacket pocket.

I pull out the crucifix that Samantha had given to me back at the house, yet I do so surreptitiously so that the Grand Master cannot see.

Predictably, he thinks that I am tiring.

He flies at me once more, open mouthed, fangs dripping all kinds of foul saliva-shit.

This time I do not engage him in the body tackle.

Instead, the hand I hold the crucifix within lashes out. I shove the cross into the Grand Master's mouth, with sufficient force to send it speeding down his vile throat.

The Grand Master swallows hard, and then stares at me in horror.

"What – have – you – done?"

"Just rammed the fear of God into you, pal. Send me a postcard from hell if you'd like."

The Grand Master backs away from me, eyes wide. His body begins to tremble in mid-air, and I could swear he is beginning to bloat.

"NOOOOO!" he screams to no one in particular.

I float a few feet away from him, and watch the paroxysm of horror begin.

The Grand Master now begins to spin on his own axis, gaining rotational speed, until he is a screaming blur.

Suddenly, he stops. His eyes meet mine. They are bulging, agonized. His body now looks like a huge melon.

"You win, man-vampire," he hisses.

And then he explodes.

CHAPTER THIRTY-FOUR

▼

I am, not for the first time, again enslimed from head to toe by the residue of a sworn enemy. I drip Grand Master goo.

I look down at the field below.

Jennifer continues to stare up at me, hissing.

And then I look to Gastroni and Kellog, as a thousand little vampiric tykes move continuously from the grand stands, onto the field, ready to take part in the human repast to come.

I dive toward them, making a mental note to myself that I am now technically flying – this time, under my own volition and steam.

Gastroni and Kellog look up as I approach them, either arm outstretched.

"Grab on!" I yell.

Gastroni and Kellog do not hesitate. As I slow to a screeching halt, just a few feet above the grass, the priest and Kellog hold fast to either arm.

I then shoot up twenty feet, well above the madding crowd of kiddy bloodthirstiness.

"Kellog, grab Jennifer," I say.

"Yes, sir!" he responds instinctively.

I fly over to where Jennifer paws at the air in an attempt to drag me out of the sky. But Kellog is swift and deft in his capture of the child, and in a second, he's holding her tight as she screams and hisses in protest.

I rise above the grandstands, and then land softly on the parking lot asphalt, only a few feet from the Esplanade.

"We only have a few minutes," I pant to Gastroni and Kellog. "After that, Jennifer is one of *them*."

"Where to?" Gastroni asks.

"Nearest hospital is County. Can you get us there quickly?"

"Not a problem, Inspector."

"Why don't you just fly her over, Dick?" Gastroni asks. "You seem to have a newfound gift."

I shake my head. "I can't. This new power – I feel it has limitations at the moment. I wouldn't make it all the way. And then I'd be forced to land and try to run her there. We wouldn't make it."

"Get in," Kellog says. "In a second, you're going to think you're flying on God's Harley."

I nod, holding Jennifer tight, as she snarls and gnashes her teeth in animal fury. Little Prick looks at us from within the car – and then at Jennifer. He yowls and disappears from sight.

"Hold on, sweetheart," I whisper to Jennifer even as she growls at me like a rabid ferret.

We're in the Esplanade within seconds, and true to his word, Kellog guns the accelerator.

And by the sweet baby Jesus, I do indeed feel like we've just taken off at light speed.

CHAPTER THIRTY-FIVE

▼

Gastroni, who has been on the phone for the past minute, hangs up and looks to me.

"They don't have any."

"Fuck me," I swear, holding Jennifer fast, as she struggles against my grip on her. "Take her, and give that to me, Father."

Gastroni hands the cell over, and takes Jennifer into his powerful arms. I dial quickly, and wait.

"This is Zelig," my captain suddenly answers.

"Captain, it's Dick Pitts. I've got an emergency ongoing."

"Pitts, Jesus – what the hell happened? Birney just hobbled in on all fours, and he's a goddamned mess."

"Yes, I'm sure. Listen, I'm rolling for County Hospital. I'm going to need some Fang anti-serum, and fast. We just called ahead, and their stock is dry."

"Who needs it? One of our people?"

"No. It's a child."

"Dick, I can't just authorize a rush-shipment of serum over there for a civilian. We're getting calls in from all points on the city compass with the same issue. Not enough serum, and inordinate attacks and turnovers."

"Zelig ... please ... this child is important," I whisper. "She's important to me."

Silence for only a second.

"I'll chopper over myself. Give me five minutes." He hangs up and I blow an invisible Wet Kiss to Zelig over the either of time and space.

Kellog drives like an insane crack-head, weaving in and out of traffic, barely missing other cars by micro-inches. Even at this mad velocity, I feel we are making slower progress than needed in the time department.

I take Jennifer from Gastroni, and stare into her eyes – eyes that stare at me in blind hate.

"We may be too late," I say, my heart sinking.

Gastroni reaches over and touches my shoulder.

"Have faith, Dick. Have faith."

On those two words, I hang all hope and prayer for my little Jennifer.

Please, Lord, please ... let just one god-damned thing go right tonight.

Amen.

Hope someone is out there listening.

CHAPTER THIRTY-SIX

▼

We arrive at County Emergency just as Zelig lands in an MV chopper. He has flown it himself, and I am momentarily surprised, until I remember that was what he used to do in that ancient thing called the Iraq War.

He exits the aircraft, a small suitcase in hand, and together with Kellog and Gastroni, myself holding Jennifer, we race into the hospital.

We don't wait to find an adequate space.

The orderlies are baffled as we lay Jennifer on the floor, Kellog and Gastroni pinning her legs, and myself holding her arms.

Zelig opens the suitcase, and produces a syringe, already fully loaded with Bioxypenicillin. He then finds an adequate vein in Jennifer's right arm, and injects her deftly with the skill of a surgical nurse.

Jennifer howls – a very inhuman howl at that, and spits at Zelig.

Zelig doesn't bother to wipe the spittle off his face. His focus is concentrated on the child's anticipated transformation.

"Are you sure we got her in time?" Zelig looks to me.

I shout above Jennifer's screams. "I don't know."

Suddenly, Jennifer ceases her quite vocal protestations, and begins to shudder. Her entire body now quivers and quakes as if she were suffering from an epileptic seizure.

"C'mon, little fighter," I hear Kellog urge. "You can do it."

Father Gastroni has his eyes closed and hands folded in prayer.

Surrounding us are doctors, nurses and orderlies, all pin-drop silent.

"Please don't die," I whisper. "Please, Jenny."

And then ... Jennifer becomes perfectly still. Her eyes are closed. Her breathing has lost the fibrillation-like panting of a wounded animal.

She opens her eyes, blinks once, and looks up at me.

"Hi, Dick. What's going on?"

I release her arms, and take her into a bear hug. I am crying openly, and by golly, if I don't see a tear run free down the cheek of crusty old Zelig.

Thank you, I whisper to whatever gods may be.

Thank you for sparing my child.

CHAPTER THIRTY-SEVEN

▼

Several hours later, following treatment given to Gastroni and Kellog for their wounds, we are at Monster Vice headquarters, answering questions. I do most of the talking, filling Zelig in on what happened at Dodger Stadium ... and outlining how Officer Curadel and his associate, Samantha, were killed in the line of duty.

I also make no small mention that the most powerful vampire on the planet – The Grand Master – is now vaporous pollutant commingling with good old familiar LA smog. To that end, I add that Father Gastroni and Colonel Kellog, as unofficial 'citizens pursuing arrest' were extremely helpful to this particular officer of Monster Vice.

I artfully avoid telling Zelig of Dracula's true identity. Father Gastroni and Colonel Kellog are likewise discreet by their silence.

When I finish, and Zelig shuts down his recording device, he stares at me.

"Alright, then. Thank you, Inspector. And thank you, Father Gastroni and Colonel Kellog. Very good work."

Little Prick is in my lap as I pet him absently with my hand, while Jennifer is seated beside me, my other hand in her own small paw.

Zelig leans in and smiles at her.

"Young lady, what are we going to do with you?"

Jennifer looks to me.

I grin and turn to Zelig. "She's with me now, Captain."

"Aren't you a little long in the tooth to suddenly become a daddy, Pitts? Doesn't suit you, it seems."

I smile – because I have a secret.

"People can change, Captain. Oh, yeah man, they can surely change."

Zelig considers that for a moment, then gives a grunt and a nod.

That is our signal that we are all free to go.

I stand up and shake hands with Kellog and Gastroni. "I'm afraid Father Ivory didn't make it," I say.

"Yes, I know," Gastroni says. "I've already made a few calls and his body is being purified even as we speak."

"Good." And for a moment, no one says anything.

It is Kellog who finally speaks.

"Damn fine working with you, Inspector Pitts. I hope it won't be the last time."

"Yes, quite so," Gastroni agrees. "You're an asset to the Cause, Dick. Remember that."

I need no reminding. Dracula and Samantha have made very clear what my responsibilities are to be.

"Until next time," I say, and then Kellog and Father Gastroni exit Zelig's office.

I look down to Jennifer.

"Want to get something to eat?"

"Sure. Let's pick up something for Little Prick, too. Okay?"

"Of course. He'd never forgive us otherwise."

I give a quick nod to Zelig. The latter allows himself a small smile of what I perceive to be admiration.

I open the door and both Jennifer and myself stare out into the vast expanse of the outer sanctum adjunct to Zelig's office.

Staring at us – or I should say – staring at me, are a hundred officers, gathered tightly together. There is drop-dead silence.

And then suddenly, there is a roar from my associates and a thunderous burst of applause.

Within a second, both Jennifer and myself are on top of some shoulders, as we are escorted out of the building to the sound of cheers and shouts of adulation.

Little Prick looks up at me with that look of his that says: *You do realize, they're all cheering for me, right?*

I laugh. And I do not stop. Not for quite awhile.

CHAPTER THIRTY-EIGHT

▼

In the following days, Jennifer and I perform a few chores. We go out and acquire two headstones, one for Dracula and one for Samantha. And though there are no coffins beneath the stone testaments to their death, as we stand in my brother's church staring down at the earth and the stone plates ... there is a feeling that our friends are with us still.

For a moment, as the sun hits the far wall of the church, I look up and think I see two figures – in fact, I am sure that they are Dracula and Samantha. I look to Jennifer, her little hand in mine, and see if she is privy to what I am witnessing.

But her concentration is on the headstones – and when I look up again ... the figures I imagined to be Dracula and my dearest love, have vanished.

My imagination again, I chide myself inwardly. It was the light, nothing more. Shadows playing tricks, even with my advanced newly acquired vampire eyes. Or a desperate hope and longing on my part that they are not really gone ... merely, as Dracula said of Pontius Pilate, in hiding, waiting to resurface to the world on another day from points far beyond and out of sight.

I pray they do indeed one day return ... if these things are allowed by the Powers At Be. It is a hope I will harbor and nurture for some time. It is the way I can honor Dracula – and love my Samantha from this side of the world – to the best of my ability.

My work is far from over. The Grand Master had contaminated literally thousands of children, and while Monster Vice went into Dodger Stadium that night to Sweep, Clear and Stake as many little blood-eaters as possible – many still escaped, and are loose in the city. Moreover, some will leave the city and commute to territories outside of Los Angeles.

The blood of these children has the mutant gene of the Grand Master running through them. Will one, or several, or many, grow into Grand Masters themselves? If so, we are then dealing with Super Vampires – as if Masters and talking werewolves weren't enough for law enforcement to handle.

I look down at Jennifer – my new vampire-killing daughter. I allow her to carry a small .22 pistol – it makes her feel safe, and she has proved her worthiness to bear arms. She has, after all, saved my life. In more ways than one.

I wander over to where my brother is buried and close my eyes. I say a prayer to a God I am not sure exists, yet all my experience and my victory over the Grand Master tells me that somehow, in some form, he does. To what purpose he utilizes my destiny, I do not yet know.

But I shall mush on.

Like the good soldier I am.

CHAPTER THIRTY-NINE

▼

And so, I reconcile myself to my new family – Little Prick, myself … and Jennifer. The war feels over to me, so many have died, and I have lost what I know to be the love of my life – Samantha. I will give myself time to grieve for her, as I will grieve with respect for the memory of Dracula. They said to me that they have moved into a different plane of existence. If there is consciousness to that plane, then indeed, I would like to believe that Sam is looking over me. Perhaps we will meet again. I hope this is the case, hope being the most powerful human virtue I possess. For the time being, I shall content myself to seeing her only in my dreams.

Beyond that, I am still a warrior for Good against Evil. Monsters still live (sort of) and breathe, and make trouble for humanity.

I am still in the fight.

I am Dick Pitts, Inspector to the Los Angeles Police Department, Special Taskforce, presently on a much needed leave.

They call me the stuff of myth, the hero of tales yet to be told and regaled, a legend in a time of a perceived apocalypse.

But I am much more than this.

I am Man.

I am Vampire.

Bigger.
Better.
A Biter.
I am Monster Vice.